WHIPLASH

"You look like you've seen a ghost, Le Page," Dan said. "What's the matter, did you think you had killed me?"

His left arm shot out and caught the gambler by the coat collar. Le Page reached for his gun. The man was too late. Dan jerked it from the holster and flung it back of the bar. Then he stooped for his horsewhip.

The lash hissed through the air and wound around the legs of the gambler. Le Page ripped out a curse of anger and pain. He flung himself down to escape the torture and was dragged back from the floor. He screamed and begged and cursed. The whip rose and fell, rose and fell, each stroke a flame of agony . . .

BORDER BREED
WILLIAM MacLEOD RAINE

POPULAR LIBRARY • NEW YORK

Chapter 1

•

BABES IN THE WOODS

THE long whiplash snapped close to the cocked ear of the off leader. Almost automatically, a string of crackling oaths poured from the lips of Dan Clifford. He never swore except at his mules. It was an axiom among skinners that shavetails could be stirred from their sloth only by bristling profanity. The expletives of the young driver were merely professional jargon. With no animus back of them, they died down into amiable advice. 'You Baldy, doggone you, git into it.'

Straight as a gunbarrel the white ribbon road stretched across the plain. At intervals rose billowing clouds of dust. From the size of these and from the rapidity of movement Dan could guess whether an ox train, a covered wagon, a stage, a buggy, or horsemen had stirred the fine powder into which trampling feet had ground the surface of the highway.

All the world, it seemed to him, was moving toward Los Piños. The adobe village had slept undisturbed for scores of years, had lain at peace in a coma of sunshine. Of a sudden Destiny had decided to make a metropolis of it. Four transcontinental lines were pushing toward Dave Shotwell's saloon, at the bar of which the drifting Southwest had been in the habit of pouring down baked throats bottled lightning. From the railheads of advancing civilization streamed a varied assortment of people using all available forms of transportation.

In the outfit to which Dan was attached were six immense freight wagons. They belonged to Ochoa and Waller, and they were carrying supplies to Los Piños. In those wagons one could have found everything from a paper of pins to a barrel of flour. The boomers rushing to the frontier settlement had not stopped to buy equipment. There would be a good market for food, clothes, lumber, hardware, and liquor.

5

The mule train swung around a covered wagon, as ramshackle a concern as Dan had ever seen, and he had looked upon some remarkable ones. The horses were so poor their bones stuck out. Broken in a dozen places, the harness had been tied with string and strips of cotton cloth. Drunkenly, the wheels sagged.

The wagon was not moving. A tug had broken, and a girl was standing helplessly holding it in her hand. She was clad in faded patched calico. Through the gaping end of a shoe Dan saw dusty toes protruding. In the wagon were two children, a boy of about nine, a girl some years younger.

Through the dust Dan caught sight of Pete Mulrooney, the wagon master. He was moving across the road to the girl. For a moment the two talked together.

The broad red beard of Mulrooney turned toward young Clifford.

'You, Dan—come here,' he called.

Pulling up his team, the mule skinner dismounted from the wagon.

The face of the wagon boss was brick red. His blue eyes, rimmed with dust so that they looked cavernous, were bloodshot and haggard, as were those of everyone who traveled this dry sunbaked trail.

'Give this little lady a hand, Dan,' he ordered. 'Fix up this tug for her so she can reach Los Piños—if this crowbait she calls a team can get her there. See you at the Elephant Corral, in case you don't catch up with us before we get in.'

Mulrooney strode back to his wagon. A long whip cracked. He was on his way.

Dan took the broken tug from the girl and examined it. From his wagon he got a hammer, rivets, and a long strip of leather. With his knife he trimmed the rawhide to the shape of a tug. After the job was completed, he looked the rest of the harness over and substituted here and there stout rawhide thongs for the flimsy string that held the pieces together.

He had worked in silence, increasingly aware that the face beneath the sunbonnet was both young and troubled. What in heaven's name was she doing here with those other children unprotected by a man?

'Where's your father?' he asked at last abruptly.

Tear blobs gathered in her eyes. 'He—died,' she murmured.

'Since you started?'

'Yes. This side of San Antonio.' The tears rolled down her cheeks.

He said, gruffly: 'You three all the family there is?'

'Yes.' She brushed away the tears and said with a wan smile, 'I'm the mother and the daddy of it.'

'You're headed for Los Piños?'

'Yes.'

'Got friends there?'

'No.'

His sympathy expressed itself in exasperation. These babes in the woods had no right to go to hell-raising Los Piños. When he had left there two months ago there had not been a dozen straight women in town. The rest were dance-hall girls, mostly Mexicans.

'What you aim to do there?' he asked, irritation in his voice.

'I don't know. I can find something to do, can't I?'

The girl lifted shy lovely eyes to his. He could see anxiety in them. Dan had not the heart to tell her what kind of place Los Piños was.

'Maybe,' he said. Then, abruptly: 'You ought to go back to your kinfolks where you come from.'

'We haven't any—none who want us,' she said.

He flung another question at her. 'How old are you?'

'Going on seventeen.'

The helplessness of her youth and inexperience was pathetic. To make matters worse, she was very pretty, would some day be a beauty. With that wild rose color in her cheeks, with that sweet sensitive mouth, with the shy appeal in the dusky eyes beneath the long curved lashes, she was sure to be the prey of some predatory male. What she needed was a father or a brother with a long blue-nosed Colt ready to flash into sight at the hint of an insult.

Though just past twenty, by the standards of the frontier Dan had considered himself a man for three years. He knew and accepted its code. You minded your own business. You asked no fool questions. If you got into a difficulty, you had to fight your way out. His slim brown body was hard as nails. The carefree way of his kind he trod with confidence.

But the plight of these young movers disturbed him. Before the boom they would have been safe enough at Los Piños. If the men there were tough characters, they had at least the outdoor virtue of respect for a good woman. Now it was different. Into the town were pouring gamblers, desperadoes, prostitutes, all the riff-raff of the untamed West.

7

For a time, until law and order could assert itself, there would be anarchy born of uncontrolled license. Doggone it, this was none of his affair. He was not responsible for it. Still, it got through his hide. He justified his concern on the ground that Mulrooney had wished this job on him.

He unhitched the scarecrows and tied them back of her wagon. This he fastened to his own outfit.

'You'll get along faster this way,' he said gruffly.

In a small, timid voice she thanked him. 'You're good to us,' she added shyly.

The mountains to the east and west were beginning to press in on the valley. The road drew nearer the river, back of which hills rose close to the stream. Soon the travelers would be among the vineyards and the orchards irrigated by winding *acequias*.

Dan was glad to be so close to his journey's end. Tonight he would make a round of the new dance halls and gambling places. He might try a fling at chuck-a-luck or twenty-one. He had been on the road for many days, with no companionship but that of his fellow mule skinners. The sap of youth flowed strongly in him. A hunger for excitement filled his veins. There was a dusky, lithe-bodied girl at The Last Chance who had turned her soft eyes on him. He had pretended not to see her advances, but if she still looked as pretty to him as she had when he last saw her . . .

When he drew up beside the river, the sun was beginning to drop toward the western horizon.

'Time for grub,' he explained. 'I reckon the kids are hungry.'

He built a fire of cow chips while she brought out her meager store of provisions. All she had left was corn meal and salt side.

'I've been expecting to get more at Los Piños,' she apologized with a blush.

Dan doubted whether she had as much as two bits left in cash. Her own dress and that of her little sister were neatly patched in half a dozen places. The trousers worn by the boy had manifestly been made from an old pair of his father's. They had been mended and added to so often that it was difficult to tell what the original pattern had been. Yet somehow, in spite of poverty and the dust of travel, the children looked clean.

From his own wagon Dan brought canned tomatoes, bacon, and coffee. While the older girl made the corn pone,

8

he took charge of the rest of the dinner. The children ate as if they were starved.

'Our name is Sutherland,' the seventeen-year-old sister said shyly. 'I am Milly. My sister is Rose. Our brother is called Tom.'

After the usual 'Pleased to meet you, Miss,' Dan mentioned his own name.

'What do you figure on doing at Los Piños?' he asked.

'I can wash clothes if there is anything of that kind to do,' she answered, in the soft drawl of the South.

He guessed they were from Tennessee or perhaps Arkansas.

'The Chinks do the washing,' he told her.

It was clear she was disappointed. The tired, slim figure drooped.

'You'll get something to do,' he comforted, though he could not think for the life of him how a decent girl of her age could earn a living for the three of them.

In the late afternoon they drew into the irrigated country adjoining the town. Here and there were one-story adobe houses and occasionally a Mexican *jacal*. The town opened below them, a haphazard little place of two or three adobe streets, some frame buildings in process of construction, and hundreds of tents scattered over the flat near the river.

Dan drove to a camping ground on the edge of the Rio Grande. He bargained with a Mexican for some greasewood which Milly could use for cooking. Before she would accept it he had to convince the girl it had cost him nothing. He would have liked to leave her money, but he knew he could not persuade her to take it. She might be a Cinderella, but she was as proud as the daughter of a millionaire.

As he drove his mules to the Elephant Corral, Dan remembered how she had always tried to stand or sit in such a way as to conceal from him the little pink toes peeping from the worn-out brogans. She was so unsure of herself that she blushed at trifles. Her gratitude for the little he had done was almost pathetic.

After supper at a Chinese restaurant he strolled round to The Last Chance. Restlessly he moved from table to table, betting a dollar aimlessly now and again.

'Señor Clifford,' a low voice at his elbow murmured.

He turned, and smiled. She was as pretty as he had remembered her. 'How is Juanita?' he asked.

'You have been away long,' she said. Her dark soft eyes offered gifts to him.

9

A man approached them. Immediately Juanita's smile became professional and rigid.

Chapter 2
•
POLLY DOBLE
TAKES A HAND

To DAN the man was a stranger, but the mule skinner knew the type. The pallid impassive face, the long soft fingers stamped him professional gambler as surely as the polished boots, the black frock coat, and the two-carat diamond in the white shirt. He was one of the human buzzards who had come in with the rush to fatten on the unwary.

'Introduce me to your friend, Juanita,' he suggested insolently.

The Mexican girl knew he had interpreted the look in her eyes when Dan had turned to her. She knew too he was not pleased. Jasper Ford had done her the honor to take an interest in her.

Obediently Juanita went through the formula of introduction. All eagerness had gone. Her face had become blank, as if she had lowered a shutter.

At once Dan recognized the name. It was known all over the frontier. Jasper Ford was a killer. He had slain at Dodge, at Kit Carson, at Leadville. Rumor credited him with a dozen victims. The eyes of the man were cold and hard, his face rigid. He was tall, slender, immaculately dressed. Many would have called him handsome.

He did not offer to shake hands with Dan. 'Not a stranger here, Mr. Clifford,' he said.

'I've been here off and on,' Dan said. 'I'm a mule skinner.'

'Interesting,' Ford drawled with cool contempt. 'And a friend of Juanita. You are lucky. Or are you?'

With the last three words the drawl vanished. A chill ran down Dan's spine. He was aware of a velvet cruelty in voice and manner. He was being warned not to trespass.

Dan said, as lightly as he could, with a wooden smile, that he reckoned he did not rank quite as a friend, since he had met the señorita only three times. He added that he was not much of a lady's man.

The gambler wasted no more time on him. He told Juanita that there were some important railroad officials in town and he wanted her to sing for them. She walked away with him.

Presently she stepped upon a raised platform, guitar in hand. She made a gesture of drawing her *reboza* about her half-bare brown bosom before she began. The song was Spanish. Translated, it ran something like this:

> Like an eagle, brave and free,
> Is my love,
> Yet he's ever unto me
> As the dove,
> Cooing,
> Wooing,
> But, eagle-like, pursuing
> When I rove.

During the storm of applause that followed, Dan walked out of The Last Chance. He had no desire to fall foul of Jasper Ford. If the man had marked Juanita for his own, young Clifford did not need to argue with himself to know that he would walk a long way around her.

He had another reason for leaving. All evening the thought of the three helpless waifs in the camp down by the river had haunted him. He had done as much as most men would have done for them, but he felt as if he had walked out and left them to their troubles.

What more could he do? He had an inspiration. Polly Doble would know how to help them. Polly was the fairy godmother of all who were ill or in need.

He found Polly sitting on the veranda of her boarding house smoking a black cigar. She was a big angular woman, mannish, and she wore her sacklike clothes as if they had been flung on her. Her face was the color and the texture of wrinkled leather. Though a mistress of vitriolic profanity, Mrs. Doble had the reputation of concealing carefully a kind and tender heart behind her rhinoceros-like exterior.

Since Dan was one of her favorites she greeted him with a burst of jovial badinage. He bandied repartee with her cheerfully, but she could see his mind was on something else. Presently, with a shrewd look out of her wrinkled eyes, she demanded to know what it was.

'Can't I come to see a lady without some other reason?' he wanted to know.

'Get out with you. I'm no lady, and it's plain as the nose

on your face you want something from me. Out with it.'

He told her about the Sutherlands. She interrupted to ask one or two questions.

'They're so poor and so helpless, such children,' he pleaded.

Polly was not so sure about that. They might be all Dan thought them, but a lad of his age was not the best judge of a pretty girl who told a hard-luck tale.

'Maybe they won't be so poor in a month,' she said dryly.

'She isn't that kind,' Dan protested.

'What do you want me to do, boy?' she demanded.

He drew a roll of bills from his pocket. 'I want you to see they don't starve. She won't let me do anything for her. She might let you because you are a woman.'

Polly waved back his money with her cigar. 'Keep it. You'll need fodder for the faro tables. I wouldn't want you to spend anything for trash like food when it ought to go to an honest place like The Last Chance.' She rose, briskly. 'Lead me to this Little Eva. I'll take a look for myself.'

They walked down the street toward the river. On the way they crossed an *acequia,* upon the bank of which was a large cottonwood. This was known as the Challenge Tree, and it had played a considerable part in the life of Los Piños. Nailed to it was a large board, and upon this men wrote unfavorable opinions of one another. Mrs. Doble had availed herself of it on several occasions to blackmail delinquent boarders and to promise them a horsewhipping if they ever darkened her door again. Fortunately Dan had no warning of how soon and how completely a notice on the tree would shatter his own peace of mind.

'This Sutherland girl says she was born in Illinois,' Dan explained as they drew near the camp. 'When she was a little trick they moved to Tennessee. Her mother died there. After a while they crossed into Arkansas. Sutherland was a renter—raised crops on shares. I reckon he was shiftless, or maybe just plumb unlucky. You know the kind, always figuring to do better somewhere else. He didn't get along and shifted to another farm. That wasn't any better. Worn-out land, the girl says. Finally they pulled up stakes and started for Texas behind two plugs so gaunt they won't throw a shadow. Like I said, her father died this side of Santone. Some freighters buried him for her. They took up a collection for the kids, and she said, "No, thank you." I don't reckon she has a plugged dime left.'

Mrs. Doble strode into the light of the camp fire. Milly

12

was washing dishes and little Tom was wiping them. They stopped work to stare at this strange visitor. In her shapeless clothes, square-shouldered and massive, the stub of a cigar protruding from her leathery face, she was a startling sight. The Sutherlands were used to women who chewed snuff and smoked corncob pipes, but one with a cigar was shocking.

Quickly Dan spoke up, to forestall if possible an unfavorable impression. 'I've brought Mrs. Doble down to see you. She is the mother of Los Piños.'

'Blarney!' snapped the landlady, and flung the cigar stub into the fire.

'This is Miss Sutherland and her brother Tom,' continued Dan.

'Thought you said there were three of them.'

'Rose is asleep in the wagon,' explained Milly in her soft shy voice. 'She was tired after a long day.'

'Think she might be,' snorted Polly. 'Now, young woman, what do you expect to do here?'

Dan tried to be helpful. 'She thought she might—'

Abruptly Polly cut him off. 'I'm not talking to you, me lad. Save your breath to breathe with.'

'I did think of taking in washing,' Milly said timidly. 'But Mr. Clifford says the Chinese do all that.'

'He doesn't know anything about it. I'll get you all the washing you want. Where are you going to live?'

'I don't know. Maybe we'll stay in the wagon. Mr. Clifford says there isn't a house in town that can be had.'

'That boy knows nothing. I have a 'dobe house at the end of San Antonio Street. You'll move into that tomorrow. It's not much—whipsawed floor, rawhide bedstead, only one window in the front room. But it is better than nothing.'

Milly was embarrassed. Color poured into her cheeks. She had no money with which to pay rent.

Mrs. Doble breezed on, apparently oblivious of her silence.

'The rent will be two dollars a month. The shack isn't worth that, but these days you could rent a *jacal* if you had it. You'll pay me after you get your business going.' Polly turned on Dan, indignant at him for being a witness of her kindness. 'What are you standing around gawking at? Scat! Be off with you!'

Dan grinned. Before he departed he left a word of comfort for Milly. 'Don't you be scared, Miss. There's not a cot in town free tonight, so I aim to roll up in my blankets

13

the other side of that knoll. If anything scares you, give a yell.'

He did not think it necessary to tell her that with the new influx of population had come men of the vilest character who would stop at nothing.

Chapter 3

•

TWENTY-FOUR HOURS TO LEAVE

POLLY DOBLE put on a campaign for Milly as thorough as that of a candidate for political office. She went into every store, every saloon, and every gambling house in town with the announcement that a straight girl not yet seventeen wanted to support herself and her little family by taking in washing. Within twenty-four hours a corner of the little house was piled high with bundles waiting to be washed and ironed.

Day by day the number grew, in spite of Milly's efforts. The girl looked at them in despair. It was nice to have plenty of work, but it was not so good to be swamped with it.

'I'll have to put up a sign saying I can't take any more,' she told Mrs. Doble. 'It will take me a week to finish the clothes already here.'

Polly reflected. It was too bad to cut off at the start so promising a business. 'Wait,' she said, and strode out of the house.

An hour later she returned, in her wake a slant-eyed Oriental with a queue reaching to his knees.

'Ah Sin,' announced Polly. 'He's going to work for you. The washing he will do, and most of the ironing. The rest you can help him with, and you and the children will collect and deliver the clothes. If anybody tries to beat you out of your pay, I'll attend to him.'

Two days later Ah Sin came to Milly with a proposition. 'Me an' you go partners flifty-flifty, missy. You catchum clothes, Ah Sin washum.'

Milly agreed to this. After they had discussed details she

asked him with a smile if they ought to put up a sign, Sutherland and Sin.

Ah Sin shook his head seriously. 'Evelybody likum bring clothes missy, but not to punk Chinese devil. We callum missy's laundly.'

So Milly went about the town with a handcart collecting and delivering laundry. Among her best customers were the professional gamblers. They were particular about their attire and they liked to wear clean linen. It was while she was taking back a bundle of shirts to his lodging house that she met Jasper Ford.

He came to the door of his room when she knocked, a tall, arrow-straight man with black mustache, hair, and eyes. The latter fastened on her so ruthlessly that a little shock of alarm set her fluttering. They were hard as obsidian, yet a curious shallow light played in them.

'I've brought your washing, sir,' she said timidly.

It was three hours past noon, but Ford was a night owl. He had been dealing faro on the graveyard shift at The Last Chance until break of day. Her knock had interrupted him while he had been arranging his tie. In his frilled shirt and custom-made boots, without a coat and vest, he was a fine graceful figure of a man.

He stepped aside, with a bow, half ironic. 'Come in, if you please.'

Milly did not move. She said, the wild rose color deepening in her cheeks: 'It's six bits, sir.'

The man ripped the paper from the package and saw that the work was good. 'Not enough,' he said, smiling at her, and drew from his pocket a five-dollar gold piece.

'I haven't that much change,' she said.

His gaze ran over her. She had on new shoes and had made herself a cheap print dress that fitted admirably her slenderness.

'Did I mention change?' he asked.

In his voice was a touch of gaiety, in his eyes a ripple of excitement that broke through the rigid coldness as the sun through clouds.

Milly put her hands behind her back and shook her head. She had no knowledge of the world to teach her how to cope with such a man.

'You can pay me next time, sir,' she murmured, and was gone before he could stop her.

As Milly walked down Deaf Smith Street in the warm sunshine, she found herself trembling. A new emotion was tingling in her. Her excitement was born partly of fear, partly of a sense that life was opening up before her. In spite of the responsibility thrust upon her, the outlook of Milly had been that of a child. A man had looked at her, and his possessive eyes had made her aware of herself. It was as startling as if he had awakened her suddenly from sound sleep.

The man smiled cynically while he arranged his cravat before the looking glass. 'She's going to be a beauty some day, if she learns how to dress,' he thought. 'Gad, I haven't seen eyes like hers in a blue moon. Shy as a faun. I'll drop around and pay her the seventy-five cents.'

He did, twenty-four hours later.

Ah Sin was in the front room ironing a shirt. He looked obliquely at Ford, quite well aware of who the visitor was. Like many of his fellow countrymen, Ah Sin absorbed much information and imparted little.

'Where is your mistress?' asked the gambler.

'Missy out.' The Oriental continued placidly to iron.

'Out where?'

'No can tell. Somewhere.' Ah Sin inspected a shirt cuff critically.

Jasper Ford reached across the counter, caught the laundryman by the queue, and brought his head down on the board with a quick jerk. Ah Sin screamed with pain.

'Not safe to be impudent to me,' the gambler said, without raising his voice. 'Chinks are cheap in this burg. For a dollar Mex I'd twist your head off. Answer my question.'

'Missy takum home laundly. Please.'

With one final twist Ford released the queue. Ah Sin massaged his neck tenderly. It would be sore for days.

'When will she be back?'

Her partner said it would be soon. She had been gone now more than half an hour.

Ford lit a cigar and stepped to the door. He could see a man and a woman walking slowly along the bank of the *acequia* toward the house. Two Mexican boys were pitching *cuartillos*. Otherwise the landscape was deserted. The gambler leaned against the door jamb and watched the approaching couple. They moved slowly, apparently interested in their talk. The woman was young and slender, the man tall. To the observer there drifted a ripple of laughter.

The cold eyes of Ford narrowed. The girl was Milly Sutherland. So her shyness was coquetry and she had already found an admirer. Whoever he was, the man would

16

have to pass out of the picture. Jasper Ford did not like competition. When reasonable men found they were in his way, they vanished inconspicuously from the field.

As they came closer, the gambler recognized with some surprise the man beside the girl. He was the mule skinner Clifford.

A few yards distant the young couple stopped. They had picked Ford up with their first glance toward the house. Both of them were surprised, both disturbed.

The smile of the waiting man was not reassuring. 'I have come to pay a little debt,' he said to the girl. 'I hope I don't intrude.'

He held out a five-dollar gold piece.

'I still haven't change, sir,' Milly murmured. 'Perhaps Ah Sin—'

'Good old Ah Sin. We have made friends already. He would do anything for me. Wouldn't you, Ah Sin?'

But Ah Sin did not answer. He was no longer in the house. Swiftly, he had fled through the back door.

'Perhaps I could make change, Mr. Ford,' volunteered Dan, drawing silver from his pocket.

'I won't trouble you,' Ford replied with chill suavity. He turned to Milly. 'At this hour tomorrow I shall bring the correct amount. You will be at home.'

'I don't know,' she said helplessly.

'Ah! Then perhaps you will set an hour.' The gambler waited, chill eyes fixed on her.

Milly dropped her lids. 'I am so busy, sir,' she ventured in a low voice.

'But not too busy to take a stroll with this mule skinner,' he suggested.

A flush burned her cheeks. 'I—met him—while I was taking back clothes.'

His smile was hateful. 'I am quite sure of it. All work and no play makes Jill a dull girl. We can't have that. Did you name the hour? Shall we say four o'clock, tomorrow?'

She had had no experience socially. Instinct warned her that this man was dangerous, but she did not know how to escape his intentions. Nodding an assent, she slipped past him into the house.

Ford gave his attention to the young man. He spoke with ominous suavity. 'Shall we walk downtown together, Mr. Clifford?'

Dan fell into step beside him. He guessed that it was

17

not going to be a pleasant walk for him, but it had to be endured.

They passed a building going up as fast as hammer and saw could put it together. Across the street two men were nailing a clapboard roof on another. On all sides of them houses were under construction.

'Town's sure booming,' Dan said, trying to bridge an oppressive silence. 'Looks like Los Piños is going somewhere.'

'The railroads won't be in for some time,' Ford said. 'A golden chance for you freighters. When do you hit the road again?'

'I'm thinking of staying here. There's nothing in mule skinning.'

'You're better away from here,' the gambler told him curtly. 'This is no safe town for you. Go with the next mule train.'

Dan resented the sharp order to get out, but he did not want to force the issue. 'I've saved some money,' he said amiably. 'Thought I would buy two-three teams and start a freighting business of my own.'

'Start it somewhere else.' Ford permitted himself a sneer. 'For one who isn't a lady's man, you cover too much territory. My advice is to get out of town. Soon. Say tomorrow.'

Dan's throat was dry. His words came hoarsely. 'I don't aim to annoy you, Mr. Ford. Looks to me like this town is big enough for both of us to—'

The killer stopped and fixed him with his cold cruel eyes.

'Your views are not important,' he cut in. 'You've had your orders. *Vamos!*'

Ford turned on his heel and walked into The Last Chance. With an icy chill drenching his heart, Dan watched him go. He had been given a day to leave. If he stayed . . .

Chapter 4

•

DAN MEETS AN OLD FRIEND

THE thing was incredible. Half an hour earlier he had been at peace with the world. Now this ultimatum had jumped out at him. He had to run away like a frightened rabbit or take the consequences.

Without intending to do it, he had managed to annoy Jasper Ford not only once but twice. Dan was a realist. He faced facts as he found them. The gambler no doubt was trading on his reputation and its effect upon a run-of-the-road mule skinner. He expected his order to be obeyed, but if Clifford stood his ground there would be a killing. Dan wasted no time in complaints at Ford's high-handed lawlessness. On the wild frontier a man's life was his own personal affair and not that of the community. That was why every man carried a revolver strapped to his hip, because he was never sure whether he would have to kill or be killed before night. Among quiet citizens such an emergency was rare, but when it came each man was his own court of last resort.

The dusty street was filled with men milling to and fro. On every corner lot was a saloon. From dance halls came the sound of tinny music. Two variety theaters would begin operations as soon as darkness fell. Los Piños devoted itself seriously to the business of amusement.

In front of the Ninety and Nine, a house kept by Madam Jeannette, Dan came face to face with an old friend. The man was a lank Kentuckian, evidently of great physical strength, rough and unkempt and shabby. At sight of Dan he gave a shout of greeting.

'Where in time did you come from, Obigod?' Clifford asked, gripping the other's great hand. 'Last time I saw you was at Dodge.'

The two had gone up the trail together with a herd of cattle. On the way, while crossing the Canadian in flood, Dan had saved Sam Jones from drowning after the horse of the Kentuckian had been knocked senseless by a floating log. The young man still remembered the promise made by the rescued man. 'I've got no money, young fellow, but if you ever get into a difficulty I'll shoot you out of it, Obigod.' Well, Dan was in trouble now, but he knew that nobody except himself could find a way out of it. A man had to shoot himself out of his own scrapes.

The two men walked into the Crystal Palace and took a seat at a table. Jones looked around him curiously.

'Some different from Dave Shotwell's old place,' he said. 'Mahogany bars and French plate glass and men behind the bars wearing white aprons and diamond studs, Obigod.'

'Yes, we had rough characters here in the old days, but even though they were tough they were men and not rats.' Dan looked inquiringly at his friend. 'I don't know how long you have been here this trip, but I don't reckon I have to tell you that half the vermin of the West has been spewed into Los Piños. The town is full of holdups and tin horns and criminals.'

'So I've heard. I don't mind telling you that I came here to get two of them. I'm with the Texas rangers.' The big Kentuckian tacked on the oath with which he larded almost every sentence, the one that had earned him his nickname.

Dan laughed, ruefully. 'I wish that one of the two you came to get was a bird called Jasper Ford.'

The ranger slanted a searching look at Clifford. 'You're not in a mix-up with Jas Ford?' he said.

'He has given me twenty-four hours to leave town.'

Jones put down his mug of beer on the table. 'Spill the story, boy.'

The young man told the facts briefly. He summed up the matter in a sentence. 'So I have to fight or run.'

The big man frowned. 'Unless someone took a crack at him first.'

Dan shook his head. 'No, sir, I don't aim to crawfish out of this and leave you to hold the sack.'

'He's sudden death, this Ford. I reckon you'd better light out for a while.'

The mouth of the mule skinner became a straight obstinate line. 'No,' he said bluntly.

'This fellow has a big rep as a killer. He's a dead shot, they claim. How about you? Are you any kind of a shot?'

'Fair to average. I'd like to take him on at fist and skull fighting, but no chance of that.'

'Boy, we've got to put our thinking caps on. Must be some way out of this. How would it do for me to go to him and promise that you wouldn't ever see either of these girls again? That might satisfy him.'

'It wouldn't satisfy me.' Dan stared bleakly at his beer. 'But I may have to do it just the same.'

'I could tell him you're just a kid and that you didn't mean to butt in on his play. We could ease you out of the jam, don't you reckon?'

'I tried to talk him out of it,' Dan mentioned. 'No luck.'

'He'll have had time to cool down by now, and anyhow I'm a ranger. Most of these slick-fingered gentry don't like for us to get on their tails. Do no harm for me to take a whirl at fixing this up with him.'

'No, if you'll stop at that,' Dan said, looking at him steadily. 'But I won't have you getting into a row with him on my account. You've got to promise you won't, Obigod.'

The ranger grinned. 'I'll be trying to duck trouble for you, not to make it for myself. This fellow is poison. I don't want him stinging me.'

Dan waited while his friend went to The Last Chance to see Jasper Ford. He did not expect it would be of any use. The killer liked to see his victims squirm. The man was confident his order to leave would be obeyed. There was not much chance that he would back down from the position he had taken.

Chapter 5

•

AN INVOLUNTARY BATH

THERE were five in the game, three of them lately arrived at Los Piños with money in their pockets. Jasper Ford held a jack full, and the betting was lively. Naturally he was annoyed when he became aware that the big rawboned fellow at his elbow wanted to speak with him.

'Don't you see I'm busy?' he asked curtly.

'Yes, sir. I want to see you only a minute.' The stranger held his ground.

'All right. You see me. Take a good look . . . Kick it ten.' Ford pushed chips into the pot, then asked a question with obvious irritation. 'Who in Mexico are you, anyhow?'

'Name is Sam Jones—of the rangers,' the big man said gently, almost apologetically.

Ford raked him with a hard, cold eye. He said nothing until the play was completed and he had drawn in the pot. This done, he rose and stepped to one side.

'Do you claim you want me?' he asked in a low, cool voice.

'No. This is private business, Mr. Ford. About young Clifford. Seems he made you sore. The kid's sorry. He didn't aim to do that. I'd like to fix it up for him with you.'

'Are you buying chips in the game, Mr. Ranger Jones?' asked the gambler, the words almost seeming to drip from his thin lips. 'Or are you sweating it?'

'I'm here as young Clifford's friend,' Jones said quietly.

21

'He hauled me outa the Canadian onct when I didn't have a dead man's chance. We're grown stuff, you an' me, but he's only a boy. I would appreciate it if you would forget that he has annoyed you. From now on he'll sure keep out of yore way.'

Ford was not in a good humor. Moreover, he did not want the impression to get around that he would weaken on a threat he had made.

'No,' he decided harshly. 'Tell him he has to get out.' The gambler went back to the poker game.

Jones returned to the Crystal Palace and reported failure.

'I figured it would be thataway,' Dan said. 'Well, I've got to hit the trail—or be killed.'

'Light out, Dan,' advised his friend. 'Nobody knows this but him and me. It won't hurt yore rep any.'

'*I* know it,' the young man replied. 'I'll know all my life that I let this wolf run me outa town because I was afraid to stay and fight.'

'Let's take a walk,' the ranger proposed. 'I'd like to see how well you can shoot.'

They went down to the river and stuck a sheet of paper on a tree. The paper was about six by eight inches. Dan stood back fifteen paces and fired five shots. One bullet hit the mark, three struck the tree, one went wild.

'Now let's see you pump lead fast as you can,' Jones said.

Dan drew and fired as rapidly as he could. Only one bullet was embedded in the bark. None had touched the paper.

'It would be fine except for two things,' the ranger pronounced. 'You're slow on the draw and you can't shoot straight. I reckon it's good-bye Los Piños for you, son.' He punctuated his sentences with repetitions of his favorite oath.

'I reckon,' Dan agreed bitterly.

He had his little round of farewells to make. There was Polly Doble. After supper he dropped around to her boarding-house. She heard the news with resentful profanity and an offer to give Jasper Ford such a tongue-lashing as he had never before had. Her honest indignation warmed Dan, but he had to decline her offer. It would do him no good to get the reputation of hiding behind a woman's skirts.

From the Doble boarding-house he walked down to the little house at the end of San Antonio Street. Milly came to the door.

'I've got to leave town,' he told her. 'Will you go for a walk with me along the *acequia*?'

'In a minute,' she nodded. 'Soon as Tom has said his prayers and got to bed.'

Presently she joined him. They walked together side by side under the stars. Both of them were shy. Neither had anything to say, at least nothing that could be expressed easily in words.

'Are you going with a freight outfit?' she asked at last.

'No. I don't know where I'm going.' He gulped out a confession. 'I've been ordered to leave Los Piños.'

'But—I don't understand—'

'That fellow Ford has given me twenty-four hours to get out.'

She was startled. 'What right has he to do that?'

Dan laughed bitterly. 'They say he has killed twelve men. That's right enough for this town.'

Milly stared at him, white-faced. 'You mean that if you don't go . . .'

'If I don't go I'll be number thirteen.'

'You poor boy,' she said, after a moment of silence. 'It's all on my account. I've brought trouble to you, just because you were kind and good to us.'

He could see her face begin to work. 'No, I had trouble with him before that. Nothing of any importance. He just didn't like me and ordered me to go.'

'Isn't there any law here?' she cried.

'A man has to make his own law. This man is sure death with a pistol, so nobody will go against him. It's all right. Don't worry about me. I came to tell you, so you would understand why I quit coming to be neighborly.'

They stood on the bank of the *acequia* looking helplessly at each other. There was nothing to be done about it. He did not want to go and she did not want him to leave, but a malign fate had decreed that he must.

The ditch was running bank full. Occasionally a wave lapped up to the edge of the path upon which they stood.

'I'll never forget how good you have been to us,' she said in a low voice. 'Mrs. Doble told me you wanted to give her a lot of money for us.'

He flushed indignantly. 'She had no right to tell you that. It wasn't anything. I figured that a loan might—'

His words died away. Someone was moving along the path toward them. Almost at the same time they became aware that the approaching man was Jasper Ford. The heart of the girl turned over. Had he come to make trouble for the lad he was driving out of the community?

23

The gambler smiled, the cold, thin-lipped smile that went with eyes implacably hard.

'It's such a divine night I decided not to wait until tomorrow,' he explained. 'Since we are going to be friends, why not begin now, Miss Sutherland? The poet Shakespeare says,

> In delay there lies no plenty,
> Then come kiss me, sweet and twenty.

He is a hundred times right. A moon, a maid, a man! What a delectable combination!' Ford turned insolently to Dan. 'You're leaving town, I understand. Tonight? Or is it tomorrow morning? How is it the old song goes? "We shall meet and we shall miss you." Life is made up of meetings and partings. You must be a philosopher, Mr. Clifford.'

Anger boiled up in Dan. The man's raffish impudence, his sneering contempt, cut at the youthful pride of the victim like a whiplash. The finger nails of the mule skinner bit into the palms of his clenched hands. He wanted to lash out furiously at the cold, derisive face.

'Los Piños is full of temptations for a young man,' the jeering voice went on. 'I think you are making a wise decision in turning your back on such a Sodom. You will carry our best wishes with you when you go.'

Dan had kept telling himself he must be careful, must do nothing rash. The impulse that flamed into action seemed to be born of no volition on his part. When his knotty fist crashed between the eyes of the gambler he was as much surprised as Ford could have been. It amazed him to see the head shoot back, to see the body catapulted from the path into the *acequia*.

The assault released in Dan forces that effected a chemical change mentally. Fear of consequences vanished. He had chosen his course and would follow it.

Ford came sputtering from the water and clung to the bank. In another moment he would be on dry land. Swiftly Dan moved forward, caught the head by the lank black hair, and soused it under the water. Presently he let it emerge for a breath of air, then plunged it down again. When at last he dragged the gambler from the stream, Ford lay on the path limp and gasping. Before he could gather his senses, Dan went over his clothes and removed from a pocket a revolver. This he dropped into his coat.

24

'I'm going to . . . kill you,' Ford said, still struggling for breath.

'Don't be too sure of it,' Dan said lightly, almost cheerfully. 'We'll know about that later. Anyway, I can't get scared at a half-drowned rat. Get up and hit the grit. You're not wanted here.'

The man rose, dripping in rivulets. He was not as imposing a figure as he had been a few minutes earlier.

'You're a dead man right now,' Ford panted, hate flaming in his eyes.

'If you get me scared I'm liable to bump you off here while it is safe,' Dan told him.

An idea came to the young man, one bold and audacious. He might as well be hanged for a sheep as a lamb.

'Changed my mind,' he went on pleasantly. 'I'm going downtown with you, Mr. Ford. We'll go to The Last Chance and get you a drink to keep you from catching cold.'

Ford looked at him venomously. 'I'm not going to The Last Chance,' he gulped.

'Yes, sir. We'll mosey right down there.' A gleam of Satanic mirth lit young Clifford's eyes. To take Ford into the gambling house in his present condition would be fatal to the man's prestige, or at least would greatly diminish it. 'You'll excuse us, won't you, Miss Sutherland?'

'I'm not going,' Ford repeated.

'Oh, yes, you're going, if I have to drag you in by the hair of the head,' Dan said, with a grin. 'Can't have you getting pneumonia, a prominent citizen like you.'

Ford tried to run. In a dozen long strides Dan caught up with him. His strong fingers closed on the back of the other's neck. The gambler twisted free and fought. Dan did not hit him a second time. He spun the man round and kicked him hard, then seized him by the shoulders and shook him until his teeth chattered.

The killer had drawn in for years the vitiated air of gambling houses. He had lived soft and easy. His muscles had grown flabby. Dan was hard as steel, toughened by years of activity in the outdoors. There was not an ounce of superfluous flesh on his supple body. A half-grown boy would have been no easier to handle than Ford.

The bully was almost sobbing with rage. He cried out again that he would kill Clifford as soon as he had a chance.

'You're shaking with the cold,' Dan told him solicitously. 'We'll hop right down to The Last Chance and get two-three drinks under your belt.'

'You'll be careful, won't you?' Milly said to Dan in a low, awed voice.

A queer jubilance sang through Dan's veins. He had felt as spiritless as a whipped cur. Now he was, for a moment at least, top dog.

'Y'betcha!' he promised. 'Don't you worry, Miss Milly. I'll be saying *Adios* for tonight.'

A prod of his knee urged the pinioned man down the path.

Chapter 6
•
DAN PAYS A FINE

THE Last Chance bulged with the milling crowd. Around the keno, faro, roulette, and chuck-a-luck tables fixed groups resisted the pressure of the more restless ones. Hard-faced dealers and *croupiers* raked in the money. The hum of voices, the rattle of chips, the shuffling of feet made a constant din.

Dan brought his reluctant prisoner through the front door and pushed him up to the platform raised above the level of the rest of the floor. The incurious glances of men drifted to them and were held by sheer amazement. Jasper Ford was known as the best-dressed man in town. Now his immaculate clothes were soggy, his hair lank and wet, his cold classical face a map of impotent fury. One of the gambler's eyes was blackened and almost closed, the other was swelling. Apparently he was here by compulsion.

In an incredibly short time the games were suspended and all attention focused on the two on the platform. There was drama there, perhaps impending tragedy. The noise died down.

'Mr. Ford took a bath in the *acequia*,' Dan explained. 'He's some chilled. I promised him a drink. Jim, will you fix him up a stiff one?'

'Someone give me a gun!' Ford cried huskily. 'I'm going to kill this Smart Aleck.'

With his left hand Dan drew the other man's revolver from a coat pocket. 'Sho! You don't want a gun. After I kicked you into the ditch I took one gun away from you. What would be the use of another to you? You hadn't ought to fool with guns. They're liable to get you into trouble.'

A hundred pair of eyes stared at them. Los Piños could not believe the obvious explanation, that the famous gunman had been manhandled by this youth, flung into a ditch, disarmed, and been dragged to public humiliation. The story was not credible, yet had to be accepted.

Ford started to leap from the platform. An iron grip caught him by the coat collar.

'Don't push on the reins,' Dan advised. 'You haven't had your drink yet.'

The raging eyes of the bad man fastened on those of one of his associates. 'Throw me a gun, Stone,' he implored.

'Obigod, I wouldn't do that, Stone,' a voice advised. 'We'll sweat the game and let them play their own hands.'

Two or three of Ford's crowd had begun to move toward the platform. Dan was relieved to see friends of his pushing through the mob. Not only was there Sam Jones. His eye picked up the wagon boss Pete Mulrooney and a huge teamster known as Yorky.

'There will be no shenanigan!' Mulrooney shouted. 'Fair play for the kid. Eh, boys?'

'That's right,' someone in the back of the hall cried.

There was a murmur of assent. Men who had feared Ford and his associates and suffered silently under their insolence were picking up courage at this surprising discomfiture of the killer.

'Is the *alcalde* of this burg present?' asked Dan.

A man pushed through the jam. 'I'm mayor. What do you want with me?' he wanted to know.

'I want to settle up. There's a fine of five dollars for throwing refuse into the *acequia*. I flung this scalawag in a while ago. Here's the five.' Dan flipped a gold piece in the direction of the mayor.

There was a roar of laughter. It died away when Ford shouted his defiance.

'Laugh on, you fools! Inside of twenty-four hours this Smart Aleck will be buried in Boot Hill. And if you get funny with me, he won't be alone.'

'So says Mr. Jasper Ford,' Dan came back with a cheerful grin.

The difference in his attitude was amazing. Half an hour ago he had been a humiliated boy, ready to scuttle away out of danger to save his life. Since then he had gained com-

27

plete poise and assurance. He was not afraid to stand up with the eyes of Los Piños on him, the focus of the town's astounded attention. He did not fear what the future would bring. This dreaded killer was not invulnerable. The fellow had been soft as putty in his sinewy young hands.

The lank ranger had pushed close to the platform. 'Ain't you gettin' pretty brash, Dan, after this hell-a-miler gave you twenty-four hours to get outa town?' he asked, loud enough for all to hear.

'He yapped around so much he got to annoying me, Obigod, so I had to cuff him around some,' explained Dan.

'Boy, you take the cake,' Jones chuckled. 'Didn't anybody ever tell you this wolf was dangerous?'

'Why, no! Is he?' Dan's face was full of innocent surprise. 'I never would have guessed it. He doesn't look thataway to me.'

Ford made a snatch at the gun in the young man's holster. Dan caught his wrist and twisted the arm. The gambler fought against the grip, could not break it, and at last collapsed with a yelp beneath the torturing pain.

'You better be good,' advised Dan. 'That's no way to act. First thing you know you'll hurt yourself.'

Again Ford cried out that he was going to kill him as soon as he could.

'Right you are, Jas!' Stone shouted. 'He has written his ticket to hell. Start him soon.'

Someone in the crowd flung out a jeer. 'I sure never expected to see a kid of a mule skinner tame that bad wolf Ford.'

'Wait till tomorrow.' Ford flung back. 'That's all I ask.'

'I reckon I better take you home,' Dan said. 'Got to put you to bed, or you'll be getting pneumonia and you won't be able to put on that show you're promising the boys. But you'd ought to take that drink first. Have you got it fixed, Jim? Mr. Ford is kinda delicate. We don't want to take any chances of losing him.'

Again someone barked out a harsh laugh and cut it short abruptly lest it prove dangerous.

A capper for the house, by name Le Page, pushed forward to the platform. He was a rat-eyed, narrow-chested man with a bad reputation as a quarrelsome, vindictive fellow swift on the draw.

'Think Jas is in danger, do you?' he sneered, looking up at Dan. 'Don't get biggity, fellow. Your grave is already dug.'

Sam Jones stood at his elbow. 'You takin' a stack of chips, Mr. Le Page?' the ranger asked, almost in a murmur.

The gambler turned on him. 'Are you claiming I can't open my mouth?' he demanded.

'Nothin' like that. But we're innocent bystanders, wouldn't you say? I'd hate to find out officially you or anyone else was inciting to riot.'

'I don't have to do that,' retorted Le Page. 'That fool mule skinner has done all the inciting necessary. At the proper time Jas will riot for about a quarter of a second and after that everything will be lovely.'

'That's yore guess.' The favorite oath of the ranger rolled out. 'Mine would be different. No can tell. But you can bet yore bottom dollar, Mr. Le Page, that the kid will get a run for his money. I'm goin' to see to that personal. This is between him and Jas Ford. A lot of bully-puss gunmen aren't goin' to start hurrahing him.'

'The thirty dollars a month you get for chasing greaser rustlers through the brush seems to cover a lot of territory,' the capper said out of a corner of his mouth. 'Too much, I'd say. Once I knew a man who lived to be a hundred minding his own business.'

'You might think that last over yore own self,' Jones advised.

What had started as an individual difficulty between two men had begun to take on a broader aspect, to define the schism in the town already felt but not openly recognized. Led by the professional gamblers, the riffraff that had swept into the town had changed it from a gay and roistering frontier village to a nest of vice. Women of loose character robbed their clients while intoxicated, thugs nightly plied their trade as hold-ups, and desperadoes committed murder without giving their victims a chance. Even the good citizens of Los Piños, with a few notable exceptions, were in favor of an open town. They gambled, with the sky the limit. They drank, some more, some less. But they objected to this flagrant flaunting of crime that disregarded so wholly the standards of the outdoor West. They were uneasy at its prevalence.

The reputation of Jasper Ford and some of his associates had daunted them. The citizens of the town were robust men, ready to fight if they must, but not willing to stake their lives against those of professional gunmen and ruffians who struck at night from the dark. Now a boy, one of no fame in the community, had challenged and made ridiculous the most redoubtable of the desperadoes. Even then they might have stood back and waited the issue if Obigod Jones had not dragged their quarrel into the light.

The bartender Jim brought to Ford the glass of whiskey Dan had ordered. Furious, the gambler seized the glass and flung it into the face of young Clifford.

Deliberately but swiftly, Dan gripped the man, whirled him round, and kicked him from the platform. Still without hurry, the mule skinner went down the steps and moved through the crowd to the door. He heard voices, some approving and others denouncing, but he looked neither to the right nor the left. Pushing through the door, he strode down the dusty street.

Chapter 7

•

DAN ACCEPTS
A CHALLENGE

DAN heard footsteps behind him and turned. His hand slid to the butt of his gun.

'Obigod, don't shoot, boy,' a voice called.

The mule skinner's laugh was pitched to a high note. Now that the crisis was momentarily past, he was feeling a reaction. 'Got to save my bullets for someone else,' he said.

Jones linked an arm in his. 'Let's go where we can talk.' He moved toward the river.

'I sure have spilled the beans.' Dan said.

The ranger chuckled. 'Spilled a whole potful of hot ones on Jas Ford and his friends.'

'They would have bumped me off right there in The Last Chance if you hadn't stood up to 'em,' Dan said gratefully.

'Maybe. But, boy, you started something.'

'Something I can't finish. The whole gang will be down on me now.'

'On you and on me too. But we've got the scalawags thinking. Mulrooney and the freighters will stand by you. So will a lot of other good citizens who have put up with a lot. You're not playin' a lone hand now.'

'I'll be playing one, won't I, when Jasper Ford turns his gun loose on me?'

'If he does. Let's wait and see. You hole up until that wolf has declared himself.'

Ford declared himself promptly. Mulrooney came to Dan with news while the boy was eating breakfast next morning.

'He's got you posted on the big tree,' the wagon boss announced.

'A challenge?'

'You done called the turn.' Mulrooney took an envelope from his pocket. 'I copied it on an old letter.'

He handed the envelope to Jones, who was eating with his friend.

The ranger read aloud.

A contemptible pup who calls himself Daniel Clifford has insulted me. I serve notice on him to go armed, as I intend to kill him at sight. At two o'clock this afternoon I shall be waiting at the corner of San Antonio and River Streets. If he has a spark of manhood he will not skulk out of this meeting.

'He gave the date and signed it Jasper Ford,' Mulrooney mentioned.

Dan put down his coffee-cup and looked across the table at a picture on the wall. He said nothing. The elation of the evening before had died down in him. He had let himself be maneuvered into a situation from which there was no escape.

'I have teams going out today,' Mulrooney went on. 'What say I get you out of town covered up in one of the wagons?'

'No,' said Dan.

'You hate to back water,' the wagon boss continued. "Nobody enjoys that, but once in a while a fellow has to crawfish. This Ford is a dead shot. He always gets his man. You wouldn't have a look-in, boy.'

'I know.' Dan moistened his dry lips with the tip of his tongue. 'But I've made my brags. I've got to stay.'

Jones looked at him and understood. He poured his coffee into a saucer to let it cool, then leaned back in his chair and stretched his long lank limbs. 'No use arguing with him, Mulrooney,' the ranger said. 'He's in a hell of a fix, but he has got to go through from hell to breakfast.'

'Yes,' Dan agreed. He remembered what Jasper Ford had said, that he was already a dead man. A chill went through him. Someone was walking on his grave.

'But he doesn't have to fight this mankiller with pistols,' the ranger said.

'What with, then? Rifles—sawed-off shotguns?' Mulrooney asked.

'No.' Jones stroked a stubbly chin. 'Dan here is the chal-

31

lenged party. This Ford claims he is a Southern gentleman. Of course the best people where he came from wouldn't spit on him, but that ain't the point. He's always made that play about his honor. We'll call it. Dan has the choice of weapons. The code Ford talks about so much says so. Good enough.'

Dan frowned at his friend, trying to get his meaning. 'If you're thinking of a fist and skull fight in a ring, you can forget it. Ford wouldn't go in for it. He would claim only ruffians fought thataway.'

'I wasn't thinkin' of that,' the ranger said, with a grin. 'How would you like to have Ford carve you with a Bowie knife?'

'I wouldn't like it,' Dan said promptly. 'Once a drunken teamster drew a knife on me and I certainly split the wind getting away.'

'Most men would feel like that.' To this the raw-boned ranger added a casual rider. 'Ford, for one, I'd bet a dollar Mex against a chew of tobacco.'

'You couldn't get him to fight in that barbarous way, even if I wanted him to—and I don't. Jumping Moses, we'd carve each other to strips. You must be crazy, Obigod.'

'My idea would be to tie a four-foot rope around the left wrist of both of you and let you go it to a fare-you-well,' Jones said equably.

'What's eatin' you?' Dan snapped. 'I'm not yearnin' to get slashed with a hunting knife. I'd rather stop a bullet if it had to be.'

'So would Jas Ford.' The ranger looked over the young man's broad, well-packed shoulders and the rippling muscles on his arms. 'You're a big husky roughneck. Ford knows all about that already. If you accepted his challenge and said you'd fight the way I'm tellin' you, he would figure you were an expert with a knife. I'd kinda help him to that conclusion. He couldn't be dragged into a ring with you.'

'He'd brush that aside and drop me with a gun first chance he gets.'

'Maybe not. This town knows if he fights you with a gun, it will be plain murder. If we work up a sentiment—and I'll see to that—he may be scared to take a chance of gettin' lynched. We'll noise it around that you're protectin' this young lady from his scoundrelly approaches.'

'No,' Dan said sharply.

'All right. Leave her out of it. This will be the proposition I'll put up, and all Los Piños will get it straight. "Fine, Mr. Ford, you're a brave gent honin' for a fight and here's one handed you on yore lap. You'll take it thataway or not a-tall!" '

'You think he'd eat crow,' Mulrooney said.

Dan shook his head. 'He'd never back down now. He couldn't.'

'He wouldn't call it that. He'd claim he was ready to fight like a gentleman, and if you were the kind of a hill-billy who wanted to go gougin' with a knife he would prefer to have no dealings with you.'

'Maybeso,' Dan agreed. 'And afterwards he would have me shot down some night from ambush.'

'Sure—if you stood around like a bump on a log and gave him a chance. I'm not claimin' he'll love you like a long-lost brother. All I say is maybe we can dig you out of the hole you're in right now.'

Jones desisted from further argument to let his point sink home. He lifted the saucer, blew on it, and downed the contents in one gulp.

The eyes of Mulrooney gleamed. He stroked his big red beard. 'Something to your idea, Obigod. I'd like to see Ford's face when he reads that Dan will fight him with knives. But I ain't so sure the boy hasn't got the right of it. Ford is a killer. He's liable to blaze away with his gun right off.'

'First thing he'd think of,' admitted Sam. 'We'd have to fix it so he couldn't. Maybe we can't. Anyhow, we won't lose anything by our bluff.'

'No,' agreed Dan. 'All right. Do we stick a notice on the tree?'

'Yes, siree. A stiff one. Get paper, boy.' The ranger piled the breakfast things at one end of the table to clear a space.

To write an answer to the challenge that suited him took Dan half an hour. The one the wagon boss carried with him to nail on the tree read as follows:

I have just been informed that a murderous scoundrel passing under the name of Jasper Ford has challenged me to a duel. I accept this, and as the challenged party hereby choose the conditions.

This morning I am having a grave dug on Boot Hill. At four o'clock this afternoon we shall fight beside it with knives, the blades to be not less than eight inches long, the ends of a five-foot rope tied to our left wrists. The one who falls will be buried in the grave. *Ahora es el tiempo.*

DAN CLIFFORD

33

The Spanish phrase had been a contribution from the ranger.

'Now is the time,' he translated, rolling the words as if they pleased him. 'Kinda sounds like a clock was ticking away the last hours for him. All gamblers are superstitious. He'll get to figurin' his luck has run out.'

'Maybe,' Dan said doubtfully. Today he was no optimist.

Sam rose. 'Got to go and fix things up. You stay right here, boy. Don't leave the house. I'll be back after a while.'

'What you got to fix up?' Dan asked.

'Lots of thing. Got to hire a Mexican to dig a grave. Goin' to buy two Bowie Knives. Want to show them to Jas Ford and see how he likes them.'

Jones departed, apparently in a cheerful mood. Dan reflected that after all the ranger was not the one who was likely to be shot. The words of a current song drifted back to young Clifford.

'He's a killer and a hater,
  He's the great annihilator,
  He's the terror of the boundless prai-ree.'

Sam was certainly taking another man's trouble jauntily.

Chapter 8

•

RANGER JONES SCORES

SAM JONES carried the problem to Polly Doble. He told the story, then made the suggestion that was in his mind.

'The boy has sure enough got his tail in a crack,' he said. 'Just one thing to do, and that is to line this town up solid as we can behind him. Ford has been making his play at this Sutherland girl. We've got to make it look like Dan is in this difficulty because he protected the girl against Ford. If we can get that across to folks, public sentiment won't let this killer murder Dan.'

'What does Dan say?' asked Polly.

'He says no. He won't have Miss Sutherland brought into it. But by crikes, we've got to play our hand for all there

34

is in it. Question is, will the girl back our play if anyone comes to her.'

'She'll do anything I tell her to do if she thinks it will help Dan.'

'Good. Well, we've got to get busy as a hive of swarming bees.'

They discussed the best way to get Dan's side of the story to the town. Polly undertook to take charge of the publicity.

She called first on Milly.

The girl listened silently and began to weep. 'It's all on account of me,' she wailed. 'That man will kill him, and he's only a boy.'

'We've got to save him,' Polly said flatly. 'You must help. I'm going to give it out that Jasper Ford was pestering you and Dan wouldn't let him. Will you stand by that?'

Milly promised that she would.

Mrs. Doble called on half a dozen friends and sent them into saloons and gambling halls with the story. Inside of two hours everybody in Los Piños had been told that Dan Clifford was going to be killed by Ford because he had tried to help an innocent girl the gambler was pursuing.

In the telling the tale grew. Ford had a bad reputation as a hunter of women, and those on the street were ready to believe anything against him. He became the villain and Dan the hero of the story.

As soon as Le Page got wind of what was afoot, he went to Ford. The gambling clique tried to stem the tide of public opinion by a denial, but few gave this credence. While the friends of the killer were still busy explaining, word came to them of the terms upon which the mule skinner had accepted the challenge.

Ford blew up in anger. He could see his prey slipping away from him and he swore not to be balked.

Into The Last Chance walked Sam Jones. Jasper Ford strode across the room to him.

'You're one of this scalawag's friends,' he said, white with rage. 'Tell him I'm going to rub him out as sure as hell's hot. He can't get away with a trick like this.'

'Fine, Mr. Ford,' the ranger said, purposely misunderstanding him. 'He'll be waitin' for you at the grave. I've bought two brand-new Bowies. Like you to look at them and see if you think they'll do. I've had them ground till they are sharp as razors.'

He opened a paper package and showed two knives. One of them he held out for Ford to inspect.

The gambler put his hands behind him. 'I'm going to kill him with a revolver—on sight—just as I said,' he announced harshly.

The ranger shook his head. 'I don't reckon so, Mr. Ford. I'm not aimin' to annoy you, but I don't reckon Los Piños would like that. A fair fight is one thing, but this boy wouldn't have a dead man's chance against you with pistols. We all know that. Now with knives, you two tied together, it would be an even-steven break.'

A dozen men were listening. None of them said anything.

'I'm a white man and a gentleman,' Ford said coldly. 'I don't fight like a greaser. I have been insulted, and I intend to kill this fellow in a civilized way.'

'All right,' assented the ranger. 'Knives are out, since you don't think that a Christian way to kill yore man. Clifford is willin' to make it double-barreled shotguns loaded with buckshot at ten paces. Anything that is reasonable will suit him.'

'No,' Ford declined curtly. 'He's trying to duck out. It don't go. I'm going to rub him out today.'

Sam helped himself deliberately to a chew of tobacco. 'Is it yore idea of a civilized Christian killin' that it has got to be a lead-pipe cinch for you, Mr. Ford?' he drawled.

'He'll have a gun in his hand,' the gambler answered angrily.

The ranger decided it was time to submit the question to public opinion. 'Would it look to you like an even break, Mr. Stevens?' he asked a bronzed blue-eyed cattleman.

Lon Stevens was a man of courage. He had fought the Comanches and the Kiowas. It was a tenet of his creed not to interfere in other men's difficulties. Yesterday he might have kept silent, but now it seemed to him that the issue was drawn and a good citizen ought to speak.

For an instant he hesitated, to find words not too offensive, then decided to speak the blunt truth.

'For all the chance he'd have, you might just as well hogtie the boy and shoot him between the eyes,' he said, looking straight at Ford.

Jones had picked the right man of whom to ask his question. None of the others present would have dared say as much, but they backed Stevens with a murmur of assent.

Furiously Ford glared at them.

The man Stone was seated at a table playing solitaire. He lifted cold eyes to ask a sneering question. 'This mule skinner is grown stuff, isn't he?'

'That's what he claims,' the ranger answered. 'Says he is willin' to prove it with a sawed-off shotgun if yore friend is afraid of a knife.'

The thin-lipped smile of Stone was skeptical. 'I'm doubting that. Call his bluff, Jas, and see him go climb a tall tree.'

'That's sure the way to find out what he would do,' Sam said.

'What's the idea in you-all getting into a sweat to protect this bird Clifford?' Stone asked, playing a jack of diamonds on his queen of spades. 'He was big enough to beat up Jas and insult him, but he isn't big enough to stand behind a gun and take his medicine.'

'There's a story about some trouble over a girl,' Stevens ventured. 'I don't claim it is true, because I don't know. But if it is, the insult did not start from Clifford.'

'The story is a lie!' Ford cried, pallid with fury.

It seemed to him that the whole town was in a conspiracy to frustrate his revenge. No doubt the Sutherland girl would back up anything Clifford said.

'If it is, all you have to do is to get the young lady to say so,' the ranger mentioned.

Stone played a card to the center. 'Men always have fought about women,' he said. 'They always will. Nothing in that to kick up a dust about.'

'Story is this isn't a woman but a girl, a decent one trying to support her little family,' Stevens said noncommittally.

'I didn't do the girl any harm,' Ford burst out in exasperation.

'Maybe it would be a good idea to find out how the young lady feels about it,' someone said.

Ford slammed his fist down on a card table. 'I'm going to kill this cuss today! That's short and sweet.'

'Wish you would come out to Boot Hill with me and see the grave, Mr. Ford,' said Sam. 'I want to make sure we're havin' it made long enough.' His gaze ranged up and down the gambler, as if he was mentally measuring his height.

Ford turned abruptly and walked away.

Chapter 9

•

REPRIEVED

DAN waited with Sam Jones in a Mexican *jacal* down by the river. They were expecting Mulrooney soon with a report as to the decision of the enemy. The afternoon was wearing along. Presently the whole town would know whether Ford was going to persist in his intention of killing young Clifford at sight regardless of the pressure of public opinion.

The threatened man was as nervous as an over-trained prize-fighter. He eased the revolver in its scabbard to make sure of an unimpeded draw. He paced up and down the dirt floor. More than once he drank from the tin dipper in the pail of water resting on a box near the door.

Sam talked, to relieve the strain. His manner was casual, his voice cheerful.

Two men passed the shack on their way uptown. Those inside heard their words.

'I've never seen Jas Ford in action,' one said. 'They claim he is chain lightnin'. Looks like this mule skinner got too brash. Jas will rub him out sure. Like to watch the rookus from a safe place if I can.'

'Ford will get the kid, I reckon,' the other replied. 'But it's a dirty business just the same. This Clifford has got sand in his craw. I kinda hate to see . . .'

Through the wattled walls Dan watched them on their way. With a sick smile he turned to his friend.

'Looks like a good time is going to be had by all—except one,' he said.

'Ford won't go through,' Sam prophesied. 'By now he knows what this town thinks. You've shoved plenty of chips in the pot for a raise. He has got to call or quit. His own crowd woudn't back him in any other play. They dassent. It would get them all in bad, and they know it. The whole caboodle might get kicked outa town, and the pickin's are too good to give up. No, sir. He'll crawl out of it.'

'I don't think so,' Dan replied. 'He's crazy mad.'

'Don't doubt it, but Stevens and the mayor have told him

straight he must quit. That girl's story did it. She went all the way for you.'

'I told you to keep her out of it,' Dan reproached.

'So you did, but I couldn't see my way to obligin' you.' Sam walked to the door and looked out. 'Here comes Mulrooney now.'

The wagon boss let out a whoop while he was still twenty-five yards away. ''S all right. The shootin' is off. Ford has done posted a notice on the tree sayin' he fights only like a gentleman and since you don't he'll have no truck with you.'

A wave of dizziness passed through Dan. He steadied himself. He knew what it was to be reprieved from impending death.

'Says for you to keep outa his way,' Mulrooney went on. 'Says he won't be responsible if you annoy him any more.'

'I certainly won't annoy him if I can help it,' Dan said fervently.

'Don't trust that bird,' advised the wagon boss. 'He's a treacherous sidewinder. Now this is all over I'd get outa town if I was you—slide out kinda inconspicuous.'

'I am going to buy three wagon teams and haul salt from the lakes,' Dan said. 'Mr. Ochoa said he would give me a contract for twenty-five tons.'

The salt lakes were on public land about a hundred miles northeast of Los Piños. For many years Mexicans on both sides of the border had taken salt from them free of cost, as had also scores of American settlers. They were looked on as community property.

'There's money in it,' Mulrooney admitted. 'If you're gettin' a fair price. You'll need a couple of skinners. I'll let you have Yorky and String Beans. They're both good game guys and friendly to you. What say?'

'I say thanks. They are the very two I would have picked,' Dan replied.

'How long will it take you to get outfitted?' the wagon boss asked. 'This town is no healthy place for you. I'd say hit the road soon as you can, and stay home nights until you can get away.'

'I've got my teams picked,' Dan said. 'We ought to get away in three-four days.'

'The sooner the quicker,' nodded Mulrooney, dragging at his red beard. 'You started out with havin' one enemy. Now you've got a dozen. Through you open opposition to the gambler element got set. Until you chirped, everything was sweet for them. They ran this town. Now they're not so doggoned sure. There are twenty birds in this town would rub you out for a dollar Mex. Don't ever forget that.'

'I'm not liable to forget it,' Dan answered. 'I don't aim to throw down on myself if I can help it.'

Sam Jones rubbed his rough chin and frowned meditatively at the young man. 'If you weren't in this trouble I'd tell you not to tote a gun,' he said. 'You're a standin' temptation to a gunman to bump you off. Too late now for you to shuck yore weapon, though. Boy, you've got to learn to shoot. Practice an hour every day. Spill a lot of ammunition. After you've burnt a ton or two and been at it ten-twenty years you may be a medium good shot. Right now I'll take you out and give you lesson number two.'

As they walked down to the river, Dan commented on one point that had surprised him a good deal and disturbed him a little.

'You went a long way to save me,' he said. 'In this country where a man has to play his own hand you certainly did a good deal of butting in. Looks like I hid back of you most of the time. I did, too."

'Were you hidin' behind me when you flung Ford into the ditch and when you dragged him into The Last Chance to show him up? Were you unloadin' yore trouble on me when you offered to fight him with shotguns? I wouldn't say so.'

'When two men get in a difficulty, folks most generally stand back and let them fight it out,' Dan continued, sticking to his point. 'It wasn't that way this time. If good citizens had kept out of this, I would have been a dead man by now. What made them go so strong for me?'

'Mostly it wasn't for you. These bully-puss gamblers and gunmen had crowded them and this was a chance to hit back.' Sam added, with a grin: 'Speakin' for myself, I had steen reasons for mixing into the rookus.'

'I know one of them,' Dan said. 'Because I happened to be the nearest guy to you one time when you and old man river Canadian were having a tussle.'

'You done mention reason number one, the most important,' the ranger admitted. 'Some of the others, if you want 'em. I'm an officer and supposed to prevent killin's when I can. For a third, I don't care for Mr. Jas Ford and his dirty friends. They have been hurrahin' this town long enough. Then there is the girl.'

'She wasn't a reason, and you know it, Obigod,' Clifford said bluntly. 'You used her as an excuse. I didn't protect her from Ford, but just happened to get in the way.'

40

Sam smoked his pipe equably. 'Not the way she told it, boy. She sure made you the white-haired lad.'

'After you primed her with a lot of lies.'

'Honest, I never saw the girl. Wouldn't know her from— from Mrs. John L. Sullivan. . . . I had a lot of other reasons, but I have forgot them.'

They set up a target and Dan blazed away at it. He fired very deliberately, drawing a careful bead.

The ranger shook his head. 'Looky here, boy. If Jas Ford gets in front of you, he won't stand around waitin' for you to get set. No sir. He'll whang away at you fast as he can without gettin' flustered. It will be strictly hurry-up business and the devil take the hindmost. Lemme have a holt of that cutter.'

The ranger made a motion as if he were drawing the revolver from a holster. One shot rang out while the weapon was still at his hip. The others were so closely spaced in time that they made almost one continuous crash. An examination showed that three out of the four bullets had passed through the paper.

'I don't see how you do it,' Dan said. 'Why, you didn't take time to aim.'

'You get so you aim by instinct instead of by sight, I reckon,' Sam explained. 'There's no time to fool around gettin' a bead on yore man while he is pumpin' lead at you. You got to be sudden if you don't want a coroner's jury sayin' you came to yore death in a mistaken effort to stop a bullet in motion. . . . Now you load up and try again. Lemme see you draw and empty that gun inside of two seconds. No matter what you hit.'

The roar of the revolver filled their ears.

'More than three seconds,' Sam announced. 'You've got to beat that.'

'I fired fast as my fingers would work,' Dan protested.

'You'll have to grease yore finger, son. Work for speed. You'll get it after a while. After that you'll have to learn accuracy. For that, it is important to be fast without hurryin' yoreself. Take a fraction of a second to steady yore arm before you start foggin'. If a guy just shoots wild, he won't puncture anything but the atmosphere.'

'You tell me one minute not to take aim and the next not to shoot wild,' Dan objected.

The ranger rubbed his chin, to help himself think more clearly. ' "Course you take aim. You look at yore mark and then you hit it. After a while you'll get what I mean. Point

41

is, you're killin' a man who is tryin' to bump you off, not lookin' over yore sights at a paper mark on a tree. It's a heap different. I never met a mankiller yet who could have won a prize as a marksman.'

Dan and his friend walked uptown as far as the junction of San Antonio and River Streets. It was impossible for the young man not to discover that all eyes turned to him. For the moment he was the center of interest. In some of the faces he read warm approval, in others tight-lipped hostility; in all of them a respect altogether new. He was no longer a kid mule skinner, but a person of importance. It came to him with a sense of surprise that none of these men knew he had been awaiting the issue with dread and dismay. What stuck in their minds was that he had laid violent hands on the notorious gunman and later offered to fight him with Bowies or shotguns.

'Got to leave you here, boy,' Sam said. 'You'll be playin' a lone hand now. Keep yore eyes peeled. You're as popular with Ford's crowd as a skunk at a dance.'

Yorky joined Dan just after the ranger had left him.

'You're sure sittin' high, wide, and handsome, kid,' the teamster said admiringly. 'I would never have figured you could drive that gambler to the tall timber like you done. When you talked about a double-pronged scatter gun at ten yards, he drew in his horns sudden."

Dan could have given him more accurate information, but he did not care to diminish any reputation he might have acquired. After all, there was some truth to Yorky's view. Ford had chosen not to fight upon the proposed conditions. The public acceptance of Dan on this new status had its effect on the young fellow. When he and Yorky walked into The Silver Dollar for a glass of beer there was a reckless *élan* about his bearing men had never noticed before.

Two men were at the bar. One of them was the capper for The Last Chance, the hatchet-faced Le Page. The other was a heavy-set man of about forty, with cold skim-milk eyes, a straight thin-lipped mouth, and a curious manner of wariness that never was absent. He was known as Zach Black.

Le Page slid a look at the newcomers.

'Look who is here, Zach,' he said, not lowering his voice. 'The boss hurrah man of our little city. Take off yore hat to him.'

A pulse of excitement began to beat in Dan's throat. He knew this man was dangerous and that his words had been a challenge, one that could be taken up or let alone. But if he side-stepped the sneer, Le Page would move to a more direct insult. The mule skinner had become a public character. The story of his meeting with this man would be all over town before the night was over.

'I'd better scratch gravel and light out, don't you reckon, Yorky?' Dan drawled. 'This piece of crow-bait here has got me scared to death. I'm so goosey I'm liable to tromp him down while I'm stampeding out of here. You tell him I'm gentle and will stand without hitching. His friend, Mr. Jasper Ford, knows I'm a lamb.'

Someone laughed. Out of the corner of an eye Le Page took in the observers. There were half a dozen of them. A stillness had fallen over their activities. One could have heard a clock tick.

'If you're claiming you scared Jas Ford, you're a liar,' Le Page spat out.

An odd gaiety bubbled in young Clifford. He had discovered he was not afraid. His voice was steady, light, cheerfully ironic, but his eyes were like half-scabbarded steel. Le Page did not make the mistake of assuming that his smile was genial.

'Trouble with me is that when I get afeared of someone, I get so jumpy first thing I know I've done him a meanness,' Dan explained. 'I wouldn't want to treat you thataway, Mr. Le Page, but I feel it coming over me. I'm scared plumb stiff. You'll excuse me if l lose control of myself and pump a couple of blue plums into you, I hope. No unkindness meant, you understand.'

Dan moved forward, to be in front of Yorky. The furtive gaze of the capper slid away from the points of steel that burned into him like live coals. He asked a wordless question of his companion Black and got no answer. That gentleman had moved back a little from the bar so that the others would have an unimpeded range. It was clear he considered this none of his funeral.

Le Page was not gun-shy, but he usually contrived to arrange his showdowns so that he had the break on his side. There was no profit in running a risk of getting killed. He hesitated.

In that split second before he made up his mind, Yorky slipped in his contribution.

'Don't you, Dan. Don't bump this guy off. You know he ain't got a chance with you.'

The words tipped the balance. Le Page decided to wait.

He could get this fellow when he was not looking for an attack.

'What in Mexico is this all about?' the pallid-faced gambler asked. 'I'm not lookin' for trouble. Have I said I was?'

The business of the house began to move once more. There was a sound of rattling chips from the poker table. The bartender began to polish again the glass that for a few moments had remained motionless in his hand. Yorky mentioned that he would like a glass of beer. Le Page had made his choice, and it was for peace not war.

'That makes everything nice,' Dan said. 'I can get over my scare, then.'

'Sure,' Yorky said with a grin. 'He's one of these live and let live lads, Le Page is. He wouldn't hurt a fly, while it was looking.'

'You in this, fellow?' Le Page blustered.

The freckled face of Yorky was a map of innocence. 'Me? Why, no! Nothin' like that. I was just sayin' a good word for you.'

'I can say for myself all the good words I need,' the gambler growled. 'Come along, Black. Let's drift. I don't like the company.'

He led the way out of the place.

'Too bad,' Dan mourned. 'He doesn't like us, Yorky. I sure am lucky he didn't jump me all spraddled out. Come up, boys. Drinks on me.'

Those present trooped to the bar.

Chapter 10
•
DAN TAKES A DIVE

DAN walked down San Antonio Street to the house where the Sutherlands lived. Milly and the children were not at home, but Ah Sin in smock and wide trousers was busy ironing some ruffled shirts.

'Missy catchum laundly,' the Oriental said.

He banged the iron down on the bosom of a shirt vindictively,

'What's the matter, Ah Sin?' Dan asked. 'Eat something that doesn't agree with you?'

'He belong Amelican devil Ford,' explained the man with the queue, referring to the garment. 'We no takum his work after now.'

It was plain that Ah Sin would have liked to have under the hot iron the cold, sneering face of the gambler. Failing that, he had an urgent desire to scorch the cuffs of the shirts. He resisted temptation, since he still had a vivid recollection of how Ford had man-handled him.

'His custom no longer wanted by Miss Milly's Laundry, eh?' Dan said.

'You killum maybe some dark night,' Ah Sin suggested.

'No,' Dan replied, almost violently. "I don't want ever to see him again.'

The ghost of a smile glimmered for a moment on the yellow face. 'You catchum dlowned rat in ditch and pullum out. Too bad.'

'You may be right at that,' Dan admitted. 'But I can't go round drowning birds I don't like.'

'He velly bad man.'

Dan caught sight of Milly and the children and went to meet them.

With a whoop Tom ran forward. 'Whoopee, Dan! You knocked the chip off'n his shoulder. He better not fool with you if he knows what's good for him.'

'Oh, I'm a wonder,' Dan said derisively.

In Milly's dark eyes there was emotion. 'Thank God,' she cried in a low voice. 'I've been so afraid for you.'

'I've been some afraid for myself,' he smiled.

'I prayed God not to let him kill you,' she murmured.

'You did more than pray. If you hadn't stood by me—if you hadn't made everybody think I had stood up for you—when I didn't really at all—'

'What did you do, then? She demanded indignantly. 'You knocked him into this very ditch because he was pestering me.'

'No. I was going to crawl out of town and leave you to fight him alone. Then all of a sudden I sorta boiled up and lashed out at him. I didn't have time to think what he would do to me later.'

'It's silly to say you didn't fight for me, because you did,' Milly protested. 'You're the funniest boy, doing things for folks and then acting as if you had done nothing.' She added, with a shy smile, a delicate color in her cheeks: 'Guess what we have for supper.'

Tom heard this last, and stood in front of Dan with his hands in his pockets and his feet wide apart. 'It's my birthday, and I'm nine years old. We've got fried chicken and a peach cobbler.'

'Are you inviting Mr. Clifford, Tom?' his sister inquired. 'Y'betcha!'

For a fleeting moment Dan recollected his promise not to be out after dark. Then he brushed the thought of it from him. He would be very careful to take a roundabout way home and avoid the busy streets where he might be seen.

'And I'm staying, "Thank you kindly, Tom." Haven't had home-cooked fried chicken for years, let alone peach cobbler.'

During supper Dan picked up information about his young friends. Their grandfather on the mother's side had been the colonel of an Illinois regiment during the war and a district judge for ten years succeeding it. Their father too came of a good family, but he was a dreamer with an absolute lack of capacity to make his way in the world. Financially he had slid from bad to worse.

'I've had quite a lot of schooling,' Milly told him. 'Pretty soon they will have to get another teacher here, maybe two or three if the town keeps growing. Would you think maybe I could get a place in the school?'

Dan looked across the table at her doubtfully. She was so young and so slim and so adorably pretty. 'Perhaps you could. I know one of the trustees,' he said.

'Would you speak for me? Or do you think I'm not old enough?' she asked timidly.

'I think you'll grow older every day,' he made answer. 'Of course I'll speak for you, though my say-so isn't important. We must get Polly Doble to see them all.'

'I'd have to take the little children on account of the discipline,' she said.

Tom said, 'Gee, I wish you was my teacher so's I could do as I like.'

A fierce gleam came into her soft eyes. 'I wonder if you could, Master Tom.' She glanced at the clock. 'Bedtime for little boys. Take yourself off, young fellow.'

'Gee, I didn't mean to start anything, sis,' protested Tom.

'You haven't,' she said, smiling at him. 'Not even yourself yet. But you are going to after about five seconds.'

Tom departed, letting it be plainly known he was an injured youth.

He left behind him embarrassment. Dan was girl-shy. He did not know what to talk about to Milly, and she was as

46

inexpert as he. After a long pause she mentioned that she was going to build a fence around the place to keep pigs from rooting up the garden.

To bridge an awkward silence, Dan gave a little dissertation on early day fencing. He explained that before the coming of barbed wire the West had been put to great straits to enclose land. On the prairies there was no timber. In Western Texas some huisache had grown and in the center of the state bois d'arc. Experiments had been made with osage orange. He recalled that one old-timer had told him an osage orange hedge could be built in four years at a cost of fifty cents a rod which would be pig-tight, horse-high, and bull-strong.

Milly looked at him demurely and said 'Thank you,' then gave a little giggle. Dan grinned, and they both burst into laughter. After that they were more at their ease. The young man deserted the absorbing topic of fences for others more personal.

When he left the house, it was by the back door. It was not likely anyone knew he was here, but he did not want to take unnecessary chances.

'Be careful,' Milly whispered.

'That's going to be my middle name from now on,' he told her.

Through the mesquite he circled to the *acequia*. Clouds were scudding across the sky. Sometimes the moon showed for a moment, then it went under again. He guessed a heavy rain was blowing up. The country needed rain. There had been a long dry spell.

The roar of a gun filled the night. A burn scorched the shoulder of the young man. He plunged forward, and his foot slipped. Into the bankfull ditch he went with a splash.

As he went under the water his mind worked in swift flashes. An enemy had lain in the bushes to murder him. The man was waiting on the bank to fire again the moment his head reappeared above the surface. He recollected that the moon had just been vanishing behind a cloud. But even in the darkness the black mass of his head could be made out.

Dan swam under the water until he had to come up for air. He had flung off his hat, and when his head emerged it pushed up into a growth of cherry bushes.

The revolver crashed again twice. The young man thought it was the end of him, but to his surprise he found no bullet had torn into him. The man on the edge of the ditch had fired at the broad hat floating downstream.

Young Clifford clung to a sapling below the water and

47

lay so that only his mouth and eyes were exposed. Above these was the heavy foliage from the drooping branches of the wild cherry trees. His one chance was to escape notice. The man might think his dead body lay at the bottom of the ditch. Dan had an almost irresistible impulse to shut his eyes. He was afraid that the light in them might attract the attention of the assassin. Nor did he want to look into the revolver when it found him and focused on his head. That instant would be unendurable.

Fear clutched at the boy's throat. To lie there helpless and wait for death to strike was horrible. He dared not move. A sound would be fatal. In the long silence time seemed to be ticking the seconds that would sweep him into eternity.

When he looked again, the man was moving slowly along the bank, the eyes in the hatchet face searching the stream. The fellow stopped just above his submerged victim and tried to push the bushes aside. From his position he could not be absolutely sure there was nothing beneath the leaves, but he could not brush the branches away for a clear view.

Dan knew the face of the killer was peering down not six feet above him. Every instant he expected discovery.

A hoarse voice said, 'Hell! He's dead.'

But the man did not move away. He stood there long terrible moments, his gaze still searching the water.

'But I reckon I'll make sure,' he said to himself with a savage laugh.

He stepped back, found a stick, and reached down to push the branches to one side.

There came a cry, in the high, frightened voice of a girl. 'Dan! Dan! Are you hurt?'

The man on the bank let out an angry oath. He dropped the stick, turned, and ran down the path toward town. The last thing he wanted was to be discovered here on the scene of a murder.

There was a rush of feet, another frightened shout of inquiry.

Dan answered, not too loud. 'Here, Milly. In the water.'

She stopped and looked down. Out of the darkness a hand came up to her. She caught it and pulled with all her strength. Dan flung a leg to the bank and rolled out. He lay in the path shaken and exhausted.

'Are you . . . hurt?' the girl gasped.

'No. Not much. One bullet burnt my shoulder.' He shuddered. 'I thought he had me. If you hadn't come . . .'

'I heard the shots. I was afraid. I thought someone . . .'

48

'You thought right. He did his best. I dived into the ditch . . . We'd better get away from here. He might come back.'

Dan rose. He put a hand on her shoulder to steady himself.

They moved toward her house. She wanted to cry out to him to hurry—hurry, for someone might be lurking in the mesquite. But she held herself steady by an effort.

Crossing the road, they walked up the path to the door. Dan opened this, stood aside to let her past, then ducked in after and dragged the door shut. He drove the bolt home. One glance showed him that the window blind was down.

The young man sank down into a rocker.

'You're hurt!' she cried, her face colorless.

'A scratch,' he answered. 'It's not that.' He looked up at her, almost as white as she was. 'It was . . . terrible. I swam under the water and came up beneath some bushes. I kept expecting him to see me. The foliage saved me, for a minute or two. Then he got a stick to brush it aside. Just then you called and he got scared. God! If you hadn't come, if you had waited twenty seconds longer—'

She said, to take his mind from that awful thought, 'Let me look at your wound. I'll have to get a doctor too.'

'Don't think so. It's just a burn—a scratch, I think.'

She helped him out of his coat and shirt. Dan was right. The wound itself was insignificant. The bullet had scorched a ridge along the flesh.

Milly washed and dressed it.

'Do you know who it was tried to kill you?' she asked.

'I'm almost sure it was a fellow called Le Page. I didn't get a good view of his face, but I could almost swear to him.'

'You'll have to stay here tonight,' Milly said.

'I can't do that.' The color came to his cheeks. 'Folks would talk.'

Pink flooded her face. 'Let them,' she said stoutly. 'You're not going out of this house till morning.'

'It will be all right for me to go after a while.'

'It will be all right for you to stay here, and you're going to do just that.'

He gave up the point. 'I can sleep on that buffalo rug on the floor,' he said.

'No, you can sleep in my bed in the room with the children. I'll sleep out here on the buffalo robe. You've been hurt, and I haven't.'

'I haven't been hurt, not to speak of. I won't take yore

bed.' He grew indignant at the thought. 'Up to you. If I stay, it will be in this room.'

'All right,' she assented. 'Have it your own way.'

She brought out blankets and arranged a bed for him on the floor.

While Milly was making his couch as comfortable as possible, Dan cleaned his revolver. He did not want it to dry while wet for fear of rust. In place of the cartridges that had been in the water-soaked weapon he substituted others. A word of advice given by Sam Jones popped to his mind. 'Keep yore gun oiled, boy. You won't need it often, but when you do, Obigod.'

Milly looked at the gun with distrust and alarm. 'It isn't Christian to carry one of those,' she said.

'No, ma'am,' Dan agreed with mock meekness. 'I'd better leave it here with you, don't you reckon?'

She stared at him accusingly. 'What would you do if—if one of these villains——'

'——cut loose on me,' he completed for her. 'I'd jump in the creek, if there was one handy.'

No smile met his. 'You take your gun and defend yourself,' she told him with a little flare of feminine ferocity.

'But you just done told me it's not Christian,' he mentioned.

'I don't care whether it is or not. You can't let yourself be murdered. Maybe I'm wrong about it's not being Christian. God helps those who help themselves.' She said a crisp 'Good night' and vanished.

It was a long time before he could get to sleep. Once in the night he awoke, to discover that a heavy rain was pouring down. He could hear it on the roof, and by a flash of lightning he saw it running down the window almost in a stream.

'We sure needed a good rain,' he murmured, then turned over and went to sleep again.

Chapter 11

•

LE PAGE SEES A GHOST

DAN rose as light was beginning to sift into the sky. He dressed and slipped out of the house without disturbing any of those in it. Rain was still falling, but there was a promise of clear weather in the sky.

The ground was soft. He sloshed through adobe mud to his ankles. San Antonio Street was deserted except for a few late revelers making their way back home unsteadily. Without incident he reached the *jacal* where he, Sam Jones, and Yorky were staying.

He had to knock on the bolted door to get admittance. Yorky came sleepily to let him into the room.

'Where in jubilee you been?' the big teamster demanded. 'We-all been worried—thought sure they had got you.'

'Nor this trip,' Dan said, with his best manner of nonchalance. 'The fellow sent to do the job kinda slipped up on it.'

By this time the ranger had wakened. 'Obigod, did the scalawags try to get you, boy?' he asked.

Dan sat down on the edge of a cot and pulled his soggy boots off. 'Did his doggondest, the fellow who tried it. It was some dark, and maybe he was goosey. Anyhow, he just creased me.'

'Then you dropped him?' Sam inquired.

'No, sir. By that time I was in the *acequia*. I figured it was time for me to take a bath.'

'Quit joshin', boy. Tell us the story, what there is of it,' ordered Jones.

Dan recounted the events of the night.

The ranger exploded in profanity. 'Didn't I tell you to stay home and keep under cover nights? What's eatin' you, fellow? By rights this killer Le Page ought to have got you. It was just luck he didn't. That's no way to play yore hand.'

'I know,' Dan admitted. 'It was that fried chicken did it. When Miss Milly gave me my invite I had to say yes. Me, I'm a plumb fool about fried chicken.' He was trying to get across

51

the impression that it was the dinner and not the hostess that had interested him.

'What do you figure on doing about this Le Page?' Sam asked.

'Want to talk with you about that,' Dan answered. 'I can't just let it ride. Got to call the turn on him. But how?'

'Sure it was him?'

'Practically sure. Couldn't swear to it in court.'

'He figures you are dead. If he saw you suddenly, he'd sure give himself away.'

'And then what?' Dan asked. 'I'm no killer. Except in self-defense I couldn't draw a gun on anyone.'

The ranger rubbed his chin. 'For a fellow buttin' into trouble much as you do, you're certainly the most harmless guy I ever see. You answer yore own question, boy. Then what? You could explain to him you were sorry to be such a nuisance, but next time he would likely have better luck.'

'No, sir,' Dan replied curtly. 'I'm going to give him something to remember me by the rest of his life.'

'Now you're shouting, son,' Yorky said.

'He's due for a cowhiding.'

'You'd have to step lively, before he got a chance to draw his gun,' Jones warned.

'I would so, unless I could bluff him out of a gun-play.'

'You want to have yore cutter handy in case the bluff doesn't work.'

They discussed the best time to meet Le Page. He was always at The Last Chance from three o'clock in the afternoon until late at night. They decided to confront him unexpectedly. In the meantime Dan was to stay in the *jacal* where he could be seen by nobody. Yorky was dispatched to Milly Sutherland to ask her not to mention to anyone the occurrences of the previous night. It was important that no advance warning reach Le Page.

The clock in The Last Chance set the time at four o'clock when Dan Clifford walked into the back door of the gambling hall. His coat was unbuttoned, but he held his left arm close to his body. He moved swiftly up the room until he reached the bar.

Le Page was standing in front of it with two or three cronies. He had been doing some private celebrating and was not quite himself. One of those with him, about to pour down a drink, pulled up abruptly, amazement written large on his face. Out of one side of his mouth he murmured a warning.

'Take a look, Jerry. Quick!'

'What at, Derby?'

The capper slid a look around. His jaw dropped. He stared, fear-filled eyes glaring out of his head. The first thought in his mind was that this was the ghost of the man he murdered.

'Goddlemighty!' he cried, backing to the bar.

Dan's eyes blazed at him the threat of punishment. The young man moved closer.

'What's the matter, Le Page?' he asked. 'Did you think you had killed me?'

'Where—where——'

'Not this time. You don't shoot straight enough.'

His left arm shot out and caught the gambler by the coat-collar. Le Page reached for his gun. The man was too late. Dan jerked it from the holster and flung it back of the bar. The mule skinner stooped and picked up the horsewhip he had dropped.

The lash hissed through the air and wound around the legs of the gambler. Le Page ripped out a curse of anger and pain. Again the whip burned his thighs like a rope of fire. He shrieked with agony.

One of his companions made a move to draw a gun.

'Don't you, Derby,' a voice advised.

Jones was at his elbow. Yorky was at the other end of the bar. He had not been there a moment before.

'We'll keep out of this,' the big teamster announced.

Le Page tried to close with his assailant, but the straight arm kept him at a distance. He flung himself down to escape the torture and was dragged back from the floor. He screamed and begged and cursed. The whip rose and fell, rose and fell, each stroke a flame of agony. When at last he flung himself down into the corner, an abject, sobbing wretch aquiver with pain, Dan let him lie where he had fallen.

'You have one hour to get out of town,' Dan told him. 'One hour. If you are here at the end of that time, it's at yore own risk. Understand?'

'Better explain what this is all about, Dan,' suggested the ranger.

The gambler Stone had just come into the house. 'This seems to be a one-man town,' he jeered. 'Looks like we'll have to take out insurance against this pest.'

'Last night this scoundrel tried to kill me from ambush,' Dan explained. 'His bullet creased my shoulder, gentlemen. I'll show you the place in a minute. Luckily for me I fell into the *acequia*. I swam under water and came up under some bushes. Before this villain found me he heard someone coming and lit out. No doubt he thought I was dead at the bottom of the ditch. That's why he was so shocked at seeing me when I came in a minute ago.'

'That's your story, is it?' Stone sneered.

'That's my story, and it's a true one. I have a witness.'

Dan slipped off his coat and shirt. He showed the furrow along his shoulder. Two or three of those present examined it.

'It's new all right,' one of the men confirmed. 'And I reckon a bullet did it. Looks thataway.'

'Might have been a quirt,' Stone said.

'If you'll examine yore friend Le Page you'll find a quirt leaves a different kind of welt,' Jones said cheerfully. 'What's eating you, Stone? Le Page got a good deal less than was coming to him. He deserved to be bumped off, the mangy yellow coyote. He's lucky to sneak out with a whoppin' and an order to hit the trail.'

'You and your friend starting to hurrah this town and say who is and who isn't to live here?' asked Stone, chill eyes fixed on Jones.

'I don't aim to let myself be dry-gulched by a wolf who hasn't sand enough to stand out in the open,' Dan said. 'Better for him to get out *pronto*.'

'And if he doesn't,' Stone suggested.

'Why, then, every time I meet him I'll give him another installment of punishment on account.'

'Unless some other wolf puts you to sleep in smoke first,' drawled Stone.

'You don't know anybody who would do that, do you, Mr. Stone?' Dan asked gently, his gaze holding fast to the eyes of the other.

The gambler laughed, with cool hardihood. 'Now this mule skinner is starting on me, boys. I'm scared. Maybe I'll get an hour to leave town.'

'Isn't Los Piños big enough for both of us, Mr. Stone?' Dan inquired. 'I didn't know there was any trouble between us. You're not taking up the cause of this yelping coyote Le Page, are you. If he is yore friend——'

'I don't make friends with that kind of riffraff,' Stone answered coolly, with biting contempt.

'Fine,' Dan said. 'Then we won't quarrel.'

He turned to the man who still lay on the floor caressing his hurts. 'One hour,' he warned.

Followed by his friends Dan turned and walked out.

54

Chapter 12

•

'THE ONLY BOY NAMED SAM MY MOTHER HAS'

IT HAD come on to rain again during the day and water was sluicing from the roofs in streams. The dirt in the street, churned to dust by scores of teams drawing heavy loads, had been ankle-deep in yellow powder. Now it was a lake of mud and slush. Some wag had stuck a sign up in the road.

No Boating Here

By Order of the Mayor

As Dan sloshed down San Antonio Street with his friends, he discovered he was ravenously hungry. All day he had been too excited to eat. Now his appetite was serving notice on him that man could not live without food.

They came to a Mexican restaurant.

'Let's eat,' he suggested.

Sam Jones was a good trencher man. Yorky had never been known to refuse food. The three of them turned in to the flat-roofed adobe building.

A fat smiling Mexican woman waited on them. She was her own menu card.

'Sopa de fideo, gallina con chile, frijoles Mejicana, chile con carne, tamales, enchiladas, tortillas, cafe,' she chanted.

'Bring the whole caboodle,' ordered Dan.

While they waited for their food, a wagon train plowed past. After it came the stage, which disgorged its contents at the office opposite. The passengers were three painted ladies and some nondescript males.

'I heard the Acme was getting in some girls,' Yorky mentioned.

The Acme was the gaming house next door to the stage office.

'We're still importing blondes and bar fixtures,' the ranger drawled.

'And Bibles,' added Yorky. 'Look. That's a sky pilot getting out.'

The men crowded to the door to see. This was something

55

unusual. Up to date the clergy had not found representation in Los Piños's motley population.

'Sure is,' Sam agreed. 'Well, he's come to a place where the Devil will certainly give him a good tussle.'

'He looks like some man at that,' Dan said. 'Broad shoulders, flat back, holds his head up. This town can use a good sky pilot.'

'Y'betcha!' assented Yorky. 'We can't always be a honkytonk burg. But, by crikey! he'll find out right soon what a strangle holt sinners have on Los Piños.'

A revolver cracked. From the wall back of the three men a trickle of dust slid to the floor. Into the adobe plaster a bullet had crashed.

Sam Jones shut the door swiftly, then bolted it.

'Le Page gettin' busy right soon,' Yorky guessed.

Dan drew the window curtains. 'I wouldn't think so. He's hardly had time. Some other bird saw us and took a crack.'

'Stone, maybe.'

'Not Stone, when he draws it will be in the open,' the ranger differed.

'Doesn't matter who,' Dan said. 'Might be any one of a dozen. Question is, what do we do?'

'You've done ordered a dinner,' Sam said. 'What's the matter with sittin' down and eating it?'

'You wouldn't go over to the Acme, if you were me?' the young man asked.

'What for?' the ranger inquired. 'Either the bird is still there, waiting for you, ready to fill you full of lead soon as you show up. Or else he beat it *muy pronto*. I wouldn't figure you had lost anything at the Acme you had to find right now. No, sir. We'll sit down and keep that engagement with the *frijoles* and the *chile* you done ordered.'

They did. The keeper of the restaurant brought in the *sopa*. She started to open the front door again, but Dan explained that they were chilly.

A grin beamed on Yorky's freckled face. 'I'm wonderin' what the sky pilot thought.' he said. 'He sure didn't have to wait long for the fireworks to begin.'

'Maybe he thought it was a salute in honor of his arrival,' Dan guessed.

The ranger looked at Dan reprovingly. 'Maybe you enjoy havin' someone plug at you. Different here. I'd take it serious. Have you bought those teams yet you were dickering for?'

'Yes. Having the wagons and harness fixed up. Be ready tomorrow.'

56

'What time tomorrow?'

'In the morning.'

'All right. You're gettin' outa town soon as the boys can get the teams hooked up. There is too much promiscuous lead bein' scattered around this town.'

'Yes,' Dan agreed.

'You're goin' home with me to the *jacal* soon as we tuck away this food. I'm hopin' I get you there unpunctured. You'll sit right there till the teams are brought round to you. When these scalawags bend their six-guns on you, that's one thing, but when they crack loose hopin' for general results, with me in the scenery, that's a heap more serious. I'm the only boy named Sam my mother has, and I don't aim to have her lose me. Understand?'

Dan said he did. He held similar sentiments about his mother's son.

When they left the restaurant, it was by the back door, after a careful survey of the landscape. Dan was glad to reach the *jacal* safely.

Chapter 13
•
THE SALT LAKES

DURING the evening word came to Dan that Le Page had taken the El Paso stage. His teamster String Beans brought the news.

String Beans got his nickname on account of his long gangling body and the way he carried it. Whether he walked or stood, he was never erect. His stoop and his slouch were as much a part of him as his shadow. He was a mild-mannered giant, and he spent a good deal of his time swapping cheerful lies about past experiences.

'By gum, boy, that galoot Le Page has done lit out,' the teamster said. 'Looks like he has had an elegant sufficiency of you. Must have changed his mind about bein' such a bad *hombre*. You sure turned out to be a hair-trigger lad.'

Dan was learning that it was a good thing not to disturb public opinion about his prowess.

'We're leaving tomorrow at noon,' he said. 'I don't look

for any trouble, but you had better have yore hogleg strapped on to yore hip, S. B. Someone may get ambitious.'

'Dad gum, so he might. You been crowdin' a bad bunch quite some. I don't reckon Jas Ford enjoys bein' made to look like a plugged quarter. If you stick around here hell will sure begin to pop.'

'You mean it will keep on poppin', don't you, S. B.?' Yorky asked with a wide grin.

'Maybeso, that is what I mean,' String Beans agreed.

From several sources it had come to Dan that he was anathema to the sporting element. He did not quite know why he was in so bad with them. After all, he was only a mule skinner who had been picked on and forced to defend himself. Why all this personal bitterness stirred up against him? Somehow with no intent on his part, and certainly with no desire, he had become a symbol of revolt against the domination of the gamblers. To maintain their prestige they had to punish him.

Dan was writing a letter to his mother. He had run away from his home at Richmond, Kentucky, to become a cowboy, lured by stories of adventure in the West. Along with thousands of others he had drifted to Texas. Here in turn he had chased longhorns through the brush, helped make up herds for the Northern market, and gone up the trail with one of Shanghai Pierce's outfits. By a lucky deal he had made several hundred dollars. This was not enough to start him in the cow business, but it would do for an entering wedge as a freighter. To learn the details he had got work with one of Ochoa and Waller's wagon trains. Now he was beginning on his own.

The letter was one designed to cheer the hearts of his parents. He told about the country and its opportunities, but he did not mention the dangers in which he had become involved. Nor did he tell them what a riproaring place Los Piños was. There was a casual sentence about the minister who had just arrived and another about the good friends he had made. How were his brothers and his sisters? Little Nelly must be a big girl by this time. What reader was she in at school? Did Dad remember the time he had recited 'Young Lochinvar' out of McGuffey's? He sent love to all the family, with a special word for his mother. If his business venture turned out profitably, he hoped to get home soon for a visit. In a postscript he added that he was sorry he had been wild and made his mother worry about him. These days were past, he promised. Now he was a safe, sane business man.

The safe, sane business man went to bed with a revolver under his pillow. There was a chance his enemies might crash the frail door during the night and he might have to get to his feet with a gun in his hand. In the morning he walked uptown with the same six-shooter strapped to his hip. He walked lightly, with a jauntiness that suggested self-confidence. His cowboy hat was slightly tilted above the bronzed boyish face. A buoyant vigor found expression in the long, lean body with the rippling muscles.

He superintended the loading of the wagons with supplies for the trip. By noon his outfit was plowing away through the muddy streets of the town's suburbs. It left the adobe houses in the rear. After a time the orchards and the fields gave place to the open plains.

Dan drew a deep breath of relief. For ten days at least he would be safe from the attacks of his enemies. The sharp angry bark of a pistol would not shake his nerves.

He could hear String Beans singing a tuneless song as he sat hunched up in a wagon seat.

'Oh, a hoss threw me off at the creek called Mud,
A hoss threw me off with the Two-W herd,
The last time I saw him he was runnin' 'cross the level
A-kickin' up his heels and a-raisin' of the devil.'

A week ago Dan had been as carefree as old String Beans. Now he had to walk a wary trail to keep from being collected by a bunch of scoundrels. Moreover, he had to begin watching expenses. He had given a chattel mortgage on his wagons and teams. A business man had to keep a weather eye out to see he didn't get skinned on a deal. He had to check up costs and sale price to make sure there was a reasonable margin of profit.

String Beans offered another verse of unmelodious song.

'Oh, old Ben Bolt was a fine old boss,
Rode to see the gals on a sore-backed hoss.
Old Ben Bolt was fond of his liquor,
Had a li'l' bottle in the pocket of his slicker.'

No more of the li'l' bottle' stuff for Dan. He never had been a drinking man, but from now on he was going to be a strict teetotaler. He was embarked on paths too hazardous for him to be what was known as a good fellow any longer. It was strange, he reflected, how circumstances drove a man to show the stuff that was in him. He had been just a good-natured boy, the most insignificant mule skinner in the Ochoa and Waller outfit. Now he was a marked man and could not walk down San Antonio Street without the eyes of men following him. He recalled a saying of Sam Jones: 'A man is like a watermelon. You can't tell how good he is till you thump him.' Until a man had been given the acid test, he did not know whether or not he could stand up under fire.

Dan did not fool himself. It had been a near thing. He had almost run away. There had been moments when he had been a quivering jelly inside. But all that was behind him. He had made his choice. From this time he would walk the way of the strong.

Travel during the first day was heavy, since the rain had been a general and not a local one. The mules were forced to get down into their collars to drag the wagons through the adobe mud. Early in the second morning they ran into dusty roads again. The pace grew brisker. The third evening Dan's outfit camped on the site of the salt beds.

The area of the lake was about one hundred acres. It looked like an ice pond, smooth and white and glistening. Over the surface was a skim of water about an inch thick.

The wagons were driven out on the lake and the salt shoveled into them. A hot sun beat down upon the men. They were stripped to the waists and rivulets of perspiration poured down their bodies. During the middle of the day they rested. The work was hard and grueling. It takes muscle to fling a shovelful of wet salt into a wagon bed hour after hour.

Within a day the hole made by those loading the wagons had disappeared. The salt water had risen to the surrounding level, new crystals had been formed by evaporation, and a fresh supply of salt replaced that taken.

Dan did not let a day pass without fifteen or twenty minutes of revolver practice. He could see improvement, both in accuracy and speed. By constant handling he acquired the feel of a gun, an intuitive touch that made for skill. He came nearer the bull's-eye, but with less consciously deliberate aim. A good deal of his money was going for ammunition. There was more than a chance it might be very well spent.

While his men shifted the salt in the wagons, to give as much of it as possible a chance to dry in the sun, Dan rode into the hills with his rifle to try for some fresh meat. Across the horn of his saddle he brought back with him an antelope.

The little cavalcade headed for Los Piños. Dan did not rush the pace. The wagons were heavily laden and there was no use in overworking the mules. Young Clifford regarded his shavetails almost with personal affection. Except for a dog he had once owned they were the first live stock that had ever belonged to him. He was a man of property, and because they were his own he thought there had never been a string of mules like these. In later years he was to become a wealthy cattleman, but no thrill of ownership would ever compare with this first one.

They camped the third night about ten miles from Los Piños. While they were sitting crosslegged at supper, two men rode up to their fire. They were a tough-looking pair, leather-faced and bowlegged. One was a squat, shifty-eyed man, with a broken nose; the other a tall, sullen fellow of few words. They gave their names as Pete Johnson and Tom Cooper. Both carried Colts in their sagging belts and looked as if they knew how to use them.

After the custom of the country Dan asked the travelers to sit down and eat. His invitation was not a very hearty one, but it was promptly accepted. During supper the host and his men kept a vigilant but covert watch on their guests. The men might be hired warriors sent out to destroy them.

They had just come from Los Piños and were on their way to El Paso, one of them explained. They were, so they claimed, cow hands on the loose looking for a job. After supper they departed, announcing they intended to travel far before they camped.

'Now I wonder what those blackbirds wanted,' Yorky said, following them with a frowning gaze. 'I'd say for a guess they were on the dodge. Looked like hard nuts to me.'

'I wouldn't quarrel with you about that,' String Beans agreed. 'If I didn't see them again till Kingdom Come, I wouldn't make any kick about that.'

'They may be riding the grub line like they gave out,' Dan said. 'But I'll bet they didn't drop in just for a square. They sized us up mighty carefully. Boys, I hate to make you stir yore stumps after we're all settled down for the night, but I don't aim to sit here and wait to see if they come back after they think we're asleep. We'll hook up and go far as Jacinto Springs.'

'What's the matter with us staying put right here?' String Beans wanted to know. He patted his sawed-off shotgun. 'If they monkey with the buzz saw, I'll fill 'em up with buckshot from old Tried and True here.'

'That would be fine if they helloed the camp,' Dan said dryly. 'But what's to prevent them from sneaking up and rubbing us out before you get yore spatter gun into action?

61

No sir. We'll fight out soon as it gets dark enough to pull our freights without being seen.'

'I sure would like to welcome them if they drift around here again,' the lank teamster mentioned reluctantly. 'Seems a pity if they are expecting us to be here for them to find the place filled with absentees.'

'You can stick around, S. B. We got business elsewhere, me and Dan.' Yorky showed his teeth in a grin. ' 'Course you'd feel some goosey waitin' around alone. Every time a hoot owl lets loose you will jump out of yore skin.'

'I reckon that's so,' String Beans admitted. 'I'll trail along with you timid lads.'

They broke camp and traveled through the darkness to Jacinto Springs. Here a small settlement had grown up around a crossroads store. There were corrals, a blacksmith shop, and a roadhouse. The mules were impounded in the corral. Two of the men slept beneath one of the wagons, the other kept guard.

Dan had the watch beginning at midnight. He had been on duty an hour or more when he heard riders coming up the road. There were two of them. They stopped at the corner of one of the corrals. The young man on guard made out the murmur of voices. He edged closer, following the fence of the corral nearest the wagons. One of the riders ripped out an oath. Dan crept closer. A snatch of words came to him.

'. . . gave us the slip . . .'

He recognized the sulky voice of the broken-nosed man Pete Johnson. The other answered, and again Dan caught only a fragment.

' . . . gone on to town likely.'

Abruptly the speech of Johnson grew sharper. 'What's that over there? Looks like wagons.'

'Betcha they're here,' Cooper said, after a pause.

Dan judged it was time to take a hand. 'Lookin' for someone, boys?' he asked evenly.

He stood in deep shadow where he could not easily be seen. There was a moment of heavy silence before one of the horsemen snapped out a question.

'Who's there?'

'The name is Clifford,' Dan answered. 'Too bad you got lost in the darkness and headed back toward Los Piños instead of following the El Paso road. It's liable to happen to any tenderfoot.'

One of the riders cursed softly. He and his companion

62

were at a disadvantage. Very likely they were trapped, with three guns focused upon them.

'It's so damned dark,' Johnson said, offering his lame explanation. 'Anyone might get lost.'

'You're right it's dark,' Dan agreed. 'Anything might happen—if a fellow wasn't careful.'

His revolver was out, ready for action if necessary. He could almost feel the hesitation of the gunmen.

'Howcome you're up so late?' the squat puncher asked.

'We didn't feel sleepy,' Dan drawled. 'And we're not up any later than you are.'

'Too late,' Johnson decided. 'I reckon we'll light and turn in here.'

'No,' Dan said. 'Not a good place. Mosquitoes are bad here. Better push on to town.'

Cooper laughed harshly. 'Seems we're welcome to beat it, Pete. This fellow must have bought the Springs, don't you reckon?'

The broken-nosed man peered into the darkness. He squinted here and there, trying to discover if the teamsters were waiting in the shadows with weapons trained on them.

'We'll mosey along, Tom,' he said abruptly. 'I never was one to stick around where I wasn't wanted.'

The two men swung their horses round and vanished. Dan did not move for a few moments, then returned to the wagons.

'Thought I heard voices,' String Beans called to him.

'Yes, we had visitors,' Dan mentioned.

'Who were they?'

'Couple of fellows who ate supper with us last night.'

String Beans sat up, as if he were hinged like a jackknife. 'By damn, why didn't you call me? Where are they now?'

'They said they would mosey along. Seems they got lost and back-tracked in the darkness.'

'Hmp!' grunted String Beans. 'Two old-timers like them!'

'I helped them to that story about getting lost,' Dan said.

'We were right,' the lank teamster nodded. 'They were warriors sent out to get us.'

'Looks like,' the young boss agreed. 'We're beginning to rate important.'

'They didn't act biggity, like they wanted to fight?'

'No. They seemed real gentle to me.' Dan permitted himself a grin. 'They were scared you boys were somewhere near on the welcome committee.'

'Wish I had been,' String Beans lamented.

He smoked a pipe, then turned over and went to sleep again.

Chapter 14

•

DAN IMPROVES THE ROAD

As DAN drew up his mules in front of Ochoa and Waller's warehouse, a man stepped forward and handed him a paper.

'What's this?' Dan asked.

'It's an attachment,' the man replied. 'I'm a deputy sheriff. Name of Larson. Been ordered to take charge of the salt in these wagons.'

'I don't get the idea,' Dan protested. 'I don't owe any money—if you're claiming this attachment is for debt.'

'I don't claim a thing, Mr. Clifford,' answered the deputy. 'You better go see Judge Harper. He issued the writ. All I have to do is take care of the salt till the matter is settled.'

'What matter you talking about?'

'I wouldn't know. See the judge.'

'I'll do that. Are you willing to leave the wagons here until I have seen him?'

'Sure. Anything to oblige. You'll find the judge up to the post-office.'

Dan turned, to walk across to San Antonio Street. Two men were standing in front of an adobe building on the other side of the road. They were watching him. The men were Johnson and Cooper. Out of the corner of his mouth one spoke to the other, using a scabrous epithet. Dan chose not to realize that the foul term was applied to him.

'You're a long way from El Paso, gentlemen,' he said derisively.

'That any of yore damn business?' demanded the tall man Cooper curtly.

'I'm just sympathizing with you for taking such a long ride for nothing.'

Dan went up the street jauntily, with the manner of cocksure confidence men had begun to notice in him. The easy stride belied his real state of mind. He was not sure one of these gunmen would not send a bullet into the flat back he had turned to them with such negligent insolence. The chances were against this. They were not likely to assassinate him in the daytime on the open street except face to face.

The young man knew this attachment must be the work of his enemies. Abel Harper was a man of no character who had been elected corruptly by the vicious element. He was known to be the tool of the gamblers.

The judge was sitting tilted back in a chair in front of the post-office. With him were several of his cronies. Leaning against the door jamb stood Zach Black, the gambler who had been with Le Page when Dan had had his first run-in with the man.

Dan stopped in front of the judge. 'What does this attachment mean, sir?' he asked coldly.

Harper took the paper and ran over it with his eyes. He knew perfectly well what was written there, but he was making an elaborate pretense to the contrary.

'It's an attachment, Mr. Clifford,' he said.

'So I see. On what grounds? Why attach my property?'

'Seems to be some doubt about whose property it is. This salt was taken from land owned by others, it is claimed.'

'I can prove I got it from the salt lakes,' Dan replied.

'That's just the point, Mr. Clifford. The salt lakes were located recently by a private party.'

Dan stared at the pink plump little man. 'Why, the lakes have been public property since the earliest days. Anyone has been free to haul away all the salt he wants.'

'So I'm told,' Harper said suavely. 'But now it has been taken up legally and of course that privilege no longer exists.'

'Who took up the lakes?' Dan demanded.

'Mr. Black here.'

Dan looked into the cold skim-milk eyes of Zach Black. The gambler returned the look steadily, warily, his thin-lipped mouth a straight gash in the face.

'Who were you acting for, Mr. Black?' asked Dan.

'For myself.'

'When did you locate this property?'

'Not very long ago.'

'I asked you when,' Dan said sharply.

'I've forgotten the exact day. You'll find it on the records.'

'I suppose you know it's dangerous.'

The heavy-set man asked a question quietly. 'Are you threatening me?'

'No. I'm warning you. Since I'm not a lawyer, I don't know whether you can make this stick legally. But you had better pray you can't. Personally, I shall abide by the law, but you ought to know there are a thousand Mexicans on both sides of the border who will feel they have been robbed of an ancient right. They won't take it lying down. You know that.'

'That's no way to talk, Mr. Clifford,' the little judge fussed. 'The law is the law. You ought not to encourage ignorant men to break it.'

'I'm not. They won't need any encouragement. This is a foolhardy business. Trouble will come of it, I'm afraid.'

'Are you afraid? Or are you hoping?' Black asked.

'Nobody has ever taken up the salt lakes because everybody has known they were free to anyone who wanted to use them,' Dan replied. 'Any man who takes them up is asking for trouble. You know that. I don't have to tell you.'

'I'll rest my case on the law,' the gambler said.

'And you claim this salt I hauled a hundred miles?'

'I claim what is mine. No more.'

'I see.' Dan looked hard at him, then turned on his heel.

He walked back to the warehouse. Larson sat on the loading platform smoking a pipe of peace with the two mule skinners.

'You win,' Dan said to the deputy; and to his men, 'We'll unload here.'

'Wait a minute,' the deputy said. 'My orders are to take this salt to the Miller warehouse.'

'Take it where you please,' Dan told him curtly. 'We're going to unload here in the middle of the road, boys.'

'In the mud?' Yorky asked.

'In the mud.'

'You can't do that,' Larson objected. 'This injunction—'

'—covers the salt, but not my wagons and my teams,' Dan interrupted. 'I'm not hauling it for you. Get busy, boys.'

'If you ruin this salt, you'll get into trouble,' the deputy sheriff warned.

'Not my fault you haven't wagons to haul it away. I need my teams for other business.'

The mouth of young Clifford was a thin, grim line, his eyes were hard and cold. Larson decided he had better get advice from the sheriff. It would be easy to make a mistake for which he would be blamed.

'Wait till I get back, boys,' he said, and departed hurriedly.

Dan did not wait a moment. He hired several men who

66

chanced to be near and strung his wagons out along the road. The shovelers began flinging the salt into the mud, each wagon being moved forward slowly to get the salt well scattered. Neither Dan nor his teamsters did any of the work. The owner of the outfit meant to finish the job he had started, and he did not propose to be hampered by having a shovel in his hand at a critical moment.

A crowd gathered. Few of them knew what was back of this strange procedure, but all guessed there was drama and perhaps tragedy in it. A man did not bring merchandise a hundred miles to fling it into the mud for no reason at all.

Among those who lined the side of the street were Johnson and Cooper. Neither of them interfered. Their instructions did not cover this contingency.

But their jeers were audible.

'Sure Shot bit off more than he can chew this time, don't you reckon?' Johnson called across the street to Cooper.

'Bound to happen sooner or later to Smart Alecks like him,' the other answered.

Sam Jones arrived and shouted a question. 'You been hired to fix up the roads, Dan?'

'I'm doing it free gratis, Obigod,' Dan replied cheerfully. 'A fellow has to be public-spirited once in a while. Seems this is Mr. Zach Black's salt. You want to thank him, not me. I'm only the humble instrument, as you might say.'

Sheriff Watts reached the scene in time to see the last of the salt flung from the tail of the wagons. He had not hurried. His sympathies were not with the lawless element. It was his opinion that the locating of the salt lakes by private parties was a dangerous business likely to lead to serious trouble. Many of the Mexicans along the border were ignorant and excitable. This interference with what they regarded as a vested right would be bound to inflame them. Moreover, the impounding of the salt Dan had hauled to town in perfectly good faith seemed to him high-handed legal robbery. The locators had put up no notice warning the public that this was private property.

Watts walked up to Dan. 'You'll have to stop throwing out this salt, Clifford,' he said. 'It is in my hands now. You mustn't touch it.'

There was a flicker of amusement in the eyes of both men.

Dan called to his shovelers not to unload the wagons.

A big red-faced shoveler rested on the handle of the tool he had been using. 'We done unloaded them. There ain't hardly a spoonful left.'

'Well, save that spoonful for the sheriff. He wants it to put in Zach Black's soup.'

Someone in the crowd started a cheer. Most of them were on the side of this young fellow who had suddenly developed into the most picturesque and audacious citizen of Los Piños. He had cut the comb of Jasper Ford, and that had never been done before. He had tossed out a careless defiance to the gamblers. Surprisingly, he still survived. This episode of the salt was one nobody less full of *verve* would have pulled off, and he did it with a cool debonair impudence that enchanted the crowd. No doubt he strutted a little, for he was still a boy. But back of his gay insolence those watching him sensed a steely hardness.

It was Sam Jones who had started the cheer, and it went with a whoop. Dan was a source of much entertainment to the ranger. Within a month he had come of age mentally. Sam had contributed to this growth by lighting some of the fireworks, but he had to admit his pupil was astonishingly apt. He knew not only how to snatch victory out of defeat, but to do it with a dramatic flair that appealed to the public imagination.

Chapter 15

•

GROWN UP NOW

DAN was paying the bill for his grandiose gesture. He had thrown into the mud the wages of three men for ten days, his own time and labor, food for men and beasts, and the wear and tear of two hundred rough miles on his equipment. But the moral victory was his. He had the laugh on the enemy. In effect, he had said: 'Black and his backers claim this salt. All right, let them gather it from the mud where I have flung it.'

It became known that Ford, Stone, and others among the gamblers were back of Black's move to locate the lakes. Through him they swore out a warrant for the arrest of Dan, charging him with unlawful entry upon the domain of another and the felonious removal of valuable property therefrom. A dozen people offered to go on Dan's bond as soon as they heard of the arrest. Among them were Ochoa and Waller, Polly Doble, and a prominent lawyer named Stephen Taft. The latter Dan engaged to represent him.

An unexpected effect of Dan's arrest was an immediate access of popularity among the Mexicans. The natives claimed him as their champion, and he became their hero overnight. As the weeks passed, they turned to him for advice. They began to consult him on all kinds of private matters. This embarrassed him, for his knowledge of affairs was very limited. But he was learning not to toss away any element of strength, and he enlisted the lawyer Taft as co-adviser. Since Taft had political ambitions, he was glad to acquire influence among the Mexican voters.

Dan dropped in at the little house at the end of San Antonio Street. Ah Sin was spraying shirts from his mouth. He rolled one up and looked at the young man reproachfully.

'You no killum devil Ford yet,' he said.

'You're sure one bloodthirsty son of Confucius, Ah Sin,' Dan responded with a laugh. 'What did Jas Ford ever do to you?'

'Him do plenty. Me fixum.'

The younger man lost his grin. 'Go slow, Ah Sin,' he said gravely. 'I don't know what's on your mind, but you'd better slip it into the discard. That fellow is a wolf. I aim to walk a long way round him.'

Milly came into the front room from the parlor.

'I'm so sorry you lost your salt,' she said after they had exchanged greetings. 'After you went so far to get it.'

Dan shrugged his shoulders. 'That's all right. My teams are busy on more profitable jobs.'

'Why did you throw it into the street?'

He followed her into the parlor. 'I don't know. Just a sudden notion. I wasn't going to let those scalawags get it after I had worked so hard for it.'

'Won't you get into trouble about it?' Milly asked.

'What kind of trouble?'

'I don't know. If you had let them have the salt, they might have thought they were even with you and let you alone in future.'

'No. They would have thought I was easy pickings. I've learned one thing. With fellows like that you have to march right up to them and call all bluffs. Honest, I think it's safer than to run—unless I ran a long way, till I was clear out of breath and Texas.'

She gave him a queer shy look. 'You're a funny boy.' A

69

moment later she corrected that. 'Not a boy now. You were one when I first met you, but you've changed. You're different.'

'Grown up now?' he asked.

'Yes. Even your looks have changed.'

'It's my mustache does it,' he said.

'Is that a mustache?' she inquired, her eyes twinkling.

He stroked the dark smudge on his lip. 'A very fine one. Or will be.'

She shook her head. 'No, the change I mean comes from inside you. The way you carry your head and your shoulders, and the look in your eye. You're not afraid any longer.'

'I sure was scared to death at first,' he admitted cheerfully.

'You were frightened, but——'

'But what?' he asked, after she had left her sentence incomplete.

Milly felt the color rise to her cheeks. What she had started to say was that though frightened he had been brave.

'Nothing. Anyway, you're not frightened now. You walk as if you'd like to knock a chip from a grizzly bear's shoulder.' The girl frowned at him, puzzled. 'I don't understand what has come over you.'

'A fellow can't quit and let scoundrels tromp on him. He has to act like he doesn't give a dad gum. The way it works out, first thing he finds he doesn't. I was reading the other day what General Grant said when some fellow asked him if he wasn't worried for fear the general on the other side would pull a trick and beat him in battle. He told the man he knew the other general was just as much worried as he was. So what was the use of fretting?'

'No use, but——how can you help it? Isn't it silly to talk about walking up to these bad men and calling their bluff? You can't walk up to a bullet fired in the night.'

'You can be where the bullet ain't,' Dan said, grinning.

'I hope you can.' Her charming mobile face betrayed an urgent anxiety. 'Oh, Dan, be careful. Don't ever give them a chance to . . . hurt you.'

'I sure won't,' he promised. 'Dan Clifford is the last man I would throw down on. You can bank on that.'

'You won't run around nights?'

'No, lady.' He changed the subject. 'Mrs. Doble tells me you're going to be a schoolmarm.'

'Yes. Beginning next week. Thank you for helping me get the place.'

'I can't honestly take that thanks, since I hadn't a thing to do with it.'

'Except talk to the directors for me.'

'They didn't give what I said any weight. I reckon Mrs. Doble is responsible for getting Los Piños such a nice school-marm.'

She wrinkled her forehead in doubt. 'I hope I'll please. Some of the parents think I'm too young.'

'You'll please,' he promised her.

Dan had no doubt of it. The delicate color in her cheeks deepened at his assurance. She was a lovely young creature, slender and immature. He thought the lights in her soft wavy hair beautiful. He liked the line of her exquisite throat and the shy gaiety that sent laughter rippling into it. A month ago she had been too thin, worn down by anxiety and lack of good food. Now she carried more weight. Her step was light and rhythmic. Energy expressed itself in the swift eagerness of her warm breathing body. The clothes had something to do with the change in her. She had been a ragged little Cinderella, in spite of her pathetic attempts at neatness. Polly Doble had got her credit at the stores. She had a gift for dress, an almost sure instinct for the fabrics, colors, and style that suited her. A man would travel far, Dan thought, to find another girl so vividly pretty as Milly Sutherland. There was a fine self-respect in the way she carried herself. She did not look like the daughter of a shiftless renter, but like the descendant of the soldier who had come back from the Civil War to become a judge in the community where he had been born and brought up.

It occurred to Dan that he had grown careless in his speech from long contact with rough men. His people were well-to-do planters. It was about time he paid some attention to his manner of talking and to the bluntness that had crept into his behavior. One did not have to be uncouth to be companionable.

Milly was still unsure enough of herself to be embarrassed by compliments. Her mind jumped at a tangent to another topic of conversation.

'I hear that Mr. Ford and those in the salt lakes business with him have sent a party to begin work and to keep off anybody else who tries to take salt,' she said.

'Yes.' Dan spoke gravely. 'There's going to be trouble. They must know the Mexicans are very excited at what they feel is an infringement of their rights. It's a foolhardy thing to do—locate this land that has been free to the public for

71

generations and has been used by thousands of people. Stephen Taft says it ought to be public domain from custom and long use, but he is afraid we can't make that stick at law. The lakes are on land subject to entry. The fact that nobody up till now has been mean enough and crazy enough to take it up doesn't affect the legality.'

'You mean that there will be fighting?'

'Afraid so. The Mexicans are a gentle people when not aroused, but back of this lies fifty years of bitterness ready to be stirred up. Ever since the days of Santa Anna and Sam Houston there has been feeling. It has been kept alive by border raids and cattle wars and bad men on both sides of the line. During the past few years the trouble has begun to die down. We haven't had dozens killed every twelve months by those of the other race. Now this salt lakes affair will start another race war if we're not careful. The Mexicans living near will all feel it's a Yankee trick to rob them of an established right.'

'If there is trouble you won't be in it,' Milly said.

'No,' Dan agreed.

But he was not so sure. It would be difficult to stay out. If he refused aid and counsel, his Mexican friends would feel that all Americans were against them and the quarrel would become a purely racial one. That would be bad.

'It may be a good thing for you,' the girl suggested. 'The more feeling Mr. Ford and his crowd stir up, the less time they will have to pick on you.'

Again Dan assented, but with the uneasy conviction that if the matter came to issue he would be dragged into the thick of it.

Chapter 16

•

STORM BREWING

DAN had taken a contract for the delivery of forty thousand feet of lumber to a contractor who was putting up a store building. He had just finished unloading a wagon when he looked up to see the Reverend Philip Washburn coming across the street to him. The road was muddy, but there was nothing finical about the way the clergyman moved. He avoided the worst of the mud, yet picked a passage without hesitation.

'You are Mr. Clifford?' the minister asked.

'Yes, sir.' Dan got down from the bed of the wagon.

'Washburn is my name.' The churchman extended a hand.

Dan liked the firm grip. He liked it that the other had not hesitated because his brown palm was soiled with brick dust.

Philip Washburn was a well-set-up young man just out of a theological seminary. He had first-class family connections in the East, but had preferred to go to the frontier as a home missionary during the earlier years of his work. It was his opinion that existence had been made too easy for him. What he needed was contact with life in the raw. That was why he had come to Los Piños rather than accept a pastorate in a church well-padded from the knocks of harsh reality.

'I saw you the day you came in on the stage,' Dan said.

'I'm surprised you had time to notice me just then,' the young minister said dryly.

'On account of the lead plum some fellow sent my way? That was only a general results shot, sir. The shooter was hoping but not expecting.'

'Hoping to do murder,' Washburn said severely, in reproof of Dan's levity.

'Yes, sir,' agreed Clifford. 'Though that's not a word we generally use here except in special cases.'

'No, you talk about trouble and difficulties and killings. A distinction without a difference. I use a good old-fashioned English word to express exactly what I mean.'

'Kill is a good old English word too, isn't it?' Dan asked. 'When my mother taught me the Ten Commandments that was the word I found in the Bible.'

'True, but out here the word has taken on the meaning of a casual offense. I am glad you remember the Ten Commandments, Mr. Clifford. Sometimes I think word of them has not reached Los Piños yet.' A smile, warm and boyish, illumined the face of the clergyman. 'But I didn't come here to preach to you, Mr. Clifford.'

'I reckon I could stand some preaching at,' Dan admitted, meeting the smile. 'I've been meaning to come and hear you, but I've been out of town. Probably you have heard some talk about me being a tough nut. The town is full of it right now. There's nothing to it, sir. I will go all the way with you in condemnation of murder. It wasn't by any wish of mine

73

I got in a jam with the gambling element. I was pushed into it.'

'I have been told you practice shooting down by the river half an hour each day,' Washburn mentioned.

'Yes, sir. Is it in your Bible that I am to let myself be murdered without lifting a hand to save my life?'

'Why not leave this part of the country?'

'Do you want all the honest men to get out and leave only the scoundrels here?'

'You must do what you think right. I'm not blaming you. That you are not the aggressor in this feud is clear. But we must stop the trouble before it gets any worse. This salt lake business is very serious. I have just heard that a Mexican has been arrested. He was in a wagon heading toward the salt deposits. These men have no evidence that he meant to go there, though the chances are he did. Those of his race are very excited about it. Something must be done. I have come to ask you to attend a small meeting to discuss the matter. They say you have influence with the Mexicans.'

'I'll come,' Dan promised. 'But you are barking up the wrong tree, sir, if you expect to handle it by an appeal to the Mexicans. They feel themselves in the right.'

Dan found a group of business men at the meeting. Among them were two or three of the more decent saloon-keepers. After some discussion the cattleman Stevens asked Dan whether he thought the Mexicans would resort to violence. The young man was surprised at the apparent respect these leading citizens paid to his opinion.

'I'm afraid there will be trouble if Ford and his crowd push their claim,' Dan said. 'All these years when a Mexican needed a little spare cash, he went to the salt deposits and sold a wagonload. Now the lid is clamped down suddenly. He is told he can't touch it. Naturally he is sore.'

'We understand that,' Stevens replied. 'Question is, How far will the Mexicans go? After all, law is law. They can't buck it.'

'They will try,' Dan answered. 'Some irresponsible fire-brands have been inflaming them. Among these is that priest Miguel. He has promised them absolution for anything they may do. Of course the best priests are doing what they can to quiet their countrymen and are urging them to submit their cause to legal decision.'

'You have influence with them, Dan,' said Waller. 'Would it be any use for you to spend several days at the different

74

villages explaining that the sentiment of decent Americans is with them?'

'I don't know. Maybeso, but not if they are choused around by Ford's bunch. The arrest of this man Chico Chaves, who wasn't within ten miles of the lakes, is a high-handed outrage. The Mexicans won't like that.' Dan voiced bluntly his view. 'If you want peace, gentlemen, work on the gamblers and try to get them to give up this scheme. Tell them what they are doing is loaded with dynamite and may blow them up. They despise Mexicans and think they can run over them as much as they please. That is a mistake. I have talked with many Mexicans recently. They are hot-tempered people when they think they are being mistreated. They will fight, unless the claim to the salt lakes is withdrawn.'

'No chance of the claim being abandoned,' Stevens said, shaking his head. 'Too much money involved. These fellows are hard characters, and they won't give up a lot of easy dollars.'

'That is true,' the minister agreed. 'I have talked with Ford and Black and Stone. None of them will listen to any appeal. They say they have a legal right to make entry, and if they were to surrender their right someone else would jump in and take it. They don't propose to let a bunch of greasers—I am using their word, gentlemen—bluff them out by threats. They talk of getting the rangers to see they are not molested.'

'That what we pay the rangers for?' growled an old saloon-keeper. 'To help these scalawags do their grabbing?'

It was decided that Ochoa, the partner of Waller, should be asked to go through the Mexican villages contiguous to the lakes, accompanied by Dan, for the purpose of trying to allay the excitement of his countrymen. Dan said he did not think their mission would be of any use, but he was willing to do the best he could.

The meeting had scarcely adjourned when the news spread that Chico Chavez had been brought to town and locked up. Los Piños became as excited as a swarm of hiving bees. The Mexicans drew together. Hot Spanish maledictions filled the native quarter. Several horsemen rode hurriedly out of town. Evidently they were going to seek reinforcements from neighboring villages. It was predicted freely that there would be an attempt to storm the jail before the night ended.

75

Chapter 17

•

DAN BORROWS A KEY

Speaking to Stevens and Waller, Dan said, 'If we're going to stop a riot, we have got to move fast.'

'Right you are,' Stevens replied. 'This town is ripe for trouble.'

'The thing is to get this Chavez out on bail,' Waller suggested. 'We can do that easy enough.'

The three men found Judge Harper and explained what they wanted. He gave them an oily smile.

'That has already been arranged, gentlemen,' he said.

'What do you mean?' asked Waller.

The fat ruddy little man had the look of a cat which had been caught stealing the cream. 'A bond for bail has already been put up,' he told them.

'Who by?' Dan wanted to know, ungrammatically but urgently.

'By Mr. Ford and Mr. Stone.'

Dan stared at him. 'What shenanigan is this?' he demanded bluntly.

Harper became dignified. 'I do not answer impudent questions, sir. I am a judge of the sovereign State of Texas and will commit you for contempt of court if you are not careful.'

'What reason did Ford and Stone give for wanting his release, Judge?' inquired Stevens.

'The same reason you gave me,' replied the judge. 'That there would be trouble if Chavez was kept in jail and that he had better be released, at least temporarily.'

'Then where is Chavez? He hasn't been seen on the streets. His friends don't know where he is.' Waller looked at the politician with sharp suspicion.

'I haven't the slightest idea where he went after he was released, nor have I any interest in that provided he does not jump his bond.'

It was clear nothing more was to be gained by questioning Judge Harper.

76

'We'd better go to the jail and find out what they know there,' Waller said.

As they walked down the street, they discussed the situation.

'I don't get what these scoundrels mean by freeing Chavez,' Dan said. 'Doesn't look good to me.'

'If they have freed him,' suggested Stevens.

Dan nodded. 'Hadn't thought of that. But you're right, I reckon. They're holding him somewhere.'

'Then they're foolin' with a charge of dynamite,' Stevens commented. 'One that's liable to blow them all to hell.'

'Sure are,' Waller assented. 'The Mexicans mean business. They are going through. Watts has sworn in a posse of a dozen men and armed them. Three-four rangers have joined him. If the Mexicans spill over, they will run into bullets.'

Sheriff Watts was at the jail. He was busy distributing arms and ammunition to his men.

'Come to join my posse?' he asked when he caught sight of the three new arrivals.

'Not exactly,' Waller replied. 'We've come to find out what became of Chavez. Seems from what Harper says that Ford's crowd got him out.'

'Yes.'

'Then where is he?'

'I'm wondering about that myself,' the sheriff answered. 'I wasn't here when they brought the order for Chavez's release. My jailor, Buck Adams, turned the prisoner over to them. They took him out the back door, claiming it was better to get him from the jail quietly on account of the feeling that had been stirred up. If I had been here it wouldn't have been that way. Chavez would have gone out the front door to his friends.'

Watts was a bronzed Westerner in the late forties, a heavy-set man with broad shoulders and bowed legs. He had been a cattleman and still dressed as one. His clothes were always wrinkled and dusty, but his boots and hat had been made by well-known firms which charged high prices.

'You don't think anything has happened to Chavez?' asked Stevens.

The blue eyes of the sheriff looked straight at the cowman. 'Your guess is as good as mine, Lon. I would say not, unless someone has gone plumb loco. He is not important. Why hurt him?'

'Then where is he?'

'He may be back with his friends by now. I couldn't say

about that.' The sheriff smiled grimly. 'This is my busy day, gentlemen. I haven't time to go look for Chavez, but I certainly would be obliged if you would find him. When his friends find he is not in the jail, they are liable to ask where he is. I'd like to be able to answer that question.'

'Maybe we're hatching a mare's nest,' Waller said. 'He may be down in some *tendejon* with his countrymen. First off, we'd better make sure of that.'

Dan offered to find out. He made inquiries of several friends among the Mexicans. None of them had seen anything of Chavez. One of them, a brother-in-law of the prisoner, said that it was impossible he could be at liberty without his relatives knowing it. Young Clifford sensed by the atmosphere that the natives were at a high tension. Chavez had to be found. If word reached them that he had been spirited away by the salt deposit locators, they would jump to the conclusion he had been murdered. Nothing could then prevent serious trouble.

On his way back to report to the others, Dan had a brain flash. He saw a chance, if his luck stood up, of getting past the immediate crisis without a battle between the Mexicans and the forces of law. It would be full of danger for him, but it might succeed.

He made it a point to walk part-way home with Waller as the merchant returned to his house. At the corner of San Antonio and Crockett Streets he stopped.

'Like to have the key to your warehouse tonight, Mr. Waller, if you'll trust me with it,' Dan said.

Waller stared at him in surprise. 'What for?'

'Rather not tell you. I'm going to have a try at stopping this riot. It may not work. Even if it does, there is danger in it. I'm making the play, not you. The less you know about it the better.'

Waller was a sober business man not given to dramatics. 'Don't you think you had better talk this over with me, Dan?' he asked. 'Two heads are better than one. I can't imagine what you have in mind, but if it is anything crazy——'

'It's not so crazy,' Dan interrupted. 'But I have to play the hand. You're not in it.'

'I can't see what you want the key of my warehouse for.'

'Our story is that I already had the key—got it from you this morning to haul those goods out to the store at San Jacinto.'

'I'm not worried about the story we'll tell," Waller replied.

'I'm worried about you, boy. What hare-brained scheme have you hatched?'

Dan shook his head. 'I haven't any information for you about that, Mr. Waller. Do I get the key?'

The merchant detached a key from the bunch he carried and handed it to the young man. 'I hate to do this,' he said. 'Maybe I'm letting you in for a lot of trouble.'

'I'm headed for it, anyhow, whether you let me have the key or not,' Dan said, with a grin. 'I'll ask one thing more. Stay away from the warehouse tonight. I'm leasing it.'

'Don't intend to burn it down, do you?'

'I'm no fire bug. Well, see you later. I've got a hen sitting.'

Waller watched him stride away with the cocksure tread so carefree and light, the Stetson hat set jauntily at a rakish tilt. The arresting thing about him was his picturesque vigor. He might be a boy in years, but it was his friend's opinion that if a bullet did not cut short his career he would play a man's part in the life of the town. Life is written in experience, not in years; and Dan Clifford was having enough of this for half a dozen men.

The older man hoped he had not done wrong in letting him have the key to the warehouse. He consoled himself with the reflection that the error, if it was one, could not be important. For if Dan had not got the key, he would have done without it. A little thing like that was not going to stand in the way of whatever reckless plan he had formed.

Chapter 18

•

'THIS TOWN IS DIS-APPOINTED IN YOU'

JASPER FORD was just stepping into the The Last Chance when a Mexican boy stopped him to deliver a note. Before reading it the gambler asked the lad who had given it to him. The olive-skinned youngster shook his head, flashed a mouthful of ivory teeth in a wide smile, and mentioned in liquid Spanish that he did not know English.

Ford shrugged his shoulders and opened the envelope. He read:

Jas, Come to my place soon as you can. I just learned something important. Don't be seen coming if you can help it.

CHRIS

When Ford looked up, the boy was vanishing round the corner. That did not matter, since he did not know enough Spanish to talk with him. The note must be from Chris Kuner, who ran a rough-and-tumble saloon near the river. The name of his joint few knew. From the number of shooting and cutting scrapes that had occurred there it was universally called The Bucket of Blood. Chris was a trusty henchman of those who ruled the lawless underworld. If he had found out something he thought was important, Jasper Ford thought it would be wise for him to discover what it was. The opinion of Ford was that within a very few hours Los Piños would echo to the roar of guns. That suited his plan. He was deliberately fomenting a riot because he wanted troops sent to oppose the Mexicans. Before the storm broke, he intended to be in the gambling house where he worked, a score of armed allies at hand.

The gambler did not go down San Antonio Street, but moved along an unlighted one which paralleled it. Night had fallen. Later there would be a moon and stars. Since he was fastidious about dress, Ford picked a way carefully along the muddy street. There had been some days of sunshine, and it was possible by going warily to avoid stepping in the mire.

He came to the place where Clifford had scattered the salt. The sight of the white road irritated him, because it brought to mind the young whippersnapper who had flouted him and made the town laugh at his discomfiture. In front of a pond of slush he hesitated, picked out with his eyes a path close to the wall of an adobe building, and began to circle the pool, his gaze still on the ground.

It was as he passed a deep adobe doorway that a shattering surprise fell upon him. A long arm reached out of the darkness and snatched him into the shadow. It slipped down and encircled his waist, pinning both hands to the body. Against the back of his head he felt the cold pressure of steel.

Ford stood stiff, an icy chill running down his spine. He felt his stomach muscles collapse.

'Relax,' a voice advised. 'Don't make a sound. Don't move.'

The trapped man knew who this was, though his eyes were turned to the wall. That cool mocking voice could not be forgotten. Ford did not cry out. He did not move. The weapon in his pocket was taken from him. His body was patted to make sure he had not another.

With a foot his captor pushed open the door. Under the

80

pressure of a firm grip, Ford moved into a large warehouse lit by a pair of lanterns. He heard the door closed behind him.

'What do you mean by this outrage?' the gambler demanded, facing the man who had trapped him.

Ford was pale but composed. The man had courage. He did not know what was in store for him, but he summoned resolution to face it.

Dan pointed to a sack of oats. 'Sit down, Mr. Ford. You're liable to be here quite some time.'

'I demand to be released,' the gambler said. 'At once. If you think you can get by with an outrage like this——'

'Twice you've used that word,' Dan drawled. 'I reckon it's an outrage when I bring you here, but it isn't when you hold Chavez prisoner. I expect you would call that a horse of another color.'

'I'm not holding him prisoner. If you don't turn me loose this instant, I'll have you bumped off before the night is over.' The voice of the gambler shook with anger.

'You don't keep your promises,' Dan told him, in the patient way one humors a child. 'You tell what-all you'll do, and it turns out to be only wind. This town is disappointed in you. It feels you don't live up to your reputation. Maybe back in Missouri—or wherever you come from—you are quite a wolf in your home town, but you don't seem to howl in Texas.'

The eyes of the gambler narrowed. He was working this thing out with his mind. That he had been trapped was clear. What for? Did his enemy mean to murder him? If so, why drag him in here when he could have shot him down from the doorway? No, there was more to it than that.

'You wrote that note the Mexican brought me,' Ford charged.

'Smart as a whip, aren't you?' Dan murmured, with mock admiration.

'How did you know I would come down this street?'

'It's the nearest way to Chris Kuner's place from The Last Chance, unless you went down San Antonio Street, and I figured you wouldn't do that. If I hadn't got you here, I would have met you as you came out of The Bucket of Blood.'

'I warned you to keep out of my way if you want to live,' Ford said angrily.

'So you did,' agreed Dan, unabashed. 'And here I am butting in again.'

'Did you bring me here to kill me? Or what?'

'I'm harmless,' Dan answered, with a gentleness that held a jeering threat. 'That is, unless you got crazy and went wild on me, so that I had to puncture you to keep you still. I wouldn't know yet whether you get tonight what's coming to you. Depends on you, I'd say. To make it short and sweet, here's where you stand. If you give me an order to Stone and Black to deliver Chavez to me, and if they do it without making any rumpus, I expect you'll leave here good as new.'

'And if I don't, you'll murder me. That what you mean?' Ford drew up his tall, slender figure, the cold eyes in his pallid face hard with defiance.

'Wrong guess,' Dan replied. 'I'll turn you over to the Mexicans and quit the game.'

'Leave them to lynch me, you coyote?'

'Would they do that?' Dan asked carelessly. 'After you have been so kind and friendly to them?'

'You know they would.' Ford glared at him. The fear of such a fate rose in his throat. It was horrible to let the mind dwell upon such an end.

'Can't tell what a crazy mob will do,' Dan admitted. 'Your view may be right. Come to think of it, I reckon your guess is good.'

'Would you turn a white man over to a bunch of Apaches?'

Dan lifted his eyebrows. 'Do you claim you are a white man?'

'I don't know where this Chavez is. We got him out of jail to stop this trouble. Then we turned him loose.'

'Where? At the bottom of some dry gulch—with a pile of rocks on top of him?'

'No. What do we care about this greaser? He's nothing to us—and nothing to you. I'm not such a fool as not to know that you are using him to get even with me.' Ford stood straight as an arrow, his eyes blazing hate.

'Use your head, Ford,' advised Dan. 'If I wanted to get even with you, I wouldn't worry about what you had done with Chavez. I'd just call in his friends and tell them you were their meat. That is all I would have to do. But I'm trying to prevent a riot in which a lot of good people will be killed, just as you are trying to bring on trouble of that kind.'

'Why would I do that?' the gambler asked sharply.

'To bring troops here to keep the peace,' Dan said, with an ironic grin. 'You're for law and order—when it helps you. If these Mexicans start making trouble they will get in bad with the Government. That's what you want them to do. Then the law will pull your chestnuts out of the fire for you. With soldiers around here your steal of the salt lakes would go through fine. The natives would be overawed. If they tried to use force, they would get the worst of it. . . . No need going into that. Point is, do you give me an order on your bully-puss friends to turn over Chavez to us? Or don't you? I wouldn't advise you either way. Suit yourself.'

Dan sat down on a large drygoods box and dangled a leg negligently. He was at casual ease, but Ford did not fail to recognize the fact that if he made a mistake based on the assumption that his captor had grown careless, he would be dropped in his tracks before he had moved a yard. The derisive gaze did not lift from him for an instant.

'I told you I don't know where—'

'Yes, I heard you,' Dan interrupted. 'Better not waste your breath on arguing. In about five minutes a man is going to knock on that door and ask for instructions. You are deciding on the orders I give him. It's your funeral, not mine. Any messages you would like sent friends or relatives?'

'You can't bluff me,' Ford said harshly.

'I wouldn't try.' Dan laughed sardonically. 'Funny the things a man will die for when he gets bull in the neck. Looking at it as an outsider, a fellow would think it didn't matter so darned much if your crowd did turn loose Chavez. But it looks like you're going to be a hero about it. Well, you'll sure get a nice long notice in the paper.'

'Say I did know where Chavez is,' Ford spoke up. 'How do I know you wouldn't go back on your bargain?'

'You don't,' Dan replied. 'I might turn the Christian over to the lions just the same. All you can do is guess. Maybe I'm a liar and a skunk. Maybe I'm a white man.'

Ford was not worried about that. He had made the point by way of insult, but he did not give it any weight himself.

'You swear to let me go as soon as Chavez is released?'

'No, sir. I tell you I'll let you go. It's neck meat or nothing with you, Mr. Ford. You're not offering conditions, but are taking any terms you're lucky enough to get. I understand you'd like to send a blue whistler to my address. But you'll have to wait for that pleasure. Right now you're playing the hand that has been dealt you, and there are no aces in it.'

'All right, you're calling the turn,' Ford said, with an ugly look of malice. 'What you want me to do—write a note to Stone and Black?'

'Yes. I'll dictate it. You can't afford to have your friends make a mistake.' Dan handed his captive paper and pencil. 'You can write on this box.'

The note was brief.

Boys, I am in a hole. They have got me. If you don't turn Chavez over to them I am to be fed to the Mexicans to be murdered. No use trying a rescue. I would be shot down before you ever got to me. Soon as you get this note give the Mexican to the messengers. I have been given half an hour. After that it will be too late. Don't try any funny business, but do as I say.

JASPER FORD

The handwriting of Ford was bold and decisive. His allies would recognize it at a glance.

The gambler read what he had written, his eyes hot with anger. 'For two cents I would tear this up and tell you to go to hell,' he snapped.

'Just as you please,' Dan told him. 'I wouldn't want to influence you. If the Mexicans rub you out, I don't reckon I'll wear mourning.'

Dan rolled and smoked a cigarette, watching his prisoner carefully, the revolver on the box beside him close at hand.

'I see a cigar in your pocket,' he went on. 'If you'd like to smoke, hop to it. We aim to give our guests all the comforts of home.'

'Don't worry about me, Mr. Cock-a-Doodle-Doo,' Ford answered. 'When I smoke up with you, it will be in a different way.'

There came a knock at the door. Dan backed in that direction.

'Who's there?' he demanded.

'Yorky and String Beans,' came the answer.

Without turning, Dan reached back and unlocked the door. His mule skinners walked into the room. They looked at Ford and at Dan, evidently surprised.

'You two havin' some kind of love feast?' Yorky asked.

The gambler saw that the teamsters had not been parties to his kidnaping. 'If you know what's good for you, boys, you'll see this fellow turns me loose at once,' he said, with a manner of curt authority.

String Beans shook his head. 'I wouldn't interfere with my boss, Mr. Ford. He would be liable to fire me.'

'It's now or never,' urged Ford. 'I'll accept no apologies later.'

'Then I reckon we won't trouble makin' any,' Yorky said, with his broad amiable grin. 'No hard feelin's, you understand, but if you and Dan have a li'l' private agreement we wouldn't want to horn in on it.'

Dan spoke for the first time.

'Boys, we want you to take this note to either Stone or Black. See both of them if you can. We're asking them to turn loose Chavez in exchange for Ford. Have your guns handy, and make sure they don't get the drop on you. If you don't, they might try to make you tell where Ford is. We are giving them half an hour. If you are not back here by that time with word that you have seen Chavez released, I am going to deliver Ford to the Mexicans. Do you get the lay-out?'

'We get it,' String Beans said. 'Don't worry about them makin' us tell. We'll keep our eyes open.'

'Fine. Scratch gravel, boys. See you later.'

Inside of the prescribed time Dan's messengers were back with word that they had personally turned Chavez over to his friends.

'Mr. Ford's friends would of liked to get on the prod,' Yorky explained, 'but they seen it wasn't no use to pull their picket pins.'

Dan turned to his prisoner with a smile of mock courtesy. 'Any time you want to go now, Mr. Ford. It has been a pleasure to entertain you.'

The gambler turned at the door for a parting shot. 'I'll certainly entertain you sometime,' he said grimly. 'And when I do——'

He left the uncompleted sentence a threat.

Chapter 19

•

DAN WALKS UP
SAN ANTONIO STREET

WITHIN a few hours all Los Piños knew how Dan Clifford had averted a riot. At every saloon and store in town the affair was discussed, always with derisive laughter except when some of the gambling clique were present. Once more the boy had scored on Ford.

At Ochoa and Waller's store some customers were talking.

'He's sure some hell-a-miler, that boy,' Pete Mulrooney cried, slapping his dusty hat against his thigh. 'Yes, sir, he'll do to take along.'

'You're damn whistlin',' agreed the cattleman Stevens. 'Every time he bumps up against Jas Ford he makes that killer look like two for a quarter.'

Sam Jones nodded. 'So he does. He pulled this off slick. We was due for a big rumpus, looked like. A nice li'l' race war, with about steen citizens killed on each side. And that crazy boy cuts loose his dog and gives that unwilling gent Jas Ford an invite to an armistice powwow. I never see the beat of him. I'll be dad-gummed if it ain't too good to be true, as old Ran Scoville said when he was told his ninth daughter had run off with the camp cook. O' course one thing is sure. Ford won't sit back on his spurs any longer. He'll land on Dan all spraddled out, immediate if not sooner.'

'Yes,' agreed Mulrooney. 'You couldn't expect him to take this without r'arin' back considerable. If I had any influence with Dan, I would get him out of here.'

'I wouldn't say Dan needed any guardeen,' Yorky commented. 'If you had seen him smokin' his cigarette and layin' the law down to Ford like he was wagon boss of all Texas, you wouldn't think that hair-trigger lad was in any jackpot. It was Ford who had his tail in a crack.'

'Is it yore notion, Yorky, that Jasper Ford is a false alarm?' asked the ranger. 'Do you reckon he got all those notches supposed to be on his gun by turning the other cheek when some guy busted him one? I wouldn't say so. If I know that wolf he is crazy to kill this very minute. We bluffed him off last time, but it won't be that way now. He'll go through from hell to breakfast. All Los Piños couldn't stop him.'

'Yes, he has got to save his face.' Stevens frowned thoughtfully. 'Not only with others. With himself, too. He has to rub Clifford out to make sure the boy hasn't got him buffaloed. Until he has done it he will be in torment.'

String Beans walked into the room. Excitement smouldered in his eyes. 'Ford has done got Dan posted on the challenge tree already,' he said. 'He aims to kill him on sight.'

'Does Dan know?' asked Jones.

'Haven't seen him this mornin',' String Beans said. 'He's been figuring on a job of hauling lumber.'

'Where?' inquired Mulrooney. 'We'd better get word to him.'

A cowboy who had ridden in thirty miles from the range and still had the dust of the road in his throat gave an order to a clerk. 'Bust me open a can of yellow clings. I'm spittin' cotton.'

The clerk reached for a can of peaches and cut the top open with a hatchet. Having poured the juice in the can down his baked throat, the cowpuncher asked a question.

'Who is this Dan bird you're powwowin' about? And whyfor does he want to get himself bumped off by Jasper Ford?'

'Name is Clifford,' the clerk answered in a low voice. 'A teamster Ford picked on. Account of a girl, they say. He sure has got himself in a jam. Looks like his chunk will go out.'

The cowboy speared half a peach and transferred it to his mouth, then gave himself to a snatch of familiar song.

> 'Don't you monkey with my lulu gal.
> I'll tell you what I'll do.'

A man came into the store by the back door. He stopped to buy tobacco. His wary gaze shifted from one to another of those present. Nobody said anything to him. The man was the gambler Black.

'Nice morning, gents,' he said.

'Sure is,' assented String Beans.

Black paid for the tobacco and walked out of the front door.

'Come to spy out the land,' Stevens said. 'Better push on your reins, Mulrooney, and warn Dan. It won't be long now. I reckon some of us better stay close to him and see he gets a fair break.'

Dan showed up in the doorway. 'Just met Mr. Black,' he mentioned jauntily. 'Seems a little close-mouthed. When I said "Good morning," the best I could get out of him was a grunt.'

'Heard any news, Dan?' blurted out String Beans abruptly.

'I get the Smith contract for the new hotel, if that's what you mean.'

'Ford has posted you on the challenge tree again,' Mulrooney said. 'Make sure yore gun is workin' good, boy.'

'When is it to be?' Dan asked quietly.

The smile had gone from his face as the light goes from a blown candle. But those watching him could see no evidence that he was shaken by the news. He stood straight, head up.

'Soon as you meet, Ford says. He calls you every black name in the dictionary.' String Beans supplied the information.

'With revolvers?'

'Doesn't say. I reckon so.'

Dan thought for a moment. 'Better get it over with soon as we can.' He turned to the cattleman. 'Will you take him a message from me, Mr. Stevens?'

'Jas Ford, you mean?'

'Yes. Tell him that in just half an hour—say at eleven-thirty sharp—I'll walk up San Antonio Street as far as Crockett. If I don't meet him, I will wait there on the corner for just ten minutes. I shall have my six-gun with me. No sawed-off shotgun. No rifle. I'll expect from him the same square deal I'll be giving him.'

One could have heard the ticking of a watch in that moment of silence following Dan's quiet challenge.

'I'll take that message, Dan,' the cattleman said.

'And I'll be there to see he doesn't slip anything over on you, Dan,' Sam Jones cried, with his usual expletive.

'*Yo tambien,*' agreed Yorky.

'Good,' nodded Dan. 'I'll be a heap obliged. Ford's pack of wolves wouldn't hesitate a minute to bushwhack me if they could get away with it. With you on the job kinda refereeing this, I'll feel more comfortable. . . . Have to say *Adios* now, gentlemen. Got a lot to do in the next half-hour.'

Dan turned and left the store. On one side of him strode Sam Jones, on the other the big red-bearded wagon boss. Already Stevens had departed to carry the message of his principal.

As they left, Mulrooney called back to those in the store, 'We don't aim to have any premature funny business before Dan is ready.'

On the way to the *jacal* Dan drew his six-shooter and took a crack at a knot on a mesquite. The bullet struck within an inch of it.

'You've certainly come along fine since that first day we went out,' the ranger said. 'You've got as good a chance as Ford now. Better, I'd say, if you keep cool. He's crazy mad at you. That won't help him any. And you've got the Indian sign on him. It's sticking in that bird's craw that maybe he'll never get his thirteenth man. He never before tangled with anyone who kept coming out on top. Betcha he's worried. He isn't usually a drinking man, but since you turned him loose last night he has done considerable. Needed something to keep him from feelin' low as a snake's tail in a wagon rut. My guess is he'll blaze away too soon. Don't let him stampede you, son. He's just a wolf you're bumpin' off. Swift, sure. But steady and deliberate. That's yore game.'

'Yes,' Dan answered.

At the cabin he gave Jones the weapon to clean while he sat down at the table to write two letters.

'I'll be driftin' back up the line,' Mulrooney said. 'Going to see yore friends are scattered here and there along Santone Street in the doors of business houses. We allow to have this on the level. See you after the rookus, Dan.'

So he would, Dan thought, dead or alive. The young man's blood ran chill. A cold lump of lead weighted his stomach. He was at the low hour before the battle. His dread was not panic. He knew he was not going to break down. Nor did he let any expression of it reach his hard grim face or contained manner.

The first letter was to his mother. It was a very difficult one to write. Unless he was killed, it would not be delivered to her. What words could console a mother for the loss of her firstborn in such a way? The other was only a note, and it was addressed to Milly Sutherland. He told her that this had been forced on him. His message was in the last sentence. 'I love you.' The three words seemed to him abrupt and insufficient. He wanted to add a great deal to them, but in the end he decided to let them stand just as they were.

He looked at his watch. 'Time for me to go,' he said, and it seemed to him that the voice which said the words belonged to someone else.

'I reckon,' the ranger said cheerfully. 'In ten minutes you'll be through with that scalawag forever. Don't worry about anyone behind you. I'll be a little ways back of you and will take care of that. Keep yore eyes peeled for Ford. Don't let anything get yore mind off that one thing.'

With a strange detachment Dan observed details during that four-hundred-yard walk. A cowboy sat on his spurs at the gateway of the Frontier Corral rolling a cigarette. Shadows rested in the hollows of the sunlit hills at the end of the street. In front of The Silver Dollar a dog was so busy hunting for fleas that it did not take the trouble to get out of his way. High above him a blazing sun rode a cloudless sky. Maybe never again would he see . . .'

No, he mustn't think of such things. He had business on foot. His gaze searched the street, right, left, in front of him. It was singularly empty. Lounging in the doorway of a saloon he saw Yorky. The teamster said, with forced optimism, 'You're gonna get him, Dan.' Out of the corner of an eye he saw two or three men at a window. Swiftly he checked and dismissed them.

Crockett Street was just ahead. He did not draw his revolver, but his fingers hovered close to the butt of it. Soon now, he knew.

He caught sight of Jasper Ford stepping from a gambling house a little way down Crockett Street. The gambler must have been waiting for him there, for his gun was in his hand. Dan drew, swiftly, and stood motionless, feet apart, his weight on the balls of them, body leaning slightly forward. Not once did his eyes lift from the man moving toward him.

The chill and the nervousness had dropped from him. Every faculty in him was keyed to intense concentration, every muscle ready for swift co-ordination. He knew, without wasting thought on it, that the gambler's face was venomous. His mouth was a thin cruel slit. In his eyes shone a fierce burning hatred.

As Ford came forward his slender body weaved slightly. He was still too far away for accurate shooting with a revolver. Tigerishly lithe, he seemed to creep closer, like a beast of prey.

Suddenly passion distorted the face of Ford. A gust of rage shook him. His gun roared.

Chapter 20

•

FROM BEHIND

From the adobe wall back of Dan a chip flew. Again there came the angry bark of Ford's revolver, and almost at the same instant a breath of air fanned Clifford's cheek.

Dan waited no longer. His finger pressed the trigger, just as a bolt of lightning struck him. The body of the boy sagged, then crumpled down in a heap.

The crack of a forty-five sounded. A man in the doorway of the bank across the street from Dan started to run, appeared to trip over his own feet, and plunged to the ground. He tried to rise, got halfway to his knees, made futile efforts with hands and feet to get up.

Sam Jones ran toward him, gun smoking, to finish the work he had started. But he was too late. Ford was ahead of him. He paid no attention to Dan, but poured shot after shot into the body in front of the bank.

'That'll be enough, Ford,' the ranger said. 'You can't make him any deader.'

Jones strode back to where Dan lay unconscious. He picked up the slack body. There was a doctor's office a few doors down the block.

It was surprising how swiftly a crowd poured out of twenty buildings. A dozen questions, answers, corrections, flew back and forth.

'Jas got him, eh? Knew he would. . . . No, he killed Le Page and was killed by him. . . . Nothing to that. Obigod Jones shot Le Page. Wasn't that the way of it, Obigod?'

'Open up and let me through,' ordered the ranger. 'I'm getting this boy to a doctor.'

'That's right. Sure. Clear the way, boys. Obigod wants to get to Doc Wilmore's.'

The ranger deposited the body of his friend on a lounge. The doctor was a gaunt old-timer with a face bony as that of a skeleton. He stood six feet six, and was as awkward and uncouth as a bear. But no woman in town had fingers more deft and skillful. Not until he had finished probing for the bullet and dressing the wound did he pay any attention to the jam of people in the street outside his office.

'We'd better carry this boy to Polly Doble's hotel,' Doctor Wilmore said to the ranger. 'He'll be in bed for weeks, and he'll need some nursing. Can you arrange to have him carried on a stretcher? Better take him out the back way and down the alley.'

'I'll 'tend to that,' Yorky said. 'I'll pick three-four of the boys and make sure no yellow coyote bites at him on the way.'

'Better send someone ahead to let Polly know,' the doctor said. 'I'll go along with you when you take him.'

'You won't let him die, Doc, will you?' the ranger said.

'He won't die, unless there are unexpected complications. The bullet plowed into the shoulder muscles.'

'From behind,' Jones said bitterly.

He sent a messenger to Mrs. Doble. Yorky left to borrow a door and to arrange for carriers. While Doctor Wilmore and the ranger waited with the patient, the physician asked how the shooting had come about.

'Everyone seems to have a different story,' he added. 'Some say Jasper Ford shot him and some say it was the man Le Page whom he horsewhipped and drove out of town.'

'It was Le Page,' Jones said. 'I don't know when he sneaked back, Obigod. Maybe he has been lying hidden. Dan should've tromped him out like a sidewinder when he had the chance. But I'm the one to blame for what happened to this boy. Nobody but me. I told him not to worry about anyone behind him, that I would be Johnny-on-the-Spot. And I let this dirty li'l' scalawag step out of the bank and plug him. The shooting had begun, and I reckon I was lookin' at Dan and Ford.'

'They say Ford killed Le Page. Was that the way of it?'

'Ford and I were pardners in that good deed,' the ranger said dryly. 'My lead whistler drapped him as he started to run, then when he was down Ford pumped bullets into him.'

'I don't understand that,' Wilmore said, frowning. 'Le Page was in his crowd. Someone told me Ford looked like a crazy man while he was emptying his gun into Le Page. The one he hated was young Clifford, as I have heard it.'

'You have heard it right, Doc. Might it be this way? Say Ford knew this little scoundrel was going to chip into the game. It might have been fixed up between them. Well, Ford sees Dan keel over and figures him dead. Then he sees me plug Le Page. He doesn't want any dying confessions, so he makes sure there won't be any.'

'Might be that way,' the doctor agreed. 'Of course he will put it that he is a square shooter and went wild when he saw Le Page do what he did.'

'Y'betcha! Mr. Jasper Ford is a gentleman of honor and would not stand for any shenanigan like that. That will be the story.'

While they talked, Doctor Wilmore looked after the comfort of his patient.

'I'll make another guess, Doc, though I can't ever prove it,' the ranger went on. 'If I hadn't got Le Page, Ford would have killed him on the spot. He sure would not have waited till his sidekick was arrested and would have had a chance

92

to talk. No, sir, his righteous indignation at such dastardly conduct would have boiled up right there.'

Dan stirred uneasily, then opened his eyes. He looked around, oriented himself, and guessed at what had occurred.

'Ford got me,' he said.

'No such thing,' the ranger blurted. 'You would of got him sure. I never saw anyone cooler than you. Le Page shot you in the shoulder from behind.'

'Le Page,' Dan murmured.

'Yep. He'll be buried in Boot Hill this afternoon.'

'That will be talk enough,' the doctor ordered. 'Save your strength to get well, Clifford.'

Yorky arrived, bringing a door that had been lifted from its hinges. With him were four other men. They stood around awkwardly while Doctor Wilmore and the ranger transferred the wounded man from the lounge to the door. The cavalcade moved down the alley, crossed the street, and headed for the hotel.

Dan was carried upstairs into a sunny bedroom. Doctor Wilmore and Polly undressed him.

'I'm sure a nuisance,' Dan protested.

'That will be enough from you, young fellow,' Polly told him severely. 'You're lucky to be alive.'

'And to have such good friends,' he added.

Polly was emotionally keyed to a high tension. She was very fond of this young fellow who had been thrust fortuitously into a spot he did not want. It was, she thought, both ridiculous and tragic that one of his age should have become a target for the anger of the evil element in town. She was thanking God he had escaped with his life, even while she had an urge to blow off in a good burst of profanity.

'You're only a kid and ought to be spanked,' she told him bluntly. 'Always getting into trouble—acting like you are Wild Bill Hickok and James G. Blaine rolled into one. Struttin' around so big and mighty. From now on you behave yourself and don't be so bumptious.'

'Yes, ma'am,' Dan promised mildly.

'Take this,' the doctor said, and gave him some liquid in a tablespoon. 'Don't pay any attention to Mrs. Doble. She barks, but she doesn't bite. We all know that.'

The doctor arranged the bandage again.

'Go to sleep if you feel drowsy,' he ordered. 'You'll do fine. I'll be back before supper-time.'

He left his patient to the ministrations of Polly Doble.

Chapter 21
•
DAN READS A BOOK

Los Piños had gossip enough to keep its tongue wagging for a pleasant exciting hour or two. Though a score of men had seen the battle from safe vantage points, the facts lent themselves to plenty of argument. There were those who maintained that Jones had joined Clifford in the fight with Ford and that Le Page had taken a hand to help his friend. This version did not get very far, owing to the subsequent fury of Ford against Le Page. Some of the gambling fraternity suggested that Jasper Ford had fought all three of the others. This, too, was seed on barren ground. Le Page and Ford might or might not be friendly, but it was certain the former would not lift a hand to help Dan Clifford. From the conflicting accounts presently the truth emerged.

The explanation of one detail was discussed by almost everybody in town. Why had Jasper Ford flung bullets into the prostrate body of the little capper with such vindictive fury? Was his white-faced anger acting? Or was he firing out of some obscure lust to kill not yet sated by the fall of his young enemy Clifford? There were many opinions. Some felt his fury was born of the fact that Le Page had come between him and his prey. Others believed he could not afford to let the public think he had plotted with the dead man to destroy his enemy and had taken instant means to wipe out such a suspicion. Not a few agreed with Sam Jones that he had finished Le Page to keep him from talking.

The duel had not ended the trouble between Ford and Clifford, since both principals were still alive. For a little while there would be a lull, then hostilities would flare up again. The locaters of the salt lakes would push their claim to sole possession. Few expected the Mexicans to give way without a struggle.

After the first days of fever and pain, Dan found it pleasant to lie in a sunny room and spend lazy days during which he dozed, ate delicacies prepared especially for him, and chatter with visiting friends. He was not yet strong enough to feel an energetic urge to be up and doing, but day by day as he built up lost blood the sap of life flowed more powerfully.

Mrs. Doble brought Milly Sutherland in to see him. The girl hung back, a little shyly. She did not know whether it was forward in her to visit a sick young man in his bedroom, but when she said as much to Polly, that good-hearted battleaxe brushed her scruples aside.

Dan put down on the quilt the book he had been reading. After the first greetings he mentioned, to bridge an awkward little silence, that he was enjoying *Kenilworth*.

'My mother sent it to me,' he explained. 'I promised myself I would read it when I busted a leg or something and got time. It's a right good book.'

Milly said she had not read it, but added that she liked Scott. She had devoured *Ivanhoe, The Fortunes of Nigel*, and *Guy Mannering*.

'I read a book once, clear through from cover to cover,' Polly told them. 'Name of it was *A Tale of Two Cities*. Told how them Frenchies went crazy in the head and had a revolution.'

'I'm glad you are doing so nicely,' Milly said. 'We were all worried at first.'

'How's the school going?' Dan asked.

'Fine, far as I know. If folks aren't satisfied they haven't told me about it yet.'

'They're satisfied,' Polly said. 'I hear you're a good teacher. All I say is I hope you don't go off and marry some young scalawag now you are sittin' pretty'

Milly's apple-blossom cheeks took on an added glow. 'I'm not thinking of any such thing. I have a family to bring up, even if anybody wanted me.'

'Hmp!' grunted Polly.

Sam Jones walked into the room, dust in every crease of his wrinkled jeans.

'How's the high-steppin' gunman of the Rio Grande?' he wanted to know. 'I'm fine, if you mean me,' Dan answered. 'But the description doesn't fit. I'm no gunman.'

'No, we-all know what you are,' the ranger came back derisively. 'Just a nice peaceable young fellow any bully-puss warrior can run on when he gets to feeling his oats.'

'You've got a lot of license to talk,' Polly cut in curtly. 'When it was only the other day you shot down that Le Page, not but what you did just right.'

'Different with me, ma'am,' the rawboned ranger claimed.

'I'm an officer of the law. This fellow had a gun out, and I had to interfere.'

'You're a fine officer,' jeered Polly. 'Nobody noticed you interfering when Dan and Jasper Ford were shooting at each other.'

'That was on the level, Mrs. Doble,' said Sam reproachfully. 'You oughta know I can't butt in when two gents have a difference. That's their private business.'

Polly exploded, with vitriolic profanity. 'I don't know any such a thing. My Bible says, "Thou shalt not kill." That's the law of the land. A lot of worthless hell-raisers go around killing each other and sometimes decent citizens, and we sit back saying it's their private business. I'd be ashamed if I was you, Sam Jones, to call myself an officer of the peace. This country won't be fit for decent people to live in until men like Jasper Ford are put out of existence with a rope. If I had my way this town would clean out all the riffraff that has come here like buzzards to feed on it. You men are a worthless lot of triflers. Nothing will be done until the women rise up and do it.'

The ranger was amused. 'You can't say, ma'am, that Dan and I haven't been doing our doggondest to clean out some of the scalawags.'

'That's not the way to do it,' Polly said, slamming a fist on a table. 'Call a mass meeting. Arm yoreselves. Close all the houses of vice and the gambling halls. Sweep the whole caboodle of devil's spawn out of town. Quit hellin' around yore own selves. Build churches and schools. Get married. Have children. Behave yoreselves.'

'I reckon you're right, Mrs. Doble,' Sam admitted. 'We'd ought to ring the bells of Heaven. I aim to repent and join the Church one of these days, after——'

'After you're all wore out and crippled and too stove up to do any more rip-r'arin' around,' Polly snapped. 'Think I don't know you, Sam Jones?'

'I think you are too hard on Mr. Jones,' Milly said gently.

'Hmp! Not half hard enough.'

'One thing I can't understand is why Ford didn't put one or two of his bullets into me when I was down, so as to make sure,' Dan remarked, by way of deflecting the talk.

'He thought you were done for when you keeled over,' the ranger replied. 'So did I. If he had taken another crack at you, he would have been on record as approving what Le Page had done. Why do that, since you were dead, anyhow? The important thing was to bump off Le Page before he could do any talking.'

'Why?' asked Milly, wide-eyed.

'I'm guessin' he knew the other lobo was going to take a crack at Dan from behind.'

'You mean he arranged it,' Polly said.

'Maybe he didn't arrange it, but Le Page had told him what he aimed to do. I can't prove that, but it sticks in my craw. I'd bet a Brazos saddle against a dollar Mex I'm right.'

'Has he done any talking since . . ."

Dan did not finish the sentence. All of them knew what he meant.

'Considerable,' said the rangy officer. 'Smooth talk—about his honor as a gentleman—and how he killed Le Page to wipe clear any stain there might be on it—and that he never hunts trouble, but won't allow anyone to impose on him beyond a certain point. Yes, I'd say he had talked a few thousand words.'

'Any more . . . threats?' Milly asked, fear fluttering in her.

Sam Jones looked at the girl. He thought her the sweetest and prettiest girl he had seen in many a day. 'No, Miss. I reckon maybe the trouble with Dan is over,' he said. In his mind he added, 'Until something starts it again.'

'I hope so,' Milly said wistfully. 'It's terrible, the way things have been.'

'It hasn't been so good,' assented the ranger.

'Even the little children in school go around saying, "I'm Jasper Ford," or, more likely, "I'm Dan Clifford," and then pretending to draw guns and kill each other. Don't you think it's awful to bring little folks up in such an atmosphere?'

'That's whatever, Miss. When little red schoolhouses and pink-cheeked schoolmarms are in, guns sure ought to be outa style,' Sam conceded with a grin. 'Put me down among the bellringers.'

'I thought you rangers were here to stop lawlessness,' Mrs. Doble bristled. 'Far as I can see you just go around making big chests and knocking down yore pay checks.'

'That's about all,' admitted the big rawboned man, rubbing his rough chin apologetically.

'That wasn't all Sam did the other day,' Dan suggested gently. 'Hadn't been for him, I wouldn't have been here.'

'Sho! Nothing a-tall to that.' Jones protested, embarrassed

by the fear of thanks in the offing. 'I just cracked down on that fellow because he was a skunk.'

Having freed her mind as to the state of affairs in Los Piños, Polly gave guarded approval. 'Some folks are so low down the only way to reform them is to rub them out,' she said.

Among those present there seemed to be no dissenting votes.

Chapter 22
•
MESSENGERS OF PEACE

THE Salt Lakes Development Company began active operations. It outfitted workmen, bought wagons and teams, and built shacks for its employees on the location. An outdoor blacksmith shop did the necessary repair work for wagons and tools. There was even a small supply store.

The Mexicans watched all this expenditure of energy sullenly. Ford and his associates were exultant.

'All you've got to do to greasers is to let 'em know you mean business,' Black said.

He was playing pool at Kelly's New York Billiard Parlor. Sam Jones was in a chair tilted against the wall, one worn-down heel of a boot hooked in a rung. He watched the gambler chalk his cue before he drawled his comment.

'Then everything is lovely. Mr. Mexican folds up and beats it.'

Black looked at the ranger. There seemed to be a hint of irony in the murmured assent.

'We've had no trouble so far,' he said.

'None so far,' Sam admitted.

Black walked round the table, made a shot, studied the lie of the balls, pocketed another. He ran the rest of the balls before he answered.

'And I'm not looking for any,' he added.

'Fine,' Sam applauded. 'You can sleep nights easy in yore mind.'

'The law is on our side.'

'Ridin' high, wide, and handsome, aren't you?'

'You don't figure they are fool enough to buck the U.S. Government, do you?'

'I wouldn't know about that.'

'If they get to annoying us, all we have to do is get Ranger Obigod Jones to read the riot act to them,' Black said.

Sam grinned. He recognized this as a hit. Nothing was more likely in the event of trouble than that he would be sent to uphold the law. His personal view of the justice of the cause would have no bearing on the matter.

An hour later word reached Los Piños that the company store building had been burned down. Shortly after this, another messenger brought the news that two Mexicans had been arrested and charged with arson. Black, Stone, and three other men, all heavily armed, set out for the salt lakes.

Two days later Lieutenant Page of the rangers sent for Jones.

'Stories are coming in about how much the Mexicans are stirred up,' he said. 'I've just heard a bunch of them are setting out for the salt lakes. Now I don't want to send a lot of rangers there. That would look as if we were expecting trouble, and I don't want to start that impression. Drift out that way, Jones, and size the situation up. If you want to take another man with you, that will be all right. Pick any of the boys who are in town.'

Sam considered. 'How would it do if I didn't take another ranger, but some citizen who stands in well with the Mexicans? Say young Clifford. The natives all along the river have kind of picked him as an adviser and leader, far as any American can be that. He has influence with them.'

'Is Clifford well enough yet to travel that far?'

'He's all right again—downtown 'tendin' to his business.'

'You could go in a buckboard if he doesn't feel up to riding.'

'Sure, but I reckon he's all right.'

'The idea is to smooth things over. Maybe you can act as a go-between, fix things up and compromise the difficulty.'

'No chance of that last. Best we could do would be to keep them from each other's throats for the time.'

'Well, that would be something. Better hit the road tonight.'

Jones looked up Dan at once and asked him go with him to the salt lakes. 'Things are liable to crack wide open.

Page wants us to sit on the lid and hold her down,' he explained.

'Or get blown up,' Dan said.

'We might, at that. There's no call for you to get mixed up any more in this.'

'Oh, I'll go and do what I can.'

Looking at this lean, tough, broad-shouldered man, Sam Jones was struck anew by the change a few months had wrought in his outward personality. All the boyishness was sloughed from his appearance and manner. He no longer depressed his nerves with over-much tobacco nor spurred them with alcohol. Physically he kept himself in the pink of condition, not wasting himself in dissipations. The look in the blue eyes had grown more imperative. The line of the clean jaw had hardened. There were times when the lips reminded one of a steel trap.

In the frontier West, facing a daily hazard of life or death, a boy might reach maturity while still in his teens. He walked into a searching test, and he came out of it with the stamp of his future character branded on him. This had happened to Dan Clifford. Chance had played its part, but his reaction to it had made him a marked man. He had become a man of influence among the Mexicans because he was master of himself and because he moved through danger with a negligent arrogance that mocked its potency. There was also a less dramatic reason. He listened, said little, used his common sense. When he gave advice, it was never based on a snapshot decision. Dan was modest, but wisdom as well as force had grown in him.

They took a pack-horse along with them. That night they camped twenty miles from town. By sunup they were on their way again. Halfway to the lakes they came on the charred remains of two wagons laden with salt. There was no sign of the mules that had drawn the wagons or of the men who had driven them. But the ground showed the tracks of many horses. Also, there were plenty of boot-marks.

From the wagons the trail of all the animals led toward the lakes.

'Hell has begun to pop,' Jones said. 'The wagons are still smouldering. Must have been fired early this morning, I'd say. If we push on our reins, we may get there in time.'

'In time for what?' asked Dan.

The ranger picked up a live coal from the burning spoke

of a wheel and lit his pipe with it. 'You guess, son,' he said, puffing to get a light.

They rode steadily, giving their mounts only as much rest as was necessary. Before dark they threw off and prepared food. The horses they picketed. After a sleep of a few hours they repacked the cross-buck and laced the lash rope in a diamond hitch. From midnight until dawn they kept in the saddle.

'Not far now,' Sam said. 'How you making it, boy? I don't want to wear you to a shadow.'

Dan was tired, but he did not say so. 'Better keep going, I reckon. We're not more than ten miles from the lakes.'

The sun was coming up over a crotch in the hills when they looked down on the distant lakes. They were still five or six miles away, but in the clear untempered light of the plains they stood out like mirrors. As the riders drew closer, buildings could be made out.

There was a little puff of smoke and presently a faint sound like the popping of a far firecracker. From the right, where Dan recalled to memory a fantastic outcrop of boulders, rose an answering puff.

'Like I said, hell is coughing,' the ranger said. 'The war has done started.'

He quickened his pace. Dan rode knee to knee with him. It came to the young man that this might prove a perilous business. Personally he was friendly to the Mexicans. Apparently they trusted him. Many of them had taken the trouble to let him know their approval of his conduct. But how far would his popularity go? If the old racial antagonism was aflame again, would not their liking for him be lost in the fact that he was a hated Gringo? They were ignorant and suspicious. They might turn on him and the ranger and swiftly blot them out of existence.

The guns were speaking more lively now. The riders were near enough to see huddles of men behind wagons and shacks. Judging by the smoke puffs, others must be lying in a ditch below the boulder field. These must be the Mexicans. Black and his men were evidently trapped among the rocks. None of them were visible.

'We been noticed,' Jones said. 'Reception committee headin' this-a-way.'

Eight or ten men on horseback were riding toward them.

'Time to declare our intentions are not hostile,' the ranger went on, and drew from a pocket a large white handkerchief with which he had provided himself before leaving town.

He waved the flag of peace. Those approaching opened up from a compact body and partially surrounded the mediators.

'Who are you? What do you want?' someone called out in Spanish.

The ranger answered in the same language. 'Like to talk things over with you, gentlemen.'

'We've nothing to talk over,' snapped the spokesman.

'I wouldn't say that, Chavez,' Jones replied amiably. 'We don't want trouble started. I reckon you feel the same way. Do no harm to have a powwow.'

'And no good. The trouble has already started. You're too late.' Chico Chavez spoke grimly.

Intermittently the crack of the guns still sounded.

'Dan and I are both friendly to you,' the ranger mentioned. 'You know what we think about this crowd roostin' among the rocks. I wouldn't say a word if this thing would quit with Black and Stone. But it won't. If you go through with this, there will be a whole mess of soldiers butting in.'

The Mexicans had closed in on them. That they were greatly excited Dan knew. Four or five of them spoke at once, gesturing to lend accent to their words.

Chavez said in English. 'Better give up your guns, gentlemen. You will be safer unarmed.'

Dan and the ranger passed over their weapons. Surrounded by the guard, they rode down to the shacks on the edge of the lakes. Here Chavez and the two Americans dismounted.

The priest known as Father Miguel came forward to meet them. He was a thin man with a gaunt, fever-ridden face. In the wild eyes there was a look that touched the borders of insanity, Dan thought. He was unkempt and dust-stained. In one hand he carried a revolver. Long since he had been unfrocked because of insubordination and unruly conduct.

'More Gringos for the sacrifice,' he shouted, in Spanish.

'These men are friends,' Chico Chavez said, also using his own tongue. 'Let me introduce them, Father Miguel. Señor Jones, a ranger. Señor Clifford, the young man who has been such a friend of our people and is a bitter enemy of the men who wish to rob us of the salt lakes.'

'That is true,' agreed a slim young *vaquero* named Juan Valdez. 'I was at Los Piños when Señor Clifford fought the man Jasper Ford.'

'Ah! We will give him back his gun and he can fight the

friends of Ford,' Miguel cried. 'We will then know whether he is our friend.'

'We have ridden a long way to try to patch up this difficulty,' Dan said, ignoring the suggestion of the ex-priest. 'I myself was arrested for taking salt and lost hundreds of dollars through the plots of these scoundrels. I do not like any of them. They have tried to destroy me. Again and again I have been shot at by assassins. You are my friends and they are my enemies. Only two weeks ago my partner here killed one of the Ford gang on the streets of Los Piños. We have come to you because we wish you to know that we are on your side, because we feel that to take the salt lakes from you is robbery.'

'*Bueno! Está bien,*' a wrinkled old fellow applauded.

The crowd around them gathered. Dan guessed that there must be between three and four hundred of them. From where he stood he saw many others crouched in the ditch. No doubt still others were posted on the far side of the boulder field to prevent the besieged from escaping. At best there could not be more than a dozen of the defenders. Unless an armistice could be arranged, the Americans were doomed.

Dan picked up from remarks made by members of the mob that the two teamsters captured at the time the salt wagons were burned had been brought here and were being held prisoners. There had apparently been a good deal of discussion as to what to do with them. The more hotheaded of the Mexicans wanted them shot out of hand, the more conservative did not wish so definitely to invite war. It was plain their fate hung in the balance.

The unfrocked priest wanted them killed. He had worked himself up into a flame of patriotic madness. Down with the Gringos! All of them. Had not God given orders to destroy the Philistines root and branch?

A heavy-set pockmarked man about forty was one of the leaders. He was the *alcalde* of a village about thirty miles from Los Piños. The ranger knew him—had in fact been on a three-day bandit hunt with him.

'Señor García, is it not possible for us to talk this over in a smaller group?' asked Jones.

García nodded. He knew there was a dangerous excitement in the air. Since he was a responsible citizen, he was all for compromise before the mob plunged into action that would involve them with American troops. Chavez joined with him, forcing the hand of Miguel.

103

Presently Dan and the ranger found themselves in a room with half a dozen other men, the leaders of the Mexicans. One or two of these were suspicious of the Americans, notably Miguel, but others did not doubt their intent in coming. Chavez knew, of course, the whole story of what had occurred at Los Piños at the time of his arrest. He told it with fiery and dramatic energy. What he said had weight. The ex-priest felt that he was losing ground. He was essentially a demagogue, and was not at his best in a small group where furious invective lacked the cheers of the multitude. Shifting his ground, he proposed that Clifford and the ranger be escorted out of the camp and set on their homeward journey. The other Americans would then be dealt with as seemed best.

Patiently Dan and his friend fought for the best terms obtainable for the besieged men. To leave them to their fate was to seal their death warrants. Two Mexicans had been wounded, one seriously, the other slightly. As the battle grew more desperate, passions would become more inflamed. If terms were to be arranged, it must be done now.

But even the most moderate of the Mexicans pressed home the advantage they held. If Black, Stone, and those with them were to escape with their lives, they must sign a solemn guaranty to release the salt mines to some Spanish-American citizen who would hold the property for the benefit of the people. It would have to be a legal release and re-entry, a transfer that would stand up against a court action to annul.

Dan had his doubts about the sanction of an agreement made under duress, but he did not voice the question. Just now his duty was to get the trapped men back to safety.

'Good,' he said. 'Let us draw up such a paper, and I shall take it to them to sign.'

García drew up the paper. He was a man of some education. The agreement contained a pledge on the part of Black and his associates to give up all claim to the salt deposits and to file the relinquishment legally as soon as they reached Los Piños. The leaders of those among the rocks were to take oath not to repudiate the bargain later.

The arrangement was not satisfactory to the Mexicans or to the two Americans in the conference. All of them were afraid that those in the development company would later refuse to go through with the deal. It would be possible, of course, to hold Black and Stone until Dan and the ranger returned from Los Piños with the relinquishment and the re-entry, but it was very likely that Jasper Ford would arrange to send back a company of rangers instead of the required paper. This would force an immediate clash, a result they were trying to avoid.

Juan Valdez went with Clifford. He spoke English, and his friends wanted to know what took place at the conference in the rocks. They distrusted Black and Stone, and some of them were not sure of Dan. After all he was a Gringo and might throw in with his fellow countrymen.

Dan borrowed the large white handkerchief of the ranger. He did not start on his errand until word had reached the Mexican snipers that a temporary truce had been arranged.

As Dan and Valdez moved toward the boulder field, the young man waved his flag. He continued to display it prominently until he was sure that those huddled among the rocks knew that this was a peace mission.

A man jumped to the top of a large rock and beckoned the envoys forward.

Chapter 23

•

STONE AND BLACK SIGN AN AGREEMENT

THE man was Stone. Apparently he had been wounded, for he had a bandanna handkerchief tied around his head.

'Swing round to the left, the other side of the flat rock,' he ordered.

Dan and Valdez did as directed and moved down a kind of alley between the boulders. The path terminated in an open walled space. Here there were half a dozen men, all armed. One lay on a coat, his arm bound with a handkerchief. The others were unshaven and haggard, their eyes sunken, the ghost of fear staring out of them. For they knew that unless unexpected help arrived, they were doomed. For nearly two days they had been penned here, cut off from food and water.

Stone said, with a thin-lipped smile of irony, 'Boys, here are some kind friends come to visit us and stay for dinner.'

'Damned if it ain't Sure Shot,' a voice called down from above.

Dan looked up. In a niche between two rocks a sentry was posted. The man was the squat broken-nosed fellow Pete Johnson.

'Haven't got lost again, have you?' Dan asked, not without malice.

Johnson laughed sardonically. 'No, Sure Shot, I'm roostin' right here and not strayin' none.'

A man broke out, in high-pitched protest. 'For God's sake, do these greasers aim to murder us? There's a million of them out there pluggin' at us, I'd say. I ain't in this. When I came along I thought—'

'Brought a gun with you, didn't you?' snapped Johnson contemptuously. 'And you been usin' it.'

'Someone has,' Dan said. 'They have two wounded men out there.'

'We're one up on them,' a young fellow in chaps said. 'Three here.'

'Maybe we'd better find out what Mr. Clifford wants, if it's not just a neighborly call,' Stone suggested.

'That's right. Spit it out. Do we get outa here alive?' Johnson asked.

'Depends on the gents who hired you,' Dan answered.

'If it depends on us, everything will be fine,' Black said. 'We're ready to vacate. I never was so tired of a place in my life.'

Dan looked at him. 'You're sure looking lank as a shad,' he said. 'I reckon you're a heap hungry *hombre*.'

'Rung the bell that time,' assented the cowboy in chaps. 'I'm so gaunt my belly button is kissing my backbone.'

Stone turned coldly on Dan. 'You can spill that message your friends gave you to deliver. What are the terms?'

'You are to sign an ironclad agreement to give up all claim to the salt deposits,' Dan said.

'They will sign anything,' the cowboy promised for his employers. 'We got itchin' feet to get away from here.'

'Who says we'll sign?' Stone said coolly. 'We're all right here. Doing fine. I'm looking for the rangers to be along pretty soon. No use getting in a sweat, Curly.'

Three or four of the men cried out a protest simultaneously. Plainly they had had enough. They had been facing the finish, despairingly, and they did not intend to fling away this newborn hope.

'If you're sitting so pretty, Stone, it is all right with me,' Dan mentioned. 'I'll be drifting along. See you later . . . maybe.'

106

A big muscle-bound ruffian seized Dan by the arm. 'No, sir. We'll make Stone sign. You wait.'

'You've thrown in with these greasers, have you?' Black demanded of Dan harshly. 'A renegade, eh? Gone in on a parternship against the whites.'

'Don't be a fool.' Dan's voice was harsh, his manner curt. 'We were sent by Lieutenant Page to patch this thing up if we can. Obigod Jones is with me. You're in a tight if ever men were. When we got here your lives weren't worth a dozen for a dime. We had a long powwow, and finally persuaded the leaders of the Mexicans to let you go if you sign up to release all claim to the salt field. Ask Señor Valdez here if I am not telling you the truth.'

'It is quite true that my countrymen would rather kill you than let you go,' Valdez said quietly. 'It is true that if you do not sign the paper we have brought, none of you will be alive when the moon comes up tonight.'

Pete Johnson came down from his post. 'You're bucked out, Stone. Nothin' to do but eat crow.'

'If you ask me, I'll say you are lucky,' Dan said. 'Father Miguel wants you rubbed out to the last man. Americans don't seem to be popular with him. A mighty little would tip the scale against you. It's fortunate you haven't killed any of them.'

'No need of any more beefing,' the big ruffian cried. 'If we can get out with our skins whole, you can bet yore boots we aim to do it. Sign that paper, Stone, *muy pronto.* You got it with you, young fellow?'

Stone looked at the big man out of cold, hard eyes. 'You telling me or asking me, Orton?' he inquired evenly.

Dan gave information, almost casually. 'If you're looking for help from the rangers, Stone, you had better cut out that expectation. Page is waiting for me and Obigod to come back with a report on this trouble. He won't move till he hears from us.'

'So you say,' cut back Stone.

The heavy rounded shoulders of Orton pushed aside those in his way. He stood squarely in front of Stone, prognathous jaw thrust forward. 'I'm tellin' you. Maybe you have gone crazy, but I haven't. Goddlemighty, don't you figure we've been through hell enough? Didn't look like we had a dead man's chance an hour ago. Now one has offered, I aim to grab it with a strangle holt. You'll sign any damn papers the greasers want. Think we want to get bumped off so Jas Ford can make a dollar? Fellow, take another guess . . .'

Curly interrupted. 'Don't push on the reins, Orton. We got to act sensible. Mr. Stone doesn't mean to be onreasonable. He knows we been spittin' cotton for two days, and he ain't dumb enough to think we can stand off much longer the whole population of Mexico and considerable of the census of Texas. Now that Clifford here has drapped down from heaven with good news, as you might say, he knows we got to take what's offered. He kinda hates to admit those fellows out there have got the dead wood on us, but seein' as he isn't a lunkhead he knows such to be the case.'

'Curly is right,' Black said, and for an instant his hooded eyes slid to meet those of his partner. 'Every man jack of us has his tongue hangin' out. We're at the end of the road. No two ways about that. I'll sign any paper you have fixed up, Clifford.'

Stone nodded. He knew it had to be. His reluctance could not stand up against the stark facts. There was no use in trying to compromise to save face. He had to take what was offered whether he liked it or not. 'All right,' he said abruptly. 'I'll sign.'

'In good faith?' Dan asked. 'You won't back out later?'

'When I make a bargain I stand by it,' Stone said harshly.

He read the paper García had drawn up. His knowledge of Spanish was limited, and he had Curly translate it into English to make sure he understood the contents.

'You ought to be a lawyer, Clifford,' he said, with sardonic sarcasm. 'We sign away everything but our shirts. If they don't give us back our guns, what is to prevent them from massacring us on the way back to town or sooner?'

'That's a chance you take,' Dan said. 'Obigod and I got the best terms for you we could. We'll be with you till we get to town—if we do. I don't know whether they will give us our guns or not.'

Stone was glad to hear that Clifford and the ranger did not mean to desert them, but his derisive comment made no such admission. 'If you are going with us, we will sure have an ace in the hole. I'll feel safe as if I was in a church listening to the Reverend Washburn.'

Black and Stone signed the document. Dan and the young Mexican carried it back to the besiegers.

As they were picking their way down among the rocks, Curly called after them. 'Burn the wind, fellows. I got a date to drink three gallons of water, even if it is so muddy I have to chew it.'

The messengers reported to the chiefs of the attackers. Word was at once sent out to all the Mexicans that the battle had been won and the Stone party was to be allowed to depart in safety. Chavez and García took great pains to impress on their followers the necessity of observing the truce faithfully.

An hour later seven or eight gaunt and unkempt men filed down from the rocks supporting a wounded man. All of them were unarmed, since they had been ordered to leave their weapons in the rocks where they had been cornered.

Hundreds of excited Mexicans watched them as they moved toward the lakes. Dan and the ranger joined the little party. Both of them knew that it would take only a spark to set the gunpowder in the souls of the Mexicans ablaze, but they felt the hated men would be safer if they stayed with them. Occasionally there was a savage yell of execration from groups of dusky young Mexicans.

'They are liable to jump us yet,' Curly said, with a rueful grin. 'These birds don't like us. Not none. I'd say, trouble ahead.'

'Nothing more likely,' agreed Stone grimly.

'I'd give a hundred dollars to be on a good horse with a pair of six-guns strapped to my side and a Winchester in my hands,' Black said.

'Might as well wish for one of Uncle Sam's cavalry regiments while you are at it,' growled Pete Johnson.

'I'll bet ten dollars to six bits Mex that if I ever get outa this jam I'll never let that slick-tongued Jas Ford talk me into another one,' Orton said nervously.

The released party sat down to a dinner prepared by the enemy. The starved men ate ravenously. Three or four young *vaqueros* dashed past the place where they sat on their heels eating. The blast of their guns was alarming.

Orton jumped to his feet. 'Goddlemighty, are they aiming to wipe us out?' he yelled.

Stone looked at him scornfully. 'Sit down, you chuckleheaded fool,' the gambler ordered. 'Don't you see they are only trying to make us show we're goosey. Thing is to let them see we don't scare.'

'We're all right,' Sam Jones said, 'unless——'

He left his proviso unfinished. Stone completed it coolly.

'Unless some of these devils get crazy with the heat and rub us out. I'm rather looking for that, and we won't have a gun in the party.'

'Dan and I are to get our guns,' the ranger said. 'So García says.'

'Then we'll be in God's pocket,' jeered Stone.

Apparently Chavez and García had doubts of their men. They selected a guard of six trustworthy Mexicans to ride along with them to make sure the Stone party reached Los Piños safely.

They arrived in town the second day after dark. Dan ate supper at a Chinese restaurant and from there went to the cabin where he lived. As soon as possible he undressed and rolled into bed. He was dog-tired. Almost instantly he fell asleep. The sun was riding high when he awoke.

Chapter 24
•
STONE DECLARES HIMSELF OUT

FORD took the news of the salt lakes defeat sourly.

'You fellows sure balled it up,' he told Black and Stone irritably.

'It would have been different if you had been there, Jas,' Stone said, with his thin-lip smile.

'If I had known what was going on, I would certainly have been there, with a bunch of rangers to show those rats where to head in at,' Ford answered harshly.

'They don't pay off in ifs,' Stone reminded him.

'This may be the best thing could have happened, at that,' Ford continued. 'I'll ask for forty-fifty rangers and clean out the whole caboodle.'

'What good will that do you?' asked Stone. 'We've lost all our chips.'

'No, sir. We're in a better position than we were before. These scoundrels have put themselves outside the law. We can sail right ahead now under the protection of the rangers.'

'Forgetting that paper we signed, aren't you, Jas?'

'No, Lou. You and Black signed it under duress. It won't stick a minute.'

'It sticks with me,' Stone replied curtly. 'When I make a deal I don't rue back on it, as young Clifford puts it, even if the other fellow has my tail in a crack.'

'You signed that paper to save your life.'

'That's right, Jas, but I signed it.'

'What's the sense in talking that way, Lou? If a stick-up threw a gun on you and made you promise to give him ten thousand dollars next day, would you give it to him?'

'A different proposition. We were in a little private war. The enemy got the dead wood on me and I signed a treaty. I'm a good enough sport to pay up when I lose. Count me out of the salt lakes proposition.'

'Not scared, are you?' jeered Ford.

The cold eyes of Stone looked very steadily into those of the killer. 'Maybe so. I've told you I'm out. If you doubt the reasons I give, that will be O.K. with me, Jas. But— I'll ask you not to doubt them out loud.'

He spoke in a low voice, with studied courtesy, and it was with the same obvious lack of stress that Ford answered. For suddenly the atmosphere had grown brittle, fraught with the possibilities of tragedy.

'Just what do you mean by out, Lou?'

'I mean that I won't have a thing to do with the lakes proposition. I have surrendered all my interest in it.'

'Did you surrender mine, too?'

'We were partners. I expected you to stand pat on any agreement Black and I made.'

'One you signed with a pistol at your head?'

'Yes, if you like to put it that way. We were taking a flier. It did not work out. What's the sense in trying to fight a nest of hornets after you have stirred them up? No profit in it. I would be through, even if I hadn't given my word.'

'But if Black and I aren't through, you wouldn't have any complaint to make about that?'

'No complaint,' Stone answered, after a slight pause. 'I would feel you hadn't backed me up when I played my hand the best I could, and I would certainly want to warn you that you will be monkeying with dynamite. Better cash in your chips and quit the game, Jas. There's bound to be a hell of an explosion if you don't. I saw these fellows out at the lake and I know how they feel. Ask Black.'

'I don't have to ask anybody about whether I'll drop my tail and crawl off like a whipped cur. This is my bone. I'm going to fight for it to a finish.'

Stone lifted his shoulders in a shrug. 'Don't believe you can get away with it. You don't know how worked up the Mexicans are. Black knows. So do I. Not one of us fellows trapped in the rocks expected to get out alive. They were

111

getting ready to rush us. If they had, we would have been wiped out. The coming of young Clifford saved us.'

'You sure must be grateful to him,' Ford sneered.

'I don't owe him any grudge for it,' Stone replied. 'Might as well lay my hand on the table, Jas. This young fellow and the ranger with him threw in with us when it looked as if we might all be wiped off the map. They decided to ride to town with us because they figured it would give us a better break. Knowing what a risk it was, wouldn't you call that white of them?'

'Was it a risk when he knew a dozen armed guards were going with you?' asked Ford contemptuously.

'He didn't know it. García and Chavez decided on that later. Another thing, while we're on the subject. These Mexicans made a bargain with us and lived up to their side of it. Their leaders made sure we wouldn't be shot down on the way home. I play a straight game, and I don't intend to let any Mexican make me feel like a skunk. So I'm doing what I promised to do.'

The obsidian eyes of Ford probed into those of the other gambler. 'Meaning that you are against us from now on?' he questioned.

'Meaning that I'm not for you or against you. I'm out.'

'The going looks tough to you, I reckon. Safer sweating the game.' The voice and manner of Ford were insulting.

Stone flushed, but he spoke quietly, his tone even and colorless.

'I didn't go into a contract to follow anywhere you want to lead, Jas,' he said. 'I'm running my own game.'

'I get you,' Ford answered, his pallid face set rigidly to keep back the anger. 'Suits me. We're through. You go your way and I'll go mine. If you want to tie up with this Clifford and his bunch, hop to it. See where you will get off.'

'Did I mention tying up with him?'

'You don't have to mention it. There are only two parties in this town. You know that. You have to be in one or the other. If you are not for me, you are against me.'

'You are making that choice, Jas, not me.'

'Nobody can play in with this fellow Clifford and with me too,' Ford said harshly.

'Seems you are making up my mind for me that I have got to line up with him,' Stone said. 'Kinda handing me my hat, aren't you, Jas?'

'Yes, sir,' the other gambler answered stiffly. 'I'd rather

112

have an open enemy than a friend who won't go through to a finish.'

The other man started to speak, then with a little gesture of resignation gave it up. He turned and walked from the room.

On the way out he met Derby, a faro dealer at The Last Chance. Derby stopped him.

'Heard the news, Lou?' he asked.

'I'll know better when you tell me what it is,' Stone replied.

'Los Piños has acquired a new citizen. Jonathan Edwards Hart has come to town.'

'When did he get out?'

'About a month ago. Soon as he got out he went down to his old hang-out in De Witt County, but there was nothing for him there. His relatives were dead, or moved out, or scared to tie up with him again. So here he is.'

'Does he mean to stay here?'

'I heard him say that down at the Brewster bar quarter of an hour ago. He studied law while he was in the pen and aims to hang out his shingle.'

'A man with his rep will have a hard time getting along no matter how much he means to walk the straight and narrow,' Stone said. 'Every man that meets him will think about his past. Every bad man will figure whether it is safe to take a crack at him. You can't kill twenty-five citizens without the ghosts of some of them rising to haunt you. Texas is no place for Hart if he means to reform. He had better light out for Oregon or California where he isn't known.'

'That's good medicine, Lou,' Derby assented with a sardonic smile. 'You tell him so.'

'I reckon I'll attend strictly to my own business unless Mr. Hart asks me for my advice,' Stone answered.

'*Yo tambien*,' agreed Derby. 'We're not in this. But Jas is, up to his neck.'

Stone's mind came to alert attention. He had forgotten that Jasper Ford had been one of the chief witnesses against Jonathan Edwards Hart at the trial of the latter for the killing of Bull Ackerman. It had been his testimony that had sent the man to the penitentiary. Now Hart was out again. Had he really come to Los Piños to settle the account against Ford? Nothing was more likely.

'Of course you'll tell Jas right away,' Stone said. 'He will have to look out.'

'Maybe Hart doesn't know Jas is living here,' the faro dealer suggested. 'Jas might slip up on him and bump him off before he knew.'

'He might,' agreed Stone dryly.

Derby passed into the room the other had just left. He blurted out his news without delay.

'Jonathan Edwards Hart is in town, Jas.'

Ford looked at him, without speaking. The muscles in his sallow jaw stood out like ropes. His body grew rigid.

'Who told you?' Black asked, after a moment.

'I saw him. Down at the Brewster. Says he has come to town to practice law.'

'What else did he say?' Ford wanted to know.

'Not much. Seems rather a silent fellow. I got the idea, sort of, that he claims to be a reformed character.'

'Didn't mention me?' Ford pressed.

'No. I was wondering if he knows you're here.'

'Some fool will tell him *pronto*. If not today, tomorrow.'

Ford stood, very erect, looking down at the table in front of him. His heavy black eyebrows met in a frown. He did not see the table. What he saw was a blond man of about twenty-five, weight one hundred and fifty, with cold, steely eyes and muscles that rippled when he moved as do those of a panther. The man was in the prisoner's box. His gaze was on the man in the witness chair who was swearing his life away. Even now Ford could feel that blazing contempt, the threat that leaped out at him like a Toledo blade. He had been sorry when Hart had escaped with life imprisonment. His stomach muscles had sunk with chill dread when the news came that the Governor had pardoned the notorious killer. Sixteen years had passed since this man had entered the penitentiary. Now he was at Los Piños, within five minutes' walk of Jasper Ford. Had he come for his revenge?

'After he has been told he'll be fixed for you,' Derby warned.

That was true, Ford reflected. Why not now, before Hart would be expecting him?

Swiftly he made his preparations. He made sure his gun was in good order—helped himself to one drink, not too stiff—gave Black and Derby their instructions. The plan was simple. It ought not to fail, and nobody could prove that the cards had been stacked against Hart.

Derby was to go to the Brewster, apparently the worse for drink, and was to seat himself at one of the small tables not too far back and close against the wall. Black would

114

walk in and join him. They were to drink, get nasty, and suddenly quarrel violently. For a few seconds the eyes of everybody would be on them. During that time Ford, waiting for the signal outside the door, would slip swiftly into the room and kill. He would call his victim by name and fire the instant the ex-convict turned toward him. No Texas jury could find guilty any man who shot down Jonathan Edwards Hart, the most desperate gunman the state had ever known.

The three men did not walk down San Antonio Street together. Each went his own way. Ford took a back street. He did not hurry. His accomplices were to pull off their quarrel at exactly ten minutes past noon. They had to take time enough to give their altercation an appearance of plausibility. Later, when men talked it over, the rumpus must have an air of sincerity.

Ford was nervous. He was staking his life against one who used to have the reputation of being the swiftest and most deadly shot in the Lone Star State. Sixteen years in the penitentiary must have taken some toll of Hart's skill and nerve. A man could not live that ghost life of furtive whispers and sly intrigue and come out the same expert nerveless fighting machine that had entered the place. Still, he must take no chances. He must be swift and sure.

From the rear Ford moved along the north wall of the Brewster. He looked at his watch. Five minutes past twelve. He stopped and made a business of pulling his trousers farther down his boot legs. When he rose his watch told him it was eight minutes past the hour.

Jasper Ford stood in front of the Brewster looking up and down the street. Every nerve in him was keyed to tension. His finger muscles ached with suspense.

Up the street walked Dan Clifford. Ford frowned. He did not want his mind distracted now at the moment when he had to concentrate on one enemy.

Dan said, with that cool, insolent aplomb that was so irritating, 'Good morning, Mr. Ford. How is the Salt Lakes Development Company getting along?'

The gambler waved him aside without answering. This was no time to bandy words with an upstart like Clifford. He had deadly business on hand.

Someone flung open the swing door of the Brewster and walked out. The man was Derby.

'He's gone,' the faro dealer said quickly. 'Left for the Doble House five minutes ago. Went to dinner.'

Ford kept his eyes on Dan. 'That so?' he said. 'Then I'll see him later. My business is not important. It will wait.'

But Dan noticed that Ford had taken the news with a deep breath of relief, that Derby was in a state of great excitement, and that he had been startled to discover that an outsider had heard his words. Moreover, Dan had caught sight of Ford a moment before the gambler had seen him, and it had seemed to him that there was an odd tense rigidity in the man's bearing. He had been under a strain, waiting for something that filled him with nervous apprehension.

For what? It had nothing to do with Dan, since he had not yet seen the young man, and in any case the sight of him did not carry dread to Ford. As Dan walked up the street, he tried to build up a reason for the excitement in the two men. He could think of none. It occurred to him that it might be a good idea to go to the Doble House and find out discreetly who had just arrived there from the Brewster bar in time for dinner.

Chapter 25

•

DAN MEETS A
NOTORIOUS CHARACTER

DAN found Polly Doble busy. She was superintending the serving of dinner. But she took time to listen to his question.

'Who walked up from the Brewster bar and reached here about two or three minutes ago?'

Polly stopped dishing up potatoes from the pot to let her suspicious gaze rest on him.

'What are you up to now?' she wanted to know.

'Nothing. I'm just curious. A few minutes since I heard a man say that someone had just left the Brewster to come here for dinner. I wondered who he was.'

'Why should you care, young fellow?'

'Maybe I'll tell you later, if it turns out to be worth telling,' Dan parried. He had begun to think that probably what he had seen at the Brewster had no significance and he did not want Polly to have the laugh on him.

'Maybe you'll tell me now. You're always poking your long nose into affairs that are no business of yours. Curiosity killed a cat.'

Dan sighed, but there was a twinkle in his eye. 'You haven't a trusting nature, Polly Doble. You look for guile where there is only innocence.'

She snorted. 'Don't I know you? You think you're smart, but I can read you like a book when you've got some devilment in mind.'

'I haven't any this time.'

He told her the incident at the door of the saloon, half expecting her to break into a loud guffaw of ridicule. But to his surprise she took it seriously. She made him go over it word for word—what they had said and how they had looked.

'You know something about this I don't,' he charged.

'Keep out of it,' Polly said explosively. 'This is none of your business.'

'If you don't want to tell me, I'll find out somewhere else,' he said with an impudent grin. '*Adios, amiga.*'

Polly slapped a ladleful of potatoes in a dish. 'Wait. I'll tell you.' She gave the dish to a Mexican girl and led him to the back door where they would not be heard. 'The man who walked up from the Brewster and got here five minutes ago must have been Jonathan Edwards Hart. He is the only man who has come from downtown in the last half-hour except yourself.'

Dan stared at her. 'Jonathan Edwards Hart. You mean —— He is here—in this house—now?'

'Upstairs—in room five.'

'But—what's he doing here?'

'I expect he's washing up for dinner.'

'I mean, what is he doing in Los Piños?'

'Why didn't you say so?' Polly snapped. 'He didn't tell me, but I've heard he means to practice law. Have you any objections?'

'I should say I hadn't. It's all right with me if he wants to start an April Fool's joke factory.' His thought reverted to the object of his coming. 'I must have been mistaken. My notion was that Ford and Derby were looking for someone.'

He used the words 'looking for' in the sense generally employed on the frontier.

'I shouldn't wonder,' Mrs. Doble said significantly.

'But they can't mean to have trouble with Hart.'

'Why can't they? If they know he has come here to get Ford.'

'But why would he do that? Hart got out of prison only

a few weeks ago. They can't have met since then. Ford hasn't been out of town.'

'They met years ago. I read a long story in a St. Louis paper when Hart was pardoned by the Governor. It told about the time he was tried. Ford swore him into the penitentiary, the paper said. There's no doubt that is where Jonathan Hart belonged, either there or on the gallows, but when he was sentenced he swore in open court that he would kill Ford if ever he got out.'

'Great Caesar's ghost!' ejaculated Dan. 'He has come to rub Ford out.'

'How do you know he has, Dan Clifford?' Mrs. Doble demanded. 'He may not know Jasper Ford lives here. Los Piños is the coming town of the Southwest. Hart may be here for just the reason he gives, that he thinks a lawyer would do well in a growing place. During his last years in prison he was a model prisoner. He was superintendent of the Sunday School, and he worked hard at his law studies. Perhaps he has repented of his sins.'

'If that's the way of it, he ought to be told that Ford means trouble,' Dan said.

'If he does. What do you know about what he intends to do? I never saw anyone who itched to get into trouble as much as you do.'

'At least he ought to be told Ford is in town, so he won't be taken unawares.'

'If Jonathan Edwards Hart has killed twenty-five or thirty men, don't you reckon he took any of them unawares? You let them do their own fighting,' she snapped dictatorially.

Dan thought this over. 'No,' he decided. 'Ford is fixing to kill him. I'm sure of that. It's only fair to let him know his enemy is here.'

'Suppose he knows already.'

'Then it won't do any harm for me to mention it.'

'I thought in this country a fellow was supposed to keep out of other men's difficulties,' Mrs. Doble mentioned acidly.

'That's right. I'll sure keep out. I'm just going to mention kind of casual that Ford is in town.'

'You'll get into it. That's what you'll do. You haven't got a lick of sense.'

'You may be right,' Dan admitted amiably. 'The way I look at it is this. Ford is my enemy as well as Hart's. I won't egg on any trouble, but if it has to come, I hope Hart wins. That is why I aim to drop a flea in his ear.'

'All right,' Polly said vehemently, half persuaded he was

right. 'But try and use what horse sense God gave you, if any.'

She flung away, to go back to her work.

Dan stayed to eat dinner, but he did not at once take a seat at the long table where the boarders dined. He wanted to sit down next to Hart.

A fair man of about forty walked into the dining-room. He was tall, slender, with a hawk nose and fierce, quick eyes. He was clean-shaven and well dressed, in a fashion not quite up to date. The hair on his head was beginning to thin.

Young Clifford took the seat next to him. There were several men at the table Dan knew. He fell into talk with them. Adroitly he led the conversation to the salt lakes controversy. The name of Ford was mentioned. The stranger showed no interest, but when Dan used the gambler's first name, the fierce eyes beneath the bushy brows stabbed a look at him.

Those present represented a cross-section of the citizenship of Los Piños. One was a lawyer, another a gambler, a third a mule skinner. Several were floaters not yet engaged in any work. A cattleman in from the ranch country rubbed elbows with the Reverend Philip Washburn. Apparently none of them yet knew that the silent stranger sitting next to Dan was the most terrible killer Texas had ever endured.

Hart made no contribution to the conversation, except to answer in the affirmative when someone asked him if he liked the young town. He spoke gently, in a low voice, as mild in manner as a Sunday School teacher. Dan would never have guessed that he was a desperado known all over the country for his efficient ruthlessness.

When Dan rose to leave the table, Hart asked him pleasantly if he might see him alone for a minute.

'Sure,' Dan said.

They passed out of the dining-room, Hart stepping aside to give Dan precedence. As they went upstairs to the stranger's room, the younger man led the way. Hart brought up the rear, ostensibly as a matter of courtesy, but Clifford realized that it was because he was accustomed not to take unnecessary chances.

Hart closed the door of the bedroom. His gleaming eyes fastened on the other.

'You mentioned a name, sir, at the dinner table,' he began, in a low voice with a gentle, courteous note. 'I gather from

119

what was said that the owner of that name is no friend of yours. I refer to Jasper Ford.'

'You are quite correct,' answered Dan. 'He is my enemy. His gang has attempted my life several times. Ford himself forced trouble upon me. I was challenged by him and we exchanged shots.'

'This Ford is a professional gambler, is he not? A tall man, with a bloodless face. If he is the man I mean, he is probably well dressed. Some would call him handsome. He carries himself with stiff dignity.'

'He must be the same man. Your description fits.'

Dan volunteered no additional information. His quiet eyes rested on those of the other man. They did not betray the excitement and interest that stirred in him. He had a feeling that this man's soul was a battlefield where opposing forces raged. Back of the fierce eyes he guessed at a great weariness, a consuming sadness. Jonathan Edwards Hart had been through the fires.

Young Clifford knew his story. Who in Texas did not? He was the son of a preacher, but even as a small boy had given evidence of the undisciplined wilderness that was to ruin his life. He was a rebel at school. Before he reached the age of sixteen, he killed a negro who attempted to bully him. From this time he ran amuck, shooting down those opposed to him. In those days after the Civil War the country was full of bush rangers. Against the federal forces left to rule during reconstruction days the defeated Confederates held bitter resentment. From other states desperadoes had poured into Texas as a place of refuge. Out of the troublous conditions were born feuds. Into the most sanguinary of these, the Taylor-Sutton vendetta, young Hart had been drawn as a violent partisan. His enemies had been as eager to destroy him as he had been to get them. Through those lawless years his gun had been forever roaring. Among scores of strong, passionate, ruthless men he stood out as chief.

In prison, his wild nature still found expression. He could not endure restraint. Again and again he had attempted jail breaks and been repeatedly flogged until his body was a horrible quivering jelly. Nothing could break his indomitable defiance.

But with the years a change came over his spirit. He began to read, to study. He conformed to prison rules, became a leader in the debating society. Under the preaching of a revivalist he got religion and later taught in the Sunday

School. Eventually he was given permission to study law. In turn he read Blackstone, Kent, Story, and Greenleaf. It was understood long before his pardon came that he was a changed man.

Looking at him, Dan wondered what the lonely prison years had made of Jonathan Edwards Hart. He thought of his father and his mother, true converts to the gospel of the gentle Jesus. Had Hart become like them? Or had he undergone only a superficial change due to emotional excitement? That the man had lost his clamorous ego, the fierce zest for evil excitement that once had driven him, Dan did not at all doubt. But had he found what Dan's mother used to call the peace that passeth understanding? Not if those sunken, hungry eyes told the truth. It seemed to Dan that they were filled with ghosts rising to torture a lost soul. Unless he missed his guess, Hart was like a rudderless ship in rough seas driven by cross-winds, now here, now there.

'I knew this man Ford in the old days,' the ex-convict said, reluctantly, as if moved by some inner compulsion to speak. 'He was on my side of a feud in which we fought, but at my trial he betrayed me and testified against me. Tell me what you know about him.'

Dan told the story of the trouble Ford had forced upon him. The older man listened, but when Dan finished, he discovered that Hart's thoughts had been busy with his own problems.

'I have made up my mind never to kill another man,' he broke out. 'The past is buried. I am a man of peace.'

'You had better let Ford know this,' Dan said. 'I think he has heard you are here and will take no chances.'

'What makes you think so?'

Clifford gave his reason. He added that Ford was likely to set the scene for a safe killing.

'Will you take a message to him from me?' Hart asked abruptly. 'Tell him I'm not looking for trouble. If he will let me alone, I'll do the same by him.'

'I'm not the man to take the message,' Dan said. 'He wouldn't believe me, but would suspect a trap. One of the rangers is my friend. His name is Sam Jones. I'll send him to you. He will tell Ford what you want him to say. If Ford knows he is safe, that you don't mean harm to him, he will probably let you alone.'

Hart smiled mordantly. 'Maybe, and maybe not. I'm Samson with his locks shorn. Someone anxious to get a reputation for killing Jonathan Edwards Hart will shoot me in the back.'

Walking downtown a few minutes later to find the ranger, Dan reflected that very likely the pardoned convict's prediction would turn out to be true. He was a shining mark for any bad man eager to find a short cut to notoriety.

Chapter 26

•

'WHY DO YOU HATE ME?'

As MILLY SUTHERLAND walked home from school, her heart was lifted with exultation merely because the sap of youth flowed fast in her strong and gracious body. To live and love was enough. It was good to have the warm sunshine kiss her cheeks, to feel the soft wind rippling through her hair. Every buoyant step was a delight. Last evening Dan had been with her. She went over in her mind his words and looks. He had said this, and she had answered that. Trivial phrases in themselves, but significant for what they did not tell. He liked her. She was sure of that. But she was in tremulous doubt how much.

The sights and sounds of Los Piños drifted to her senses. She caught a glimpse of the yellow muddy river on its turbulent way to the sea. A heavy wooden-tired two-wheeled Mexican cart drawn by burros lumbered past. There came to her a whiff from a native goat meat market. An olive-skinned baker carrying a large osier basket filled with cakes cooked in an outdoor clay oven gave her a smiling *'Buenos dias, señorita.'* She heard the music of saws and hammers busy converting a sleepy village into a metropolis. In the shade of an adobe wall two cowpunchers sat on their heels and rolled their own, regardless of a painted sign, *'No se permite fumar.'* A snatch of their indolent drawling talk came to her ears. Evidently they had met after a protracted separation and were chewing over old times, to use their own vernacular.

'I reckon Shep Dubbs is still borrowin' chewin' tobacco,' one said.

'No, sir,' the other answered. 'Old Man Trouble camped on

122

his trail and he lit out sudden for parts unknown, not waitin'
to shake hands with his enemies, seein' he had no friends.'

Milly blushed when she thought of what a sight she must
have been when Dan first met her. She remembered with
shame the little rosy toes peeping from her shoes. Cinderella
was all very well in a book, but in real life it was something
different. Dan was getting to be an important man now and
it was humiliating to know that he had seen her as patched
if not as ragged as a Mexican beggar.

A suave voice broke into her musing.

'Why do you hate me, Miss Sutherland?'

Jasper Ford had his hat off and was bowing from the
waist to her in his dignified fashion.

Milly was snatched abruptly back into the present. Her
eyes registered alarm. It was absurd, she told herself, to be
afraid of him. In open daylight, before all Los Piños, he
could do her no harm, even if he had any such intention.
Yet at sight of him something very like fear took her by the
throat. At the bottom of her heart she knew the dread was
not for herself but for another.

'I do not hate you,' she told him in her low throaty
contralto. 'Why should I, since you are almost a stranger
to me?'

'And have done you no harm,' he added, his dark eyes
fixed on her.

'That is true,' she admitted.

'Yet you let it be known I had insulted you. By a lie
you injured my reputation in this town, to protect the worthless mule skinner with whom you are in love.' He spoke
harshly, stung into fury by the thought of his enemy.

Milly drew her slender body to its full height and looked
at him. 'You are insulting me now, are you not?' she said.

'Are you going to marry this fellow Clifford?' he demanded.

The color poured into the cheeks of the girl. 'I will not
discuss my business with you, sir,' she told him haughtily.
'Please let me pass.'

Ford knew that he was making a mistake. He had stopped
her on an impulse, to satisfy his thwarted vanity. Nearly
always he had been successful with women. He was handsome, and he carried himself with an air. His dark reckless-
ness, his sinister reputation, helped to create an air of mystery
about him. He knew when to blow cold and when hot. As
a brand to be snatched from the burning, he had charmed
more than one good woman who had discovered her mistake

too late. This girl was a beauty, ardent, shy, sweet as a wild rose. To feel that she preferred a raw young fellow like Clifford to him filled him with fury. He felt it to be an incredible outrage, one that could be explained away if he could only get her to listen.

The gambler choked back his anger. 'I am wrong. When I think of the insults I have endured from this whippersnapper, my blood boils. You could not look at him twice. I realize that. He is not a gentleman.'

'And since you are one, of course you will let me pass when I ask it,' she mentioned, not without irony.

'Since you do not hate me, I offer you my friendship,' he insisted. 'You are alone, in this rough place, without father or brother to protect you.'

'I do not wish your friendship,' she said bluntly. Then, lest his anger turn against Dan Clifford, she added more gently: 'Your ways are not my ways. It is impossible for me, alone as I am, to meet strangers outside my narrow circle. The school trustees would not like it. I am in a position where I must be discreet. You will see that, I am sure.'

He saw it, plainly enough. He was a professional gambler, of unsavory reputation with women. A young woman of good position could not accept him as a friend and retain her social standing. He was outside the pale. This he knew and resented. Because she was unattainable, unless she was willing to pay the price of becoming *déclassée,* his urge was more imperative.

Defiantly he said, 'I have power in this town and can guarantee that no friend of mine will suffer because of gossip.'

'I shall not ask you to make good such a guaranty,' Milly said quietly, knowing that his boast was impossible. 'I cannot be too careful. It is expected of a teacher. You know that, Mr. Ford.'

'Why waste your time in teaching?' he asked. 'Old maids should do that, not beautiful girls like you. Let someone else do the prosy work. A lovely young lady ought not to be soiled by it. Your place in life is to inspire some man to better things.'

Milly did not answer him. She had caught sight of the Reverend Philip Washburn and she hailed him as a deliverer.

'Oh, Mr. Washburn, may I see you a minute about the church social?' she called, at the same time walking past Ford to join the minister.

124

The face of the gambler darkened. He turned abruptly into the nearest saloon.

Washburn made no reference to Ford, though the fact that he had been talking with Milly shocked his sense of propriety. The two discussed church affairs for a minute or two. Presently Milly broke through to what was on both their minds.

'He stopped me and I could not get past him,' she explained. 'He offered me his friendship and I told him I could not accept it.'

'You did right,' the minister told her warmly. His eyes had rested on this young woman often with approval, and he was likely to think that anything she did was right. 'The man is evil, and he has an amazing effrontery to speak to you at all.'

'He is dangerous,' Milly said. She did not add what was in her mind, that her fear was for Dan Clifford and not for herself.

'Yes,' agreed Washburn. 'He is the head and front of the vicious element in this town. It looks to him as leader. Last night a man was shot down by a hold-up on a side street. Two others were robbed. Every day there is lawlessness of one kind or another and nothing is done about it. We need strong, energetic officers. There was a meeting yesterday of some citizens at the office of the mayor. It was decided to ask young Clifford to become marshal of the town.'

'Oh, no!' Milly cried. 'He's been through trouble enough. Don't ask him to do that. They hate him now, Ford and his men do. If you make him marshal, you'll send him to his death.'

Washburn looked at the girl's white, frozen face. For weeks he had been trying to make up his mind whether to ask her to marry him. He knew now the answer to the question was of no importance. He did not have to consider whether she would make a good minister's wife or would fit happily into the group where he would lead his life after this frontier experience was past. Taken unexpectedly, Milly had betrayed her secret. Philip Washburn knew he was not in the picture.

'He may not accept it when it is offered,' the young parson said gently.

The girl found no consolation in this. 'He will, too. You know how foolhardy he is. He has some queer kind of notion that a man mustn't run away from danger.' She exploded with feminine ferocity. 'It's fine business, isn't it, for a lot of leading citizens to ask a boy of twenty-one or -two

125

to run so terrible a risk while they sit back and clap their hands comfortably?'

'They feel he is the best man,' the minister said, and knew it was no sufficient explanation for Milly Sutherland.

'Of course!' Milly cried scornfully. 'Someone else is always the best man to send into a death trap.'

'It isn't as bad as that,' Washburn protested. 'Surely not. We shall all be backing him.'

'But he is the one they will . . . will . . . kill,' she wailed.

'I don't think so. He will come through all right. I feel it.'

Milly bit her lip and turned abruptly away to keep breaking down on the street. The sunshine had lost its warmth and the day grown harsh and chill.

Chapter 27
•
DAN TAKES A JOB

DAN looked round on the little group with a sardonic smile. 'Wouldn't some of the rest of you gentlemen like the job?' he asked. 'I don't want to hog the honor.'

The mayor said, sheepishly, 'You're the only man in town for the place.'

'Why?' Dan wanted to know.

'You've proved to these scoundrels you are not afraid of them. The feeling is you've got them on the run. Los Piños is with you strong. Ford and his crowd know that. You'll start out with a big enough advantage so you could beat any other fellow from the chunk.'

'And where will I end up?' Dan said grimly. 'In a box on Boot Hill?'

'I don't say that being marshal of a wild town is as safe as sitting on a fence and chewing plug tobacco,' the mayor admitted. 'You'll have to keep your eyes peeled.'

'Or be too dead to skin,' Lon Stevens added. 'No use denying that if you take this job and don't lie down on it, you'll have a man's work cut out for you. Already you are poison to these fellows. They'll get you if they can.'

'What's the matter with Jonathan Edwards Hart for marshal?' Dan suggested. 'You claim you want a man who is tough, dead game, and quick as greased lightning. He fills the specifications every way from the ace. Why pick on a tenderfoot amateur like me'

'He isn't at all the kind of man we want,' Philip Washburn said quickly. 'As I understand it, we want law brought to Los Piños, but we don't want a lot of men killed, even those who are enemies of the public. To appoint Hart, even if he would take the place, would be to serve notice that we were going to have a carnival of shooting. But I don't think it is fair to ask Mr. Clifford to carry this burden alone. I am a man of peace, but I believe it my duty to fight for the right. If Mr. Clifford calls on me to serve on a posse to help arrest criminals, I shall not shirk the task.'

"Good for you, parson,' Waller applauded. 'That's the way to talk. We'll all give Dan our support.'

'Mostly moral support, don't you reckon?' Dan drawled.

He knew it was all very well for these friendly citizens to offer their backing now. They meant what they said. But when he walked up to a gun to arrest a desperado, he would be alone, just as he would be when he walked down some street at night with no assurance that an assassin was not lying in ambush a few yards away to destroy him.

Lon Stevens tugged at his mustache, smiling at Dan. 'Young fellow, that's whatever. You'll be playin' a lone hand most of the time. No use loadin' you about that. We'll help if you call on us. But the way it is liable to be is that trouble will jump up at you when you're not lookin' for it. I'm not strong for sawin' off this job on you. If I was you I wouldn't take it.'

'Nor I,' chimed in the minister, catching sight in imagination of Milly Sutherland's white, strained face. 'You are too young for the place, and you haven't had enough experience. I think we had better get an older man.'

'I'm as old as I was last night when you figured I would do, Mr. Washburn,' Dan remarked.

'I hadn't given the matter enough consideration then.'

'Why ask this young fellow to do what we don't want to do ourselves?' Stevens demanded abruptly. 'I don't like it.'

'But you're on the committee inviting me to butt into this trouble that is ready to jump up at me,' Dan said.

'Sure I am. We need a good marshal. If you want to take it, that will be all right with me. But I wouldn't want to send you in blindfolded.'

127

'I'm a business man,' Dan reminded them. 'I can't afford to quit after making a good start.'

'You wouldn't have to do that,' Waller explained. 'Get another teamster. All you need to do is rustle up business and give your men orders. Won't take half an hour a day. You can do it while you are on duty.'

In the undercurrent of his mind, while Dan was protesting to the committee, he debated the question pro and con. He believed he could clean up the town, if he could escape the bullets of the thugs. In that proviso lay the nubbin of the whole thing. Bat Masterson, Pat Garrett, Ben Daniels, Billy Tilghman, and many other frontier officers were still alive. Wild Bill Hickok survived his term of office, and so did Dallas Stoudenmire. But all of these were famous fighting men. Dan had no record at all. Also, there was another side to face. Ed Masterson, brother of Bat, had been shot to death at Dodge. So had Tom Smith at Abilene. Dan could name a dozen brave officers who had gone under in the line of duty along the skirt of the frontier. No need to fool himself, as Lon Stevens had said. If he put on the marshal's star, he would be flinging out a challenge to his enemies. By fair means or foul they would get him if they could.

'I name my own deputies,' Dan said.

'Fair enough,' the mayor agreed. 'How many?'

'Two will be enough now. More if the town grows fast.'

Stevens nodded. 'You'll need two.'

'I'm to have a free hand,' Dan went on. 'No pets of the administration I am expected to let alone.''

'Nary a pet,' the mayor said, with a grin.

'I'll take the job, for three months,' announced Dan. 'By that time we will have made a good start on the clean-up or I'll be known all over town as a four-flusher.'

There was an alternative. Dan thought of it, but did not give it voice. He might then have gone the way of Tom Smith and Ed Masterson.

The news spread swiftly. An hour later, Dan met Lou Stone in front of the Lone Star wagon-yard.

'Congratulations, Mr. Clifford,' the gambler greeted him ironically. 'I hear you have a job.'

Dan said blandly, 'Don't congratulate me, but the city, Mr. Stone.'

'Perhaps you're right. There are good jobs and bad jobs.' Stone lifted an eyebrow appraisingly. 'You haven't been what the insurance companies call a good risk for some time. Probably they won't rate you a better one now.'

128

'Just a friendly warning?' Dan asked, with a touch of answering sarcasm.

'You might call it that,' Stone assented. 'I could name some who won't throw up their hats and yell at your appointment.'

'Including Mr. Stone?' Dan said lightly, his eyes steadily on the other.

'Not including Mr. Stone,' answered the owner of the name quietly. 'I'll put my cards on the table. For myself, I like an open town. It's good for business.'

'Especially your business,' Dan slipped in.

'Right, but for others too. A certain amount of helling around is good for a growing city like this. It brings in men with money who want to spend it. We give them the entertainment they ask for in exchange for their patronage. But I don't hold with murder and robbery. So I'm supporting you, Mr. Marshal.'

'That's bully,' Dan drawled. 'It's good citizens like you I am asking to aid me in cleaning up the town.'

A ghost of a smile flickered across Stone's impassive face. 'I sure appreciate your approval,' he said.

'My approval doesn't extend to all your friends,' Dan carried forward. 'Unless, of course, you can convert them to your way of thinking.'

'Did I give you a list of my friends?' the gambler inquired carelessly, in fact so indifferently as to stress the remark.

Dan took care not to show his interest. He guessed that there was a cryptic meaning in what the gambler said.

'I reckon maybe I could name one or two of them,' Dan ventured casually.

'You would probably ring a bull's-eye first shot, but I would give even money you miss.'

'How about Jasper Ford, your partner?'

'He isn't my partner. He was, in the salt lakes business.'

'Not now?'

'Not now. I signed a paper quitclaiming any rights I had. Jas didn't see it my way. So he is in, and I am out. I don't reckon you could call him my friend, either. We had a difference of opinion, and we have gone different ways.'

'Shook hands and said *Adios*. That the way of it?'

'Said *Adios*, but didn't shake hands.'

'Funny,' Dan said. 'I had you both pegged right. I kinda expected you to stand by your agreement with the Mexicans and I was dead sure Ford wouldn't.'

'Smart as a whip, aren't you?' Stone jeered.

Dan did not resent the sneer. He knew that Stone considered himself a tough and hardboiled *hombre* and he did not expect him to make any admission in words that he had changed front. None the less it was clear, not only that he had quarreled seriously with Ford, but also that he no longer held any hostility to Dan. If he still sparred with him, it was only to save face.

As he walked down the street, an idea jumped at Dan and stopped him dead in his tracks. Why not ask Stone to be one of his deputies? Very likely he would not accept. The offer would have to be put to him diplomatically. But if he could be persuaded to take the job, it would be a blow to Jasper Ford and his clique, since it would be tantamount to an open admission of the fact that the gamblers no longer held a united front against the reform element.

Dan found a note waiting for him at the *jacal*. It was signed by Milly, and it said that she wanted to see him at once.

Chapter 28

•

DAN BECOMES ENGAGED —AND DISENGAGED

THE first words of Milly were, 'You're not going to take it.' She flung them at him like a blow.

He nodded. 'Yes, I'm taking it.'

'Why? So you can show off and let everybody see what a big man you are? So you can strut around and say, "Who's afraid?" '

Dan was startled at her ferocity. He could not understand it any more than he could guess the reason for her injustice. She ought to know him well enough to see that if he became an officer, it was because he felt it to be his duty. His resentment at her words was keen.

'Maybe that's the reason,' he said stiffly.

'You told me yourself that you had been lucky in your trouble with Ford. Do you expect always to be so?'

'I wouldn't know about that, but I can hope, can't I?'

She ignored his answer. 'While you were just a private citizen, you could stay home nights and not give these

130

ruffians a chance to shoot you down in the dark, but as marshal you can't do that. You have to walk up and down the streets, passing dark alleys a dozen times every night. Very well you know what will happen.' She frowned at him, severely, in her best teacher manner.

'Why, no, I don't, but since you seem to have it all worked out, maybe you'll tell me,' he retorted flippantly.

'You can't do this crazy thing, Dan,' she insisted sharply. 'Your friends ought not to let you. It's a—a kind of vanity. Why should you take this job more than anybody else? Unless you want to be pointed out as another Wild Bill Hickok.'

'That must be it,' he said, anger in his heart.

'I don't understand you any more,' Milly went on, with a little gesture of despair. 'I used to think I knew you, but now——'

'Shows how we fool ourselves,' he agreed, with a laugh that held no mirth. 'I thought I knew Milly Sutherland, but I sure don't. The girl I figured I knew was my friend, and she acted like she believed in me. Anyway, she didn't allow that all I wanted to do was grandstand and throw out a big chest. My mistake, I reckon.'

Milly realized she had gone the wrong way to persuade him. She had waited so impatiently for him to come, under such a stress of anxiety, that her nerves had betrayed her. She had attacked instead of conciliating him. Now they were quarreling, and that was the last thing she wished to do.

'I want to be friends,' she said miserably. 'The things I said I don't mean. I am afraid for you, terribly, so I tried to make you mad. I don't know why I did.'

His anger was swept away instantly. He held out his hand, and her small warm palm rested in his. The touch of her flesh, the look in her shy soft eyes, set the blood racing through his veins. Somehow she was in his arms and he was kissing her. There was a wordless interlude during which they spoke to each other as lovers have since the world began, with kisses, caresses, laughter, and the gift of eyes.

They came to earth again, and to a rift in the happiness that had sunk all differences.

'If I had known in time, I would have turned down this appointment,' Dan said.

'You can tell them your plans are changed,' Milly murmured, smiling up at him.

Her words were like the shock of a plunge into icy water.

Dan knew he must convince her, and he doubted whether it was possible.

'I have promised them, sweetheart,' he said gently.

Milly drew back from his arms. 'You don't mean that you'll still go ahead with it?' she asked swiftly.

'I've got to now. Don't you see that if I quit, after giving my word, everybody in town would think I was scared?'

'What of that, since you know you're not?'

'I can't go around feeling that everybody thinks me a skunk. When I promise to do a job, I have to go through with it.'

'Because you are afraid to be thought afraid? Oh, Dan, wouldn't that be cowardly? It's much braver to do what you think is right.'

'That's the point, honey,' Dan explained. 'I'll be doing what I know is right for me. Don't you see I can't go back on a bargain and put the blame on our love? That would be a poor way for us to start.'

'Would it be a better way for me to live every day through in fear lest you be killed?' she asked, a quaver in her throat.

'I'd hate to have you do that,' he said in a low voice. 'I want to bring you happiness.'

'How can I be happy if I never know when I am going to be called to a doctor's office to find you lying dead? And even if it wasn't as bad as that, if you had to kill somebody else, wouldn't his blood stand between us?'

Her big eyes looked at him appealingly. Never in his life had he so much wanted to give up to another. But he could not do it. He lived by the code of the frontier. Having pledged himself to a dangerous task, he had to go through to a finish.

Dan caught her hands and held them tight in his, looking down into her eyes. 'I'm sorry, girl. Anything else in the world you ask, I will do for you. But I can't do this. I hate to go against your wishes, but I have to decide this for myself. A man will do to ride the river with, or else he won't. Explanations don't go. When you have given your word you have to stand up and take your medicine.'

'And it doesn't matter how much you make me suffer?'

'Yes, that matters a lot,' he said humbly. 'I never expected to have luck enough to get you. Now I have to hurt you. I wish to God I didn't have to do that.'

She met his eyes directly, her chin up. 'But you are

going to do it, to save your silly pride. I'm less important than that.'

'Can't you see it's not what I want to do, but what I have got to do?' he cried desperately.

She pulled her hands from his. 'Very well. You have made your choice. I'm not going to marry a man who insists on being murdered or becoming a murderer, just because he is afraid to do right. It's a good job we understand each other in time.'

'You mean that, Milly?' Dan asked, very quietly.

'Yes,' she cried, her voice breaking. 'I mean every word of it. You can't have me and this job too.'

For a moment he did not speak. Then, 'I'm sorry,' he said, and turned away, picked up his hat, and walked from the house.

Chapter 29

•

A HOLD-UP

JONATHAN EDWARDS HART was a marked man. When he walked down the street the eyes of those in sight followed him. Back of the fixed regard, he felt, were curiosity, disapproval, speculation, even a vivid anticipation. With his past in mind, Los Piños was waiting for the roar of guns. It would be anticlimax until he killed again or was himself killed.

The man had not reckoned on his past, except perhaps as an asset to bring him clients. But he could not escape it. He never spent five minutes in the company of others without knowing it was hovering in the background. Clients did not come. They were afraid of him. In his very gentleness they found a threat of explosive violence. Safer to limit intercourse to polite formalities.

Hart had been simple-minded enough to suppose that the announcement of a changed life would be accepted at face value. He knew better now. The brand of Cain was on him. He had to walk a lonely path apart from his fellows. No kindly human companionship would ever be his.

He brooded. At times loneliness engulfed him. As an

133

escape he began to drink. By this time he was aware that more than one bad man in Los Piños had an urge to kill him. When they met, Hart read the furtive longing in their eyes. Only fear of him restrained them. Though he had given out that he would never take life again, they knew he still carried a gun.

Through some officious fool word reached Hart that Ford had boasted to his friends that he had frightened off the great killer. Though this rankled, Hart made no comment. He was still determined not to return to his old manner of life.

It was when he went into depressions that he drank most. In liquor his mind slipped back to old grooves. During such periods he was mentally a desperado once more.

After drinking heavily he walked downtown one night. Wild thoughts were surging in his brain. Since he could not make a living as an honest man, why not collect it by force? Why not show Ford he was not afraid?

At San Antonio and Crockett Streets he met the new marshal, Dan Clifford. This young man was one of the few with whom Hart had established a friendly relationship. Dan had moved up to the Doble place from the *jacal*, and the two occasionally spent an hour together in one of their rooms.

The keen eyes of the marshal made note of the other's condition.

'Don't you think you had better go home, Mr. Hart?' he suggested gently. 'You look feverish. I don't think you're very well tonight.'

Hart laughed. "No, son. Going to have some fun. Tired of sitting in my room alone. There's life in the old dog yet.'

'What kind of fun?' Dan asked amiably.

'Don't know. Haven't decided. Paint the town maybe.'

'Not too red,' the marshal mentioned.

'Just pink,' agreed Hart. 'Place needs waking up. . . . Come and have a drink.'

Dan did not drink, but he did not say so. He gave the legitimate excuse that he was on duty.

'Thasso. Well, see you later, young fellow.'

Clifford watched him go. Hart walked with perfect steadiness. He had control of his muscular co-ordination. Yet Dan was disturbed. It was in his mind to follow the other, but he had just been called to the lower end of town to look after some drunken annoyer. In a town like this a man trod his own way. One could not close-herd a character like

134

Jonathan Edwards Hart. He might be heading for trouble. That was his business. In making his suggestion Dan had gone to the very limit permissible.

Fifteen minutes later a tall, slender man walked into the side door of The Last Chance. He wore a muffler and his hat was pulled well down over his eyes. Quickly he stepped to the stairway, which led to the private rooms above where the big games were played. From the landing a passage ran to the back of the building. Light showed through a transom above one of the doors. He heard the click of chips, the voice of a *croupier* asking if all bets were made. His fingers eased the gun at his hip. Over his face he arranged a bandanna handkerchief with eye-holes prepared. A moment later he was in the room, standing with back to the closed door, a forty-five in his hand.

Six or seven men were in the room standing or seated round a roulette table. In front of them were piles of blue, red, and white chips. Conveniently at hand were small service tables upon which rested cigars and liquor glasses. In the air was a heavy drift of smoke.

The *croupier* looked up and saw the masked man. His startled face brought the others to attention. They stared silently at the man with the gun.

'Take it easy,' the hold-up advised. 'Reach for the roof, gents, and don't get excited. I don't aim to hurt anyone unless it is necessary. Line up against that wall with yore backs to me. No, don't monkey with a gun, Mr. Ford. That would be bad medicine.'

Jasper Ford had dropped into the room for a few minutes to see that the game was moving properly. He asked a futile question.

'Is this a hold-up?'

'You guess,' the robber advised grimly. 'Redhead, collect all weapons, and be sure you don't miss any.'

A red-headed cowman relieved the others of their revolvers.

'Toss them out of the window,' ordered the bandit. 'Yore own too. That's good. Now line up with the others.'

The masked man stepped to the check-rack and stuffed into his pockets the gold and bills he found there. Moving backward to the door, he felt with one hand for a key. The other hand held the forty-five trained on his victims. His fingers withdrew the key from the lock. He opened the door, slipped the key into place outside, and made sure by turning it that there was free play.

135

'Sorry I had to interrupt, gents,' he murmured apologetically. 'Consider it an emergency contribution for charity. I'll say good night.'

The door closed behind him. In the lock the key grated. Those inside the room heard the slap of running feet.

By this time the gamblers had awakened to violent action. One flung open the window and cried out to the world what had taken place. Another cursed fluently, not repeating himself once as he poured forth a vitriolic stream. Others flung themselves at the door and broke it down.

They poured downstairs, a stream of them, noisily explanatory. The man they wanted was apparently not in the well-filled saloon. Someone remembered that a man had passed across it to the side door. There were men in the street, but none of them seemed to be the one who had just come out from The Last Chance.

A crowd gathered, eager to hear details of the hold-up. Among them was Jonathan Edwards Hart. In his low, courteous voice he asked if any of the gamblers could describe the robber. At the moment his eyes chanced to be resting on Jasper Ford.

Several of those who had been in the room offered details. The bandit was tall, big, dark. He had been masked.

Ford said nothing. His black eyes held fast to those of Hart.

Chapter 30

•

DAN MAKES AN ARREST

DAN CLIFFORD walked into the office of The Last Chance and nodded a little stiffly to Wilkins the proprietor and to Jasper Ford.

Suavely Wilkins said, 'Take a chair, marshal.' Ford said nothing.

Dan brushed some papers aside and sat on a corner of the desk, one foot on the floor, the other dangling. He looked at his enemy, whose hard eyes were fixed on him.

'I don't reckon you have arrested the hold-up yet,' Wilkins continued amiably.

'Not yet,' Dan answered.

Ford laughed unpleasantly. 'Nor won't,' he said.

'Until I know who he is,' Dan added.

'If you don't know, you're too dumb to be marshal,' Ford told him bluntly.

'I have talked with every man in the room, except the bandit, and not one of them can tell me who the fellow is, or if they can they won't,' Dan countered. 'Perhaps, now you've had a night to think it over, you can help me to his name, Mr. Ford.'

'Maybe I can,' the gambler replied.

'Fine. Swear out a warrant, and I'll bring him in *pronto*.'

'You claim you don't know who did it?' Ford jeered.

'How would I know, since I wasn't there, when half a dozen of you who were can't tell me?'

'I can tell you.'

'We're on our way,' Dan said lightly. 'Give the gent a name.'

'When I want him taken care of, I'll do it myself,' Ford said, his voice heavy with meaning. 'I'll not expect one of his friends to do the job.'

'So he is a friend of mine?'

'Tell him for me I hope he enjoys what he got.'

Dan shook his head. 'I wouldn't know how to reach him, unless I posted it on the challenge tree—one of those to-whom-it-may-concern notices. Sure you don't want to whisper the name?'

'No need to do that. You know as well as I do.'

'You talk as if I was a kind of silent partner of his,' Dan said, apparently reflecting aloud. 'Sure I'm not the bird who stood you up, Mr. Ford?'

'You have an alibi. When you left him, five minutes before the hold-up, you walked down to old-town. It was a good out, with a dozen men to swear to it.'

'Too carefully planned, you think,' Dan said, smiling cheerfully. 'Maybe I stopped and asked someone the time, so as to make my alibi copper-riveted.'

'What's the sense in chinning this way, boys?' reproached Wilkins. 'You know doggoned well, Jas, that Mr. Clifford didn't have a thing to do with this. He says he'll arrest the robber if you'll tell him who to go after. Fair enough.'

Ford's black orbs gleamed at the marshal through narrow-slitted lids. 'Would you arrest Jonathan Edwards Hart if I told you he was the man?' he asked.

Dan did not bat an eye. 'If you'll put it on paper—swear

out a warrant for him. Do that, and I'll agree to have him at the sheriff's office in half an hour.'

The mind of the gambler worked swiftly. Why not? If he sent one enemy against the other, there would be trouble. Hart would never let himself be taken alive. He would kill this officious fool almost certainly, and there was a reasonable chance that Clifford would destroy him.

Ford rose from his seat, abruptly. 'I'll take you up on that. If you're the white-haired lad you claim you are, in half an hour you will have Hart arrested and in jail.'

Within a quarter of an hour Dan set out, armed with a warrant for the arrest of Hart. It was just dinner-time. The ex-convict would probably be at the Doble place.

Dan had not seen Hart since they had separated last night just before the hold-up. He believed that the man was guilty. Jasper Ford was the first man to mention his name in connection with the hold-up, but there had been a strange reluctance on the part of several whom the marshal had questioned to tell all they knew. They were keeping back something. He felt sure of that. Very likely a suspicion they were afraid to voice. There was danger in even a whisper that tied up the name of Hart with the robbery.

The marshal understood, of course, why Ford had sworn out the warrant. He hoped that Dan would be killed in trying to serve it. There was a chance the gambler might have his wishes fulfilled, but not if Dan could talk himself out of trouble.

In answer to his knock, Hart came to the door of his room. Dan walked in, and on invitation took a chair. He thrust his hands deep into trouser pockets and tilted the chair back. His waistcoat was open. The young man had dropped belt and revolver on his bed before calling on his neighbor.

He smiled, cheerfully, and spoke his little piece with friendly pleasantness.

'I have a warrant for your arrest, Mr. Hart, sworn to by Jasper Ford.'

Hart sat up, his body rigid, keen eyes fixed on the officer.
'For what?' he demanded.
'For holding up The Last Chance roulette game.'
'He says I did it?'
'Yes. He sent me here in the hope that you would kill me.'
'Does he claim to have recognized me?'
'Yes.'
'Do any of the others?'
'No.'

Hart looked at Dan, silently, frowning at him. The marshal's guess was that the man had had a bad night and a worse morning. Plainly he was suffering from the morning-after effects of heavy drinking. In his sunken eyes Dan read, or thought he did, some anguish of remorse. Spurred on by liquor, he had yielded to a mad impulse. In doing so he had closed the doors of hope behind him.

'Where is your gun?' Hart asked abruptly.

'In my room,' Dan replied. 'What do I want with a gun?'

'Do you expect to arrest Jonathan Edwards Hart without a gun?' the ex-convict inquired harshly.

'My idea is to arrest you with your own consent, Mr. Hart. I wouldn't have much luck doing it any other way. Ford swore to the warrant only to put me in a hole. Of course, he would like to get you in trouble. I'll admit that. But when it comes to a showdown, I am not sure he will stand pat.'

'He wants to put me behind the bars again,' Hart said bitterly. 'I'll never go to prison. I would far rather die.'

'I don't know the facts about this hold-up,' Dan said, in a quiet matter-of-fact voice. 'Since you haven't been proved guilty, I assume your innocence. Would you object to my searching the room? If I find none of the money taken, it would be a point in your favor.'

Hart waved a hand. 'Go ahead. Search all you like.'

Dan was relieved. He had not expected so ready an acquiescence. His search uncovered no cache of gold and bills.

'Shall we eat dinner before we go?' Dan asked, taking it for granted that Hart had consented to the arrest.

'If you like. I am not going to be locked up. Understand that. If Ford stands to his story, bail will have to be arranged for me.'

'We can talk about that when the point comes up,' Clifford said casually.

After dinner the two walked downtown side by side. They turned in at the courthouse. In the sheriff's office they found not only Watts but Judge Harper. Both of them were willing to oblige this tall, grim man with a record of killings equaled by no other desperado in Texas. To think of making an enemy of Jonathan Edwards Hart filled the flabby judge with panic. He was lined up as an ally of Jasper Ford, but he affirmed repeatedly that there was no personal feeling on his part. To prove it he offered to go on the prisoner's bond. This might not be strictly legal, he admitted, but his confidence in

Mr. Hart was such that he would strain a point. Lou Stone was passing the courthouse and Sheriff Watts called him into conference.

'The bond has been fixed at a thousand dollars,' Watt explained. 'Judge Harper will go on it, but we need another surety. Do you know anybody who would sign?'

'I'll sign it,' Stone said. 'I don't suppose Mr. Hart intends to run away, and some day I might need a bondsman myself, even as good a citizen as I am.' He smiled cynically at the marshal.

'Much obliged, gentlemen,' Hart said quietly. 'No, I don't aim to run away. I'm going to stay and make this cur Ford eat his oath.'

'Legally, of course,' Dan said.

Hart assented. 'Oh, of course. When he thinks it over he will see he was mistaken.'

Judge Harper slid a quick look at the notorious killer. He was wondering what the man meant to do.

Chapter 31

•

FORD CALLS ALL PRESENT TO WITNESS

JUDGE HARPER carried the news at once to Jasper Ford. The gambler received it with no pleasure. His scheme had not borne the expected fruit. Clifford was still alive and Hart was at liberty. Moreover, the ex-convict now had a new definite grievance against him. It was all very well for Hart to give out that he would never kill another man. He had said, too, that he was a reformed man, but he had put on a mask and held up the roulette game at The Last Chance.

Ford made Judge Harper repeat the story, especially that part where Jonathan Edwards Hart had mentioned his name.

'Just exactly what did he say?' he demanded. 'Give me his very words.'

'Said he wasn't going to jump his bond, that he meant to stay here and make you eat your words.'

'What words?'

'The ones in which you claimed to recognize him as the bandit.'

'Then this Clifford made him soft-pedal what he had said?'

'Yes. Clifford put in that, of course, he meant to make you retract by legal methods.'

'And Hart said then?'

'He said sure he would be legal.'

'How did he look when he was saying that?'

'Looked mighty sour to me, as if he had said too much and was backing water so as not to warn you.'

'It's your opinion he intends trouble for me?'

Harper made a gesture with his white pudgy hands disclaiming responsibility. 'How do I know what he meant, Jas? Maybe he is as full of religion as he claims he is. Maybe he is glad to have you swear out a warrant that is liable to put him back in the penitentiary. But if I was in your shoes, I wouldn't feel right comfortable. You're the only man who can, or at any rate will, identify him as the hold-up. If he gets rid of you, he is in the clear.'

'You think I'm in a jam.'

'I didn't say any such thing, Jas,' the judge denied petulantly. 'I don't know how the mind of a man like Hart works. They say he has killed thirty or forty men. One more probably wouldn't make much difference to him, unless he really has been converted. I'd worry, if I was you. But I'm naturally timid, a man of peace. Maybe if you would say you had made a mistake about recognizing him, he would forget all about it.'

'He hasn't that kind of a memory,' Ford said grimly. 'No, sir. It's Hart or me one, and I don't intend it to be me. I'm going into a hole for a few hours, some place where I can't be found. When I come out of it, I'll be the hunter and not the hunted.'

'You're going after him?' the judge said, fear in his voice.

'I'm going after him, before he goes after me. Keep your trap shut, and don't do any talking.'

Now that he had prepared the ground for trouble, Harper was filled with panic. He might be drawn into danger.

'For God's sake, be careful,' he urged. 'And whatever you do, Jas, don't bring me into it.'

'You're a chicken-hearted scoundrel, aren't you, Harper?' jeered the other. 'Without the pluck of a louse. Too bad you are so fat. It must interfere with you when you run away.'

'I don't claim to be any kind of a hero,' the little man admitted equably. 'I duck trouble whenever I can.'

'Well, you won't duck it if you open your mouth before I have fixed Hart,' the gambler told him savagely.

Ford kept to a private room at The Last Chance. He conferred with Black, Pete Johnson, and Tom Cooper. All he asked of them was to keep him informed of the movements of Hart. At the showdown he intended to play a lone hand. He meant, if it was possible, to do the job with a minimum of risk to himself.

Not until night had fallen did he emerge from seclusion. Word had just been brought to him by Cooper that his man was at the Tivoli drinking.

'Celebrating the hold-up of yore roulette game,' Cooper had suggested maliciously.

'If things break right, I'll celebrate, too, before the hour is up,' Ford had answered with cold cruelty.

He was glad that Hart was drinking. A man looking for immediate trouble keeps himself sober.

As on the previous occasion Ford took the back way. Just back of the Tivoli a squat, heavy-set figure loomed out of the darkness. The man was the shifty-eyed Pete Johnson.

'He's in there now,' Johnson said. 'Up at the bar having himself a good time. Just before I left he was claiming that liquor is the only stuff to drown yore sorrows in. He's sure pouring them down the hatch. It's his night to howl. Had one with him myself. He don't look to me like a man who is on the prod to get him a guy before breakfast.'

'Been drinking a lot, has he?'

'Quite some. Clifford was in a while ago and tried to get him to drift back home, but Hart told him he was old enough to look after himself.'

'How many up at the bar with him?'

'I dunno. Three or four, maybe. They come and go. He's treating liberal.' Pete permitted himself a derisive grin. 'Seems to have plenty of money today.'

'At which end of the bar is he standing?'

'About eight or ten feet from the front door.'

'Isn't keeping his eyes peeled for trouble, you think.'

'He wouldn't know trouble if he stumbled against it—not tonight.'

'Drop in again and make sure he is still at the bar,' Ford said.

Johnson disappeared through the swing doors and reappeared.

'Still there,' he reported.

'Facing which way?'

'Elbow on the bar, with his back to the door.'

Ford nodded, silently. His lips were a thin, hard gash

in his white face. The eyes of the man blazed with a cold, deadly light. He drew his revolver and held it under the left flap of his Prince Albert coat, then pushed through the swing doors into the barroom.

Hart was at the bar with two other men. In his hand was a dice box. He had just rolled the ivory cubes to the mahogany top of the bar.

'Four sixes to beat,' he said, a little thickly.

They were the last words he ever spoke. The roar of a gun filled his ears as he sank to the floor. Ford had shot him through the back of his head.

Confusion filled the Tivoli. Men screamed, shouted, ran for cover.

Ford stepped forward and looked at the body lying inert and slack in front of him. A muscle in a sprawling leg twitched. The gambler flung two more bullets into the huddled figure.

He raised a hand for silence. 'I call you all to witness he saw me in the looking-glass and reached for a gun.'

'Sure,' a frightened bystander murmured.

'Tell the sheriff I'll be at the office of The Last Chance if he wants me,' Ford announced. He added, to suggest the right point of view to those present: 'Hart threatened my life today. No man in the community was safe while he terrorized it. Only last night he robbed our roulette game. I had to kill him in the public interest.'

The killer turned and walked from the room, an erect and dignified embodiment of justice.

Through the back door Lou Stone, newly appointed deputy marshal, walked swiftly into the Tivoli. His broad shoulders pushed a way through the crowd. Reaching the fallen man, he knelt on one knee to make an examination.

'Who did this?' he asked quietly.

Half a dozen men started to tell him at the same time. He silenced them and named one he knew to give him the facts. While the man was talking, he pulled Hart's gun from the holster, then broke and examined it to see how if any shots had been fired from it. The cylinder was empty of shells.

Hart had been unable to live up to his promise to reform, but he had kept faith with himself in one particular. Though he had carried a gun in the hope of deterring other killers, he had made it impossible for him to take a life with it.

Chapter 32

•

THE NEW MARSHAL FUNCTIONS

AN HOUR after the death of Jonathan Edwards Hart the money taken from the upstairs roulette room at The Last Chance was recovered by Polly Doble. She found it in a sack that had been dropped into a rainwater barrel placed to catch the flow from the roof. Her guess was that Hart had leaned out of his window and flung the sack into the barrel. No doubt he intended to retrieve his loot later, when the hunt for the bandit had spent itself.

Mrs. Doble at once hunted up Dan Clifford and turned over to him the wet sack and its contents. She found him with one of his deputies, a gambler whom she knew by sight named Lou Stone. They were having a little argument. Upon her arrival this was discontinued, or at least postponed.

The finding of the money apparently established the guilt of Hart. Dan locked it in a table drawer.

Polly was under an impression that Dan had been just ready to leave the office at the time she entered.

'What are you going to do about this killing?' she asked.

'We're going to arrest the murderer,' Dan said.

'You'll be careful,' she begged.

'We're always careful.'

'He's dangerous. If you don't go about it the right way——'

'We'll go about it the right way,' the marshal gave assurance.

Stone smiled sardonically.

Looking at Dan Clifford, so competently sure of himself, Polly was impressed anew with the swiftness with which the marching days had made a man of him. Not only had he come of age mentally. His shoulders seemed broader, his chest deeper. There was power in the grace with which he moved. Few men in Los Piños were his equal physically.

He had capitalized his strength. Though he carried a gun, he had never drawn it in making an arrest. As yet this had not been necessary. His reputation and personal presence had been enough. On one occasion he had jounced around a bit an offender who had showed fight.

As soon as Mrs. Doble had gone, the two men renewed their argument.

'Better change your mind and let me go along with you,' Stone urged. 'Especially if you aim to arrest Ford with his gang around him. They're celebrating tonight, and they won't take kindly to an arrest while they are roostered.'

'I don't want a fight with that outfit,' Dan explained. 'If you go with me, they will think we are there prepared for trouble. If I go alone, they will understand I am not trying to arrest him by force.'

'Fine, if they are all sober enough to figure that out and if none of them happens to be on the peck,' the deputy said. 'You're betting on a long shot. Use your brains, young fellow. That gang hates you. They won't ask anything better than a chance to bump you off.'

'Which they would get if you and I walked in to cut Ford out of the herd.' Dan shook his head. 'No, Stone. I've got to reason that Jasper Ford is not a fool and that he will see it is bad medicine to kill an officer come to arrest him for this Hart business. He knows no jury in Texas is likely to convict him for rubbing out a man with the record of Hart. I look for him to come along with me as peaceable as Mary's little lamb.'

Stone shrugged his shoulders. 'All right. Have it your own way. Maybe you are right. Anyhow, you're the boss in this office. Only, if you want to do all the work yourself, I don't see any need of having a couple of deputies.'

The two men walked down the street together. Out of the Tivoli came a heavy-set broken-nosed man. He gave a whoop, dragged out a gun, and fired it at the sign of a Chinese restaurant. The man was Pete Johnson, very much in liquor.

'I'll take care of this,' Dan told his deputy.

He moved forward swiftly, with a catlike tread. Johnson turned, caught sight of him, and gave a yell of derision.

'Well, well, if it's not the tough marshal himself,' the drunken man jeered. 'Sure Shot strutting around and playing Big Chief.'

'Put up that gun,' ordered Dan curtly.

'He says for me to put up my gun.' Johnson laughed contemptuously, his wavering weapon pointing more or less directly at the officer. 'If I don't he'll likely put me in the calaboose.'

Dan's fist lashed out and caught the man on the chin. Johnson went back as if a battering ram had struck him. He

145

hit the ground at full length. Before he could move, Dan put his boot on the outflung wrist, rested one hundred and eighty pounds on it, and stooped to remove the weapon.

The marshal called to his deputy. 'Mr. Stone, will you take this man to the jail and lock him up?'

Johnson sat up, groggily. 'What did you hit me with?' he asked.

Half a dozen loungers had seen the knockout. In the ensuing half-minute that number had increased to forty. Any kind of disturbance could draw a crowd in Los Piños day or night. The newcomers asked questions. Those present from the first satisfied their curiosity.

'This hell-a-mile marshal knocked out Pete Johnson and took his gun from him. Pete was loaded up with tarantula juice and had started to howl,' String Beans explained.

'Clifford was quick as chain lightning,' another cried, with enthusiastic admiration. 'While Pete was holding a gun on him, he knocked him cold with one punch. You never saw the beat of it. He cut loose like a Missouri mule.'

Dan turned and walked away without any comment. He had discovered that a certain aloof indifference helped to maintain one's prestige. That his reputation was much greater than his merits as a fighting man, he was very well aware, but he took a good deal of pains to do nothing to diminish it. No longer was he a hail-fellow-well-met companion to half a hundred casual acquaintances. At times it was difficult to hold to it, but he managed to maintain a manner of polite and slightly austere reticence.

The marshal found the man he wanted at the office of The Last Chance. With him were the proprietor of the place, Wilkins, Black, Derby, Cooper, and one or two other choice spirits. They were celebrating the victory of Jasper Ford.

Someone knocked on the door and Wilkins called to come in, not troubling to rise.

'Must be Pete Johnson,' guessed Cooper.

Dan was already walking into the room. He nodded casually to those present. For Cooper he had a special word.

'Pete can't come, Tom.'

That he was a focus of resentful eyes Dan knew. In this crowd nobody in Los Piños was less welcome.

'Why can't he?' demanded Cooper sullenly, a glass in his hand.

'He got a little too noisy and I had to put him where he will cool off for a few hours,' Dan said placidly.

'And Pete let you do it?' Cooper snarled.

'Why, yes,' Dan replied mildly. 'You know I've been appointed marshal, Tom.'

'Does that entitle you to go around arresting anyone you don't like?' Derby wanted to know.

Cooper cut in again. 'I don't believe Pete let you arrest him without putting up a scrap. He wouldn't be scared of a whole parcel of fellows like you.'

'He wasn't scared, Tom, but he was some groggy,' Dan explained. 'Pete is a rambunctious kind of bird and had to be knocked cold before he would understand.'

'Who knocked him cold?' persisted Cooper.

'I thought I mentioned I was marshal,' Dan said, smiling cheerfully at the rawboned ruffian.

'Did you come here to tell us you have arrested Johnson?' Ford asked harshly.

The marshal was standing. The others were still sitting, with the exception of Cooper, who had jumped to his feet at sight of Dan.

'No, Mr. Ford, I came here to arrest you.'

The two principals looked at each other. Their hard eyes clashed, the gaze of neither yielding in the least.

'What for?'

'For killing Hart.'

'He had threatened my life. He was reaching for a gun when I fired.'

'If so, the court will no doubt free you.'

'I killed him in self-defense. Do you think I'll let an upstart like you arrest me for it?'

Except the two talking, nobody else spoke. The outsiders did not move. They did not make a sound. This was a personal issue. Ford would not thank them if they interfered.

'I reckon you will,' Clifford answered, his voice low and even. 'You claim this killing was justified. It would be bad medicine to make a good case bad by resisting arrest."

'This is a frame-up of my enemies. I won't stand for it. You are making a bluff, I suppose, that Hart didn't rob this place.'

'No, I wouldn't say that. I think he did. Fact is, the money he took was found a little while ago.'

'Where?' asked Wilkins.

'In the rain barrel below his window. He must have used that as a hiding-place in case his room was searched.'

'Someone must have,' Black said, with obvious meaning. 'Someone who boarded at the Doble place.'

Dan nodded thanks. 'Much obliged, Black. We won't need to go into that now.'

Ford envisaged the situation. If it were true that Hart was practically proved guilty of the hold-up, his own case was better than it had been. He had not only killed a desperado, but one who had already reverted to his evil ways. Practically he was in the clear. By killing Hart he had done the town a service and saved the officers danger and trouble. To have shot anybody else in the back would have been fatal. Even now there would be talk criticizing the way he had destroyed his enemy, but there could be no serious trouble about rubbing out a man with so terrible a record.

'No, Black,' said Ford, with crisp decision. 'Hart did that hold-up job. I recognized him. That is why I shot him. He had run amuck and was too dangerous to let live. Any day he might have killed some good citizen.'

Dan suppressed swiftly an impulse to smile. This was no time for levity. Some of these men had been drinking heavily. He could count on Wilkins to oppose any resort to violence, providing he had time to register opposition, but Cooper might start trouble at any moment and one or two others of those present were of uncertain disposition.

'That is true,' the marshal said suavely. 'You can't tell when a killer will strike again if he is used to taking human life.'

The cold eyes of Ford probed into the wooden face of his enemy. What did the fellow mean? Was this a dig at him instead of at Hart? If it was, he decided to let it pass.

'I'll surrender for trial if you will send one of your deputies here,' the gambler announced.

'Why bother my deputies, Mr. Ford, since I am already here?' Dan asked, after a barely perceptible hesitation.

'Because I am not going to let you arrest me. That's why.'

Dan felt himself hardening. He did not intend to leave the room without taking Ford with him. That all present were watching him he was aware. He felt their eyes stabbing at him. This was the hour of acid test for him. If he let Jasper Ford bluff him now, it would be taken as a sign of weakness. His face betrayed nothing. When he answered, his voice was cool, his manner imperturbable.

'Not much point to that. You can walk down the street beside me as well as you can beside Stone.'

'If I was in his place, I wouldn't go a step with either one of you,' Cooper broke out angrily.

Ford looked at him. 'Maybe I can handle this, Tom. Mostly I play my own hand.'

Cooper subsided.

'I have told you what I will do,' Ford went on, speaking to Dan. 'Take it or leave it.'

Iron grating in his low, even voice, Dan said, 'I won't take it and I won't leave it.'

The shallow obsidian eyes of Ford glittered. 'No?' he said, almost in a murmur.

'I represent the law,' Dan remarked, speaking so deliberately that his words seemed to be spaced. 'I came here to arrest you, and I am going to do it.'

Into the momentary silence that followed, Wilkins broke with a hurried protest. He could not afford a killing here, especially that of a law officer who stood high in popular esteem. It would mean the end of business for him at Los Piños.

'Wait a moment, gents. We can fix this up. Don't go off half-cocked. Listen to me.'

Ford said nothing. He did not lift his gaze from the marshal.

Nor did Dan shift his steady gaze when he answered briefly, 'I'm listening.'

'You don't want trouble, Jas,' explained Wilkins, losing no time. 'In this Hart business you are one hundred per cent to the good. Leave that lay as it stands. A difficulty with the marshal over that is bad medicine, like he has done mentioned. We know that.' The owner of the place turned to Dan. 'Now, Mr. Clifford, as I understand it, you are not hurrahing Jas?'

'I'm arresting him,' Dan said. 'Call it anything you like.'

The voice of the owner of The Last Chance was oily with unction. 'Any officer who looks for the chance can kill offenders and drag them in dead. But you are building up a rep as being the kind that doesn't use a gun to get yore men. That's fine. Tom Smith of Abilene was that way. Game as they come.'

'And one of the guys he started to arrest bumped him off,' Cooper cut in with a jeering laugh.

Wilkins did not dwell on that point. 'All you want, Mr. Clifford, is for Jas to surrender. If he gives you his word he will be at the sheriff's office inside of half an hour, will that be all right with you?'

Swiftly Dan came to decision. 'Make it fifteen minutes,' he modified.

149

"All right, fifteen minutes. That suit you, Jas?'

Ford nodded. 'Get this right, Mr. Smart Aleck Marshal. I'm going because I'm in the clear and not afraid of all the officers in Texas. I was justified in getting Hart. The law can't touch me. I'm not surrendering because you have butted in with your say-so. I'd send you to hell on a shutter first.'

'I don't care why you come, if you come,' Dan said, meeting him eye to eye.

The young officer let his hard gaze travel slowly from one to another of the men in the room.

'Thanks for your help in supporting the law, gentlemen,' he told them derisively.

He turned and walked from the room. The eyes of the men followed his jaunty progress. His walk was as light and carefree as that of a buck in the rutting season.

'By God, he takes the cake,' Black swore.

In their hearts the others agreed with him. In the end he might lose, but he would go down fighting.

'You going down to give yourself up, Jas?' asked Cooper, with an insulting lift of the lip.

'I'm going to do just that, and you're going with me,' answered Ford, fixing him with his black eyes. 'We're going down the street together, all of us. We're going to show this town we stand as a unit.'

Within a few minutes Ford and his associates marched down San Antonio Street eight strong. Bond was accepted without demur. The sentiment of those in authority was that Hart was better dead if he had been about to resume his old wild ways. They might not approve of the manner in which he had been assassinated, but that was after all a detail. One could not be expected to be too punctilious in dealing with a man who had back of him such a record as that of Hart.

Chapter 33
•
DAN MEETS A
YOUNG LADY

DAN met Obigod Jones in front of the courthouse.

'I've been ordered to take twelve rangers with me to the salt lakes country,' the lank sergeant told his friend. 'We're setting out today.'

'To protect the rights of Ford and his company, I reckon,' Dan said.

'Yes, sir. That's a fine use for Texas rangers, to help a bunch of crooks get away with their steal.'

Dan nodded. No use to tell Jones, what he already knew, that legally the locaters were within their rights.

'More trouble brewing?' he asked.

'Y'betcha! Have you seen Stone's notice in the paper, that he is no longer connected with the company in any way?'

'Yes. Too bad Black and Ford couldn't see it his way.'

'Riding for a spill, those buzzards are,' the ranger predicted. 'Well, see you later, son.'

Dan turned up Houston Street. Presently his heart did a flipflop. A young woman was walking toward him. He lifted his hat and stopped.

'Good evening, Miss Sutherland,' he said, a little stiffly. He was not sure how familiar one ought to be with a girl to whom one had been engaged about three minutes in days past.

Milly said, 'Good evening, Mr. Clifford.' A tide of color had swept into her face. Otherwise she was quite composed.

'May I walk with you a little way?' he asked.

Her face registered a surprise that was wholly artificial. 'If you like.'

He shortened his stride to match her steps. In no haste to speak, he walked beside her in silence.

'We're having very nice weather,' Milly said in a small formal voice.

'I haven't been killed yet,' he said abruptly.

'No. That's very nice.'

'Nor killed anybody.'

'How long have you been marshal?' she inquired politely.

'So you're not taking back any of the things you said about me?"

'Does it matter what I said? I'm only a schoolmarm, and you are the great Dan Clifford.'

He was surprised at her bitterness. He did not know that she had lain in bed and wept more than once when she was sure the children were asleep. It broke her heart to know that she had driven away the man she loved. It was not her fault, of course. She felt sure of that. How could she marry a man who would choose so turbulent a way, one with the likelihood of death at the end of it, in preference to the safe, sane road of love?

Dan thought her the loveliest thing under heaven and

the most unreasonable. He had been unhappy at her condemnation of him, without knowing anything he could do about it. Now he had joined her on impulse, in the hope that time had softened her judgment. Apparently it had not.

His voice hardened as he inquired how the children were. They talked of outside things. She had moved, she explained, to a cottage two blocks farther up the street. The old place was being used for the business. Ah Sin had taken another Celestial in as partner in her place. She still had a minor interest in the concern, which was still called Miss Milly's Laundry. Yes, thank you, she enjoyed teaching. That and looking after her family kept her very busy. She had not much time for anything else except her church work. The Reverend Philip Washburn was a fine young man, devoted to his work and to his people. Milly felt he would do a great deal of good at Los Piños and was glad Mr. Clifford agreed with her.

'He sure loves his people, at least a portion of his congregation,' Dan drawled, watching her out of the corner of an eye. 'I hear he is figuring on getting married. That would increase his usefulness, wouldn't you say, if he picked the right girl?'

Into the girl's cheeks there came a little glow of added color. 'No rumors of that kind have reached me,' she said primly; then added with some tartness, 'But then I don't have time to loaf around all day and listen to gossip.'

'You'd certainly know if it was true, you being so interested in the church,' Dan replied innocently. 'Still, seeing him around here and there, I would say he plays favorites among his people. Not that I blame him. He would make a nice, tame, peaceable husband too.'

The eyes of Milly blazed at him. 'No doubt Mr. Washburn would appreciate your interest in his affairs if he knew, even though you never come to hear him preach.'

'Whether he would henpeck easy a girl couldn't tell till she had tried,' he concluded thoughtfully.

Milly stopped abruptly. Her little fists were clenched, her slim figure rigid. 'If you are quite through insulting me, Mr. Clifford, I can get along without your company,' she said furiously.

Dan felt a swift compunction. 'I didn't mean to do that,' he said gently.

'Then you succeeded very well without meaning it,' she told him, flying storm signals.

They had reached her gate. Swiftly she unlatched it and

moved up the walk to the house. Without looking back, she shut the door behind her.

'Now whyfor did I talk thataway to her?' Dan asked himself dejectedly. 'None of my business if she and the parson are friends. She would sure do better marrying him than me. Howcome I to bring him into it?'

He grinned ruefully, for he knew the answer when he asked the question. He had seen them together and was jealous.

Chapter 34
•
'KEEP UP THE
GOOD WORK, DAN'

STONE sat in the little office of the marshal opposite Dave Shotwell's saloon and glanced over the news columns of the Los Piños *Courier*. Occasionally he read aloud an item to his chief, who was employed in cleaning his revolver. The boots of Mr. Stone were on the edge of the table, his chair tilted back at a perilous angle.

> The social held last evening by Saint Barnabas Church was a great success. After a pleasant hour of conversation ice cream and cake was served to all and sundry. More than a hundred were present and a good time was had by all. Our popular young teacher, Miss Milly Sutherland, was chairman of the committee of arrangements and saw to it that the inner man was filled to repletion.
>
> Ground has been broken for the church building at the corner of Deaf Smith and River Streets. At present services are being held at Shotwell Hall. All are invited.

Having read this to Dan, Stone waited for a comment. The marshal was squinting down the barrel of his weapon and apparently had not heard it.

'I reckon *popular* is right,' Stone drawled. 'The boys are certainly wearing a path to the little lady's door. I'm putting my money on the sky pilot. He is the pick of the field, and unless I'm 'way off, Miss Milly knows it.'

After a moment Dan said, with no enthusiasm, 'I wouldn't doubt you are right.'

'He is a good guy and a square shooter.'

'No argument there,' Dan admitted briefly.

While Marshal Clifford was making his rounds Tuesday night some ruffian fired at him from an alley but fortunately missed. The young officer is not popular with gentry of this sort because of his efficient work in cleaning up the town. During his régime hold-ups and other crimes of violence have decreased fifty per cent. Keep up the good work, Dan. The good citizens of Los Piños are with you.

Stone added, sardonically: 'You're getting a lot of bouquets these days, Marshal. If one of these sure-shot alley-cats gets you, the town will certainly give you a bang-up funeral.'

'That will be nice,' Dan grunted, beginning to load the weapon.

'I notice the odds have changed in your favor,' the deputy said. 'When you took office the betting was four to one against you, but a fellow can't get better than even now.'

'I have only got one foot in the grave, you might say,' Dan commented.

'What beats me is the way your mind works,' Stone volunteered. 'You spend hours cracking away at a mark, and then when you go to arrest someone you never draw a gun.'

'We're not trying to blast this town into decency. Soon as the boys find it is getting civilized and won't stand for crime, they will fall into line.'

'And Jas Ford will probably run the Sunday School,' jeered Stone.

'I'm not expecting to reform Ford,' Dan said.

'What you expecting to do with him?'

'I wouldn't know right now.'

Stone resumed his perusal of the *Courier*, to break out a few moments later with an answer to his previous question. 'You won't have to do a thing about Jas. He has declared himself a good citizen looking only for justice. Listen here.

Jasper Ford, now president of the Salt Lakes Development Company, greatly deplores the new outbreak of violence on the part of those who oppose the operation of the company. He says that he and his associates hope to employ a considerable number of laborers, teamsters, and office men. He feels that in all justice the Government should back him up against the lawless element which has set itself against progress.

Dan delivered himself of an apothegm. 'If those that holler for justice the loudest had it done to them the jails would be a lot fuller.'

'There are going to be some graves fuller one of these days,' Stone said seriously. 'Won't be much longer now until there is a big explosion. The Mexicans feel that Ford's crowd have the State and the Governor back of them. So they have. Jas has been working all the influence he has at Washington too. If the rangers and the natives have a clash, I'll expect to see U.S. troops move in. The feeling is getting more bitter every day. Jas is as stubborn as a mule. He means to bull it through in spite of hell and high water.'

'Yes,' assented Dan. 'I've a notion that one reason he and his friends have laid off me is because he wants to keep his rep bright and shiny with the authorities so that when the blow-off comes he won't be classed as a bad man too tough for them to support.'

'Were they laying off you Tuesday night?' Stone asked dryly.

'That might have been some bird playing his own hand,' Dan suggested. 'You can't close five or six places for too raw stuff, as we have done, without making some enemies. Most of the rapscallions connected with them we drove out of town, but we could not get them all rounded up. You know that.'

'Sure I know it. Didn't three of them jump me last week down at Ochoa and Waller's wagon yard and pump four or five shots at me? If it hadn't been so dark they would have collected me too. No names mentioned. Everybody too busy sending blue pills. But that is no proof Jas Ford's fine Italian hand is not shuffling the deck.'

'Well, he'll go too far some day.'

Dan buckled on his belt, set his wide hat at precisely the right angle, and sauntered out to see how the town was getting along.

The upper end of it was getting along very well apparently. Real estate offices seemed to be doing a rushing business. A brick bank building was going up on Crockett and San Antonio Streets. Scrapers were removing dirt for the new hotel. His eye could pick out a score of frame stores under construction. A wagon train of mules bringing in supplies moved down the street. The new sidewalk was crowded with hurrying pedestrians. The Gateway City, as the town had dubbed itself, gave every evidence of prosperity.

Slowly Dan moved down San Antonio Street, stopping here and there to chat with acquaintances who opened conversation. It was in front of Dave Shotwell's saloon that the cowboy called Curly, one of the men rescued by him at the salt lakes, gave disquieting information.

'That fellow Pete Johnson, the one you cracked down on and sent to the calaboose, is at The Bucket of Blood tanking up,' Curly said. 'He claims he is looking for you. His side-kick Cooper is with him, and he is chipping in with a lot of "Amen, brother!" stuff. Better keep yore eyes skinned, Marshal.'

'Expect I had better have a talk with them,' Dan said quietly. It was impossible for Curly to guess that back of the officer's imperturbable manner raced a swift panic.

'Take someone along with you when you do yore talkin',' advised the cowboy. 'Or two or three. Pete is sore as a boil. Claims you took advantage of him when you laid him cold and now he is out he aims to stop yore clock. The way I size it up Cooper figures on sitting in too.'

'Did he say so?'

'I gathered he was fed on raw meat and r'arin' to go. They're damned sidewinders, both of those buzzards. Johnson came from the Strip,[1] sudden. So fast his bronc's belly was draggin' the dust. Killed a deputy U.S. Marshal. There's a noose waiting for him at Fort Smith, I understand. He's a sure-enough bad *hombre* and wears 'em low. I wouldn't want to scare you or anything, but don't think there won't be fireworks when you meet. Someone is going out in smoke. I'm pluggin' for you, Marshal. Take a whole passel of sheriffs with you and blast these wolves off'n the map.'

'How do you know Johnson came from the Strip and killed a marshal?' Dan asked.

'Cousin of mine drifted down from the neck of the woods. Soon as he saw Johnson he recognized him.'

'What was the name of the officer he killed?'

Curly shook his blond head. "Search me. How would I know?'

'Your cousin reliable?' Dan wanted to know. 'Not given to telling windys?'

'No, sir. When he says a thing is so, you can bet money on it.'

'What d'you mean, there's a noose waiting for Johnson at Fort Smith? Was he tried and convicted?'

'Yes, sir. And broke jail later. No two ways about that. My cousin showed me a reward poster for him. His name was John Peterson then. But the picture on the bill is the

---

[1] The Cherokee Strip, at that time a resort of bad men.

spittin' image of Johnson. You get yore posse and hop to it, Marshal.'

Dan was no spendthrift of words. He said 'Much obliged' nonchalantly. The cowboy did not know that his heart had turned over, plunged down like a plummet into a region of ice.

As Dan walked away, still with that air of jaunty *insouciance* which was one of his chief assets, he was engulfed in chill dread. The wind from the hills was like a whetted knife. He shivered. The breath of death was fanning him. Crags of fire were in the sunset. They held no warmth, no promise of a glorious day tomorrow.

Tomorrow! Would there be any tomorrows for him? Would he ever see again . . .

Abruptly he dragged himself out of despair. He had to go through to a fighting finish. There was no way out of that. The safer course was to call on Stone and his other deputy to help him when he met these gunmen. If he did that, his prestige would be gone. A threatened man cannot run to his friends for aid, not when his official duty is to stand up to hardy ruffians. No, he had to play a lone hand. Desperately he longed for the backing of a tough, hard man such as Stone was, but he knew he would never go and ask for it.

Dan flogged his failing spirit with a whip of self-contempt. Why was he always such a quaking jelly inside during the interval between the appearance of danger and the moment when he must grapple with it? Why did he always have to spur himself on to face peril, unless it came upon him so unexpectedly that he had no time to be afraid?

He squared his shoulders and took his light-footed way toward the Bucket of Blood. Anyhow, he would keep up the bluff as long as he could.

Chapter 35

•

'BEST DAMN MARSHAL EVER WAS BORN'

CHRIS KUNER'S notorious resort stood on a bluff just above the river. A cynical critic had once guessed that it had been placed there for convenience, in order that patrons who had been slugged and robbed could be disposed of more easily.

This was an exaggeration. The proprietor was not squeamish, but he drew the line at murder. An occasional impulsive killing was quite a different matter.

The building was adobe. A stairway ran up the outside of the south wall to the second story. At the sixth step there was a window lighting the saloon. The day had been warm and the window was still open.

Dan did not walk into the barroom. He soft-footed up the stairway and looked down. Six or seven men were in the place. One lay on a bench asleep. Others sat at a table, beer mugs in front of them. In front of the bar, their backs to him, stood Johnson and Cooper. The bartender, Bill Grogan, polished the mahogany with a cloth.

' 'Nother of the same,' Johnson said huskily.

'Make it two,' Cooper approved.

Grogan turned to fill the order.

Now was the time, Dan told himself, while the bartender was facing the other way and could not give warning. He eased a leg over the sill, swung the other one across, and dropped on his toes to the floor. At his entrance one of the men at the table sat erect. Noiselessly Dan padded swiftly across the floor.

Johnson was standing nearest the door. He became aware of someone at his right and turned to look. What he saw startled him.

'Sure Shot!' he cried, and gulped out an oath.

From where Dan stood, close to the entrance, his eyes could cover the whole room unless someone walked into the place behind him. His brain stabbed out impressions. The men at the table were outsiders and would not bother him. Grogan was not likely to take a hand. This was none of his business.

'I hear you are looking for me, Pete,' the marshal said, a touch of challenging contempt in his voice.

Johnson made up his mind instantly. He would call for a showdown. But not just yet, not while this alert young devil stood at his right hand, supple fingers hooked in belt an inch or two from the butt of the six-shooter. All the advantage of position lay with the marshal. Clifford could drill him before his hand closed on a weapon.

'Who said I was looking for you?' demanded Johnson harshly.

'A little bird whispered it to me. . . . Don't you, Cooper. Keep your hands on the bar.'

158

'He's a damn liar,' the squat broken-nosed ruffian burst out explosively.

Someone pushed through the front door and stood on the threshold, evidently held there by the knowledge that he had walked into drama. Dan' did not lift his eyes for a moment from the two men in front of him. His back was to the door. A shiver ran up and down his spine. If the man behind him was an enemy a bullet might crash into him.

'Friend, whoever you are, keep coming,' Dan said, and was surprised at the cool lightness of his voice. 'There's a chair at the table where the other boys have reserved seats. It's for you. Take it.'

The man walked down the room and did as he had been told. Out of the corner of an eye Dan recognized Curly. The cowboy had returned in order to be present when the marshal and his posse arrived. He had not been able to keep away from the anticipated excitement.

'So he's a liar, Pete,' Dan continued. 'You're not looking for me. Different here. I'm sure looking for you. On account of that little matter of the U.S. Marshal you killed in the Strip.'

'It wasn't in the Strip.' The denial leaped from Johnson before he could realize that it was a confession.

'Not in the Strip?' Dan said. 'My mistake. Some other part of the Nation?' His revolver leaped from the holster. 'Put 'em up, Mr. John Peterson. You're my prisoner.'

Johnson stood motionless, uncertain what to do. He had no intention of letting himself be dragged back to the gallows. Far better take a chance with this fellow. But not while he was covered. The thing to do was to play for time and the hope of a break.

'You claim my name is Peterson?' he said sulkily, his slitted eyes watching the officer.

'I don't care what your name is. Reach for the roof.'

'You got a warrant for my arrest?'

'You're looking into it.'

'You can't pull that on me, fellow. I know my rights.'

Dan's steel-barred eyes were hard as jade. 'Put up your hands,' he ordered, his voice almost a purr.

He read the outlaw's mind, knew he was waiting for the moment to strike. Presently the guns would roar. Dan was as certain of that as he could be of anything in the world that has not yet come to pass. He too was ready. An officer of the law, he could not shoot until one of these men made the first move.

159

Awakened by the cessation of noise at the poker table, the man on the bench sat up and blinked back to consciousness of his environment. At sight of the three at the bar his eyes popped. 'By granny!' he yelped.

'Keep yore shirt on,' Curly advised warningly.

Taking advantage of the distraction, Cooper made his error. He snatched at his gun and dragged it out.

Dan fired, across the shoulder of the shorter outlaw. So close was the margin of time that Cooper's gun roared twice before his lank frame collapsed. Buckling at the knees, the man slid to the floor along the front of the bar. One of the bullets from his gun struck the window jamb, the other plowed through the ceiling.

Johnson tried to draw. Before his hand had fallen to the weapon in his belt, Dan pistolwhipped him across the temple. He went down like a pole-axed steer, rolled over on his back, and lay still.

For a moment the others in the room did not move. The climax had leaped at them with paralyzing swiftness.

Dan looked down at Cooper. The man's body, unbelievably long, lay stretched on the floor, arms outflung limply. The Colt's forty-four had dropped from his hand. A thin trickle of smoke rose from the barrel. Through the forehead, halfway between the eyes and just above them, a neat hole had been bored.

The man on the bench jumped to his feet. 'Goddlemighty, I'm gettin' outa here,' he cried, excitement high in his voice.

'Sit down,' Dan told him crisply. 'The trouble is all over.'

From a pocket Dan took a pair of handcuffs and fastened them to the wrists of Johnson. He confiscated the weapon of the man and made sure he had no other gun concealed about his person. The forty-four of Cooper he also recovered.

'Take care of these guns, Curly,' he said. 'They will be wanted for evidence.'

The cowboy came forward, eyes big with admiration and amazement. 'Never saw the beat of it. You were that quick, that sure. Drilled Cooper right through the head.'

'You saw him reach for his gun before I fired?'

'Y'betcha. I'll swear to that till the cows come home.'

The marshal leaned against the bar, his forearm resting on the polished top, fingers still clutching the revolver that had just driven life violently from the body of a lusty man. A sickness ran through his vitals. He felt white and shaken. It

160

was in his mind that he must not let these men know he was close to prostration. His lips tightened to a thin line. He tried to fight down the waves of nausea that submerged him.

As if from a great distance he heard a babble of voices. Words came to him, standing out from lost sentences. He saw heads weaving about, disassociated from bodies. The room tilted, righted itself.

'Here's where one of Cooper's bullets hit,' a man was saying. 'Must have whizzed right past the marshal's ear.'

The room was filling with men. They crowded forward to see. Dan gave a curt command.

'Stand back everybody.'

The crowd left an open space, the center of which held Dan, the handcuffed prisoner, and the body of the dead man.

The eyelids of Johnson fluttered open.

'What happened?' he asked presently.

Four or five began to tell him, all talking at once. The gaze of the handcuffed man fell on Cooper, slowly shifted to the marshal.

'You rubbed him out,' he said.

Dan gave him a handkerchief. 'Better wipe the blood from your head,' he suggested.

Johnson looked at the bandanna sullenly, then lifted it to his head with his manacled hands. Presently his eyes found a man he knew.

'Go tell Jas Ford,' he said, in sulky despondency.

'Tell him what?' the man asked.

'That this wolf here—Sure Shot—has killed Tom and got cuffs on me.'

Dan added, quietly, 'And that I mean to keep them on him.'

Again there was a gabble of voices, out of which words and sentences rose. 'Bet yore life he will . . . Best damn marshal ever was born . . . Crazy as a bedbug . . . Hell, just lucky . . . Hurrahing the boys . . . Waited till Cooper cracked down on him . . . All wool and a yard wide, that boy.'

The marshal caught sight of Sam Jones coming through the door and called to him. 'This way, Obigod. Here's a prisoner for you—wanted at Fort Smith under name of John Peterson to keep a date for his own hanging. Take him off my hands, will you?'

Ranger Jones pushed to the front. 'At it again, you young ripsnorter,' he said with a grin. 'Sure I'll take care of this

161

blackbird. You can give me the details later. Has someone gone for the coroner?'

The coroner bustled into the place. He was an important little man and liked to be in the public eye. At the instigation of Jones he held an inquest on the spot. The witnesses were heard. Dan told his story.

The jury brought in almost immediately a verdict that the deceased had come to his death by getting in the way of a bullet propelled from a pistol held in the hand of Daniel Clifford in the rightful discharge of his duty.

The room and the street outside were filled with people. As the verdict reached them they broke into cheers. Jasper Ford was among those present, but he did not lift his voice in protest. This did not seem to be the hour to challenge the marshal's popularity.

At the first chance Dan walked into Chris Kuner's private washroom and locked the door. He stayed there fifteen minutes, very sick.

Chapter 36
•
THE ROAR OF THE MOB

JASPER FORD sat motionless, his frozen eyes fixed on a half-empty bottle in front of him. He did not see the bottle and scarcely felt its former contents within him. The spirits had given him no warm glow. He was busy thinking, and his thoughts were a curse. Events were not going in a way to suit him. The world had turned sour for him.

From Lieutenant Page of the rangers he had just heard disquieting news. Sam Jones had ridden in from the salt lakes with word that there had been a clash between the company workers and a small group of Mexicans in which two of the latter had been killed. The trouble had arisen so unexpectedly that the rangers had been unable to forestall it. Ford supposed that the town would soon be buzzing with angry natives.

He needed all the strength he could summon, and just at this time that damned marshal had killed Cooper, and started Johnson on his road to the gallows. Of all the infernal luck!

Not once but a good many times of late a bell of warning had rung in him. He had made a good stake at Los Piños. It was time to get out. A man could easily outstay his luck. He could see the cards being stacked against him. This upstart Clifford had shuffled them, with the result that the feeling of the town had crystallized in favor of law. No longer was he a czar in the underworld. Stone had deserted. Those he ruled had lost confidence in him. They did not tell him so, but he could read it in their shifty looks, in what they did not say.

Time to be hunting fresh pastures. Of that he had no doubt. But he was a stubborn and an avaricious man. He could not bring himself to run away and leave Clifford cock of the walk. Nor could he bear to give up the salt lakes proposition, knowing that an easy fortune was within reach.

It might be wisdom to fall in line with public opinion and give orders to his followers to cut out the rough stuff. There always came a time when a frontier town swept out the riff-raff. Why not join in and direct the clean-up? No need for it to include legitimate business such as reputable saloons and gaming houses. If he went into a law-and-order movement vigorously, he might recover lost ground. Some of the thugs and prostitutes allied to him would be furious, but he counted that negligible. Of course, when the proper time came he would rub out Clifford, without risk to himself if possible.

He poured out another drink, swallowed it, and corked the bottle. With a rag he flicked the dust from his shiny boots. Before a looking-glass he straightened his black tie and brushed his hair. Into the latter was coming a sprinkle of gray. He did not like that, for he had reached an age when youth was slipping away. For such a man age held no compensations.

As he stepped out on the sidewalk, he saw that darkness was falling. One by one the street lights began to shine. He stood a moment, uncertain which way to go. It was his intention to take a leisurely walk before reporting at The Last Chance for duty. He decided to stroll past the house of the Sutherland girl. She might perhaps be in the garden. It still irritated him that his attentions had been so politely but firmly declined. That a slip of a girl, fresh from the backwoods of Arkansas (or Tennessee, he was not sure which) should repulse him was an annoying absurdity.

He became aware of a distant buzz of voices, borne to him by the evening breeze. The night life of the turbulent young city had got under way, no doubt. But as he drew closer he realized that this was something special. The humming was like that of a hive of angry bees, insistent and sustained.

He guessed there had been trouble. Perhaps some one had snuffed out a life in a saloon. It was a little early in the evening for that, but the unusual was likely to happen.

The clamor grew. He heard individual voices, though he could not make out words. Coming to the corner of the street, he looked up Houston. A mob that filled the street was moving slowly toward him. A swift dread caught at his stomach muscles. They were Mexicans.

He was standing under the street light of a store. A high voice shrieked out recognition. Fifty others took up his name and flung it savagely into the night. To Ford it seemed that the tide of humanity poured at him like a wave of water from a cloudburst.

Appalled by the fury of it, he turned to run. Fear winged his feet. But before he had covered fifty yards, he knew they were gaining on him. He could hear the thud of the pursuing mob. The leaders were almost on his heels. Furiously his heart pounded. He knew that in the hands of the infuriated Mexicans he would not last three minutes.

A sharp command reached him. 'This way, Ford!'

Two men had just come out of a hardware store. One of them caught him by an arm and almost flung him through the doorway. 'Keep going,' he was told. The man was Dan Clifford, his companion Stone. They slammed the door shut behind him and stood in front of it.

Ford raced down the aisle of the store to the back door. Looking back, he saw a jam of men at the entrance through which he had just come. They were piling up fast. He heard angry voices, shrieks of malediction, the sounds of struggle. Then he was out of the building, scudding down the alley.

The front door of the store must have crashed or been opened, because as he looked back through the darkness he saw a spate of dark figures pour through the back door. Some of them at least were following him. He heard excited cries and curses, knew they were gaining on him again.

He went over a fence like a cat, dodged in and out among the trees of a small orchard, and flung himself across another fence. It seemed to him that he could hear shouts in every direction, but he dared not stop. He plunged through an open stretch of weeds and bumped into one of his hunters.

The man caught at his coat and raised a shout. With the barrel of his revolver Ford knocked him down. He took another fence and crossed a cow pasture, his lungs bursting with the strain of his desperate flight. His legs were buckling under him. He could go no farther. Drawn by a light in a kitchen, he opened a back door, to see a young woman standing by a stove with a skillet in her hand.

He cried, panting for breath, 'Save me!'

Chapter 37
●
A SELF-INVITED GUEST

MILLY's slender figure moved about the kitchen with a swift, efficient grace. She heated vegetables, beat up biscuits, and baked a custard. No motion was wasted.

Yet the underflow of her thoughts was not on the work. She brooded over the unhappiness that had swept over her. The prophecy made by her had been verified. In the course of duty Dan had been forced to kill a man. She knew, as all Los Piños did by this time, that the slain man had been an outlaw and that the marshal had been obliged to fire to save his own life. As an officer, no blame whatever attached to him. None the less the crook of a finger had created an impassable gulf between them. There was blood on his hands. That it was by no choice of his own made no difference, since he had elected deliberately to follow the path leading to this result.

It was time, she decided, to call the children in from play to wash up for supper. The door opened behind her. Without turning her head, Milly started to give orders.

A voice, choked for want of breath, cried 'Save me!'

Milly whirled, skillet in hand. She stared, in startled amazement. Jasper Ford was standing, his back to the door, ghastly fear staring out of his eyes.

'Save you from what?'

'The mob—outside—Mexicans!' he gasped.

She asked no more questions, did not waste a second. An excited shout in the street confirmed what the gambler had said. A hubbub of voices reached her. Turning, she led the way into the bedroom and pointed to the homemade wardrobe which contained the spare clothes of the family. Ford was crossing the floor to burrow deep among the dresses as she hurried back into the kitchen.

A knock came on the door while she was reaching for the skillet. She opened the door, a pulse of excitement beating fast in her throat.

Three Mexicans were standing there. They hurled a spate of Spanish words at her.

Milly shook her head.

'Pardon, señorita,' one explained in English. 'We look for a man—that villain Jasper Ford. Is he here?'

The girl made a pretty picture of indignant virtue. 'A man in my house—above all, the man who once insulted me! Why would he be here, sir? Do you mean that I am not a good girl—that I let such men visit my house?'

'No—no—no, señorita. He ran somewhere for safety. He can not be far away. We thought—perhaps——'

'——that he would come to me!' She flung out her hands in dramatic scorn and anger. 'Why, I ask you? Why? Do I not hate him from the bottom of my heart?'

'I told you he was not here,' one of the Mexicans said to his companions. 'Do we not know about the trouble this girl had with him? Never would he come here to hide.' He spoke in his native tongue, but Milly caught enough in words and gesture to make out what he was saying.

'Sí, Pedro,' another assented. 'It is true, what Juan says. Vamenos.'

'The front door is locked,' Milly mentioned. 'There is no way this evil man could have got in, except by the kitchen, and I have not been out of this room.'

'Sí, sí, señorita,' agreed the man Juan apologetically. 'We did not think he was here, but in case he came in and was compelling you to hide him——'

He concluded with a lift of the shoulders.

'When you catch this man, so bad, so full of sin, I hope you will punish him as—as he should be punished!' Milly cried, her eyes flashing with feminine fury.

Juan promised for all of them that Jasper Ford would never trouble her after this night. He was trapped. There was no escape for him. The end of his long crooked trail had been reached.

After the door had closed on them, Milly returned to the bedroom. Ford heard her coming, made sure she was alone, and came out from among the clothes. He tried to

166

achieve a manner of dignity, difficult under the circumstances.

'Have they gone?' he panted.

'Yes.' She stood near the bed, a small glass lamp in her hand, looking at him with a white face of cold distaste.

'What did you tell them?'

The pride in the lifted head, in the slender, erect figure, gave a whiplike lash to her scorn. 'The truth, as far as I could—that you are an evil man whom I detest. I asked them why you would come here, since it is well known I am no friend to you.'

Dread was still riding him. Milly could see that while he talked with her he was listening to the sounds outside, that his eyes had made sure the curtains were drawn.

'If you are no friend of mine, why did you not give me up?' he asked. 'You like me better than you pretend.'

'Your vanity is hard to kill,' she said contemptuously. 'I wouldn't give a dog up to a mob like that. Listen.'

Out of the night a howl of execration lifted to them.

The eyes of the man darted to the windows, to make sure their shadows did not show. 'Are the doors locked?' he asked.

'Not the kitchen door. If I locked that—and some of them came—they would know I was hiding you. Shall I lock it?'

He paid no attention to her mockery. 'Better not. If they find me——'

His lip twitched. He did not finish the sentence.

She was as empty of sympathy as a young Portia. 'What have you done now, that they are hunting you to put an end to you?'

He attempted a look of injured innocence. 'Nothing, Miss Sutherland, upon my word. They and their friends break the law trying to cripple a legitimate business enterprise in which I am a partner. In an attack upon our property, two of them were killed day before yesterday. I am in no way to blame. If you consider this fairly——'

'Hadn't you better consider a more urgent question?' she interrupted, with a little gesture that swept his defense out of consideration. 'Soon—in a minute or two—the children will be here. What do you mean to do? You can't stay here.'

'I must stay here, for the present,' he pleaded. 'You wouldn't throw me out to those wild beasts.'

'No, I wouldn't. Probably it is what you deserve, but I don't want to be responsible for what would happen.' Her pale face reflected the anxiety that still filled her bosom. 'The point is that if the children know you are here, and if the Mexicans come back again, you would be discovered. They would betray you without meaning to tell.'

'Then they mustn't know I am here.'

'How can they help knowing it? This is the room where they sleep. If I keep them out of here, they will know something is up.'

The children came pounding into the kitchen. They called Milly excitedly, eager to tell the news ready to burst out of them. The young woman left Ford and joined the little folk, closing the door behind her.

'What is it?' she asked, trying to smile at them.

'They're hunting for a man, Milly!' cried Tom. 'Golly, if they find him!'

'And they're searching everywhere. They think he is near, 'cause he couldn't hardly have got away,' Rose contributed.

'When they get him they're going to hang him or shoot him or something. Jiminy!'

'Wait a minute,' begged Milly. 'What is it all about? Who is hunting for who?'

'About a million Mexicans, sis. They're looking for that man Jasper Ford. Seems he killed a lot of men and ran away.'

Another knock sounded on the door.

Chapter 38
•

'SOMEONE ELSE
AT THE PARTY'

MILLY felt the pulse in her throat beating again. She picked up a pan of biscuits and put them in the oven, at the same time telling Rose to go to the door.

Into the room walked Dan Clifford. He carried himself with stiff embarrassment. Only once since the killing at Chris Kuner's place had he met her. Then she had passed him with a formal bow.

Now she rose swiftly from the place where she had been crouching before the oven and cried out a question, misgiving in her heart.

'What have you been doing?'

His face was bruised and bleeding. An eye was swollen. Above one brow there was a cut. The coat he wore had been torn to rags. Through a rent in one sleeve the smooth, supple muscles of the upper arm showed.

'Got in the way of a stampede,' he said somberly.

'What you mean, Dan?' Tom asked, big-eyed.

'Another fellow and I got a notion we could stop about fifty milling Mexicans. They stomped us down some.'

'Something about this Ford business?' Milly said, her eyes on Dan.

'There has been trouble at the salt lakes,' Clifford explained. 'Two Mexicans killed by company men. Word has just reached town and a mob jumped Ford.'

'He got away?'

'For the moment. They're hot on his trail.'

'You helped him escape,' Milly guessed.

'Stone and I.' A rueful grin spread over his disfigured face. 'They mussed us up some.'

'Did you fight the Mexicans?' Tom wanted to know, in a hot glow of admiration.

'No, Tom. I see you have got to know all about it. Ford was coming down the street, with a hundred Mexicans hotfoot after him. We yanked Ford into Shanley's store and slammed the door shut, we being on the outside. They landed on us all spraddled out. What they wanted was to get us out of the way so they could follow Ford. We kind of stuck around and they had to claw us up some and drag us down. They busted the door and went right over us. Now you know all about it, boy.'

'Gee! I wisht I had been there,' Tom regretted.

'I would have given you my place free gratis,' Dan said. He turned to Milly. 'Thought maybe I had better drop in and stay awhile. These fellows are some excited. They wouldn't do you any harm, I reckon, but it is just as well to make sure they don't worry you.'

'It is nice of you to think of us,' Milly said in a proper little voice. She felt safer with Dan in the house, but she did not know what his reaction to the presence of Ford might be.

'You came just in time for supper, Dan,' Tom said joyfully.

'We would like to have you stay if you would care to join us,' Milly added, reinforcing her brother's invitation primly.

Dan accepted, reluctantly. He guessed the offer had been forced on Milly. Under the circumstances he took no pleasure in joining the family, but he did not see how he could well refuse.

'Everybody wash up,' Milly ordered, flinging a towel at Tom on her way to open the oven door.

Presently they were all seated at the kitchen table, since the kitchen served also as a dining-room. Dan had his back to the bedroom. Tom faced him. The sisters were at the top and bottom. The children were so full of excitement they kept the conversation going. Milly contributed only formal talk. Dan answered questions, but except for that at first remained silent.

'Does it hurt you, where they beat you up?' Tom asked, his mouth full of biscuit.

'Not much,' Dan answered. 'Tomorrow it will hurt like sixty, especially if I let a smile crack my face.'

'Let's go out right after supper and scout around, Dan,' proposed Tom. 'Maybe we could find this fellow Ford.'

'What would you do with him if you found him?' Dan wanted to know.

'You're not going to leave this house tonight, Tom,' his sister Milly told him decisively. She looked at Dan. 'What would *you* do with him?'

'Nothing,' Dan said promptly. 'I haven't lost him.'

'You wouldn't turn him over to the Mexicans, now you have had time to think it over?'

He shook his head. 'I don't reckon I would. He deserves killing for sure, but I couldn't do that to any human being, even though it would be a heap better for this town if he was out of the way for good.'

'Would you help him to escape if you had a chance?' Milly persisted.

'I'd hate to, but I expect I would if it was wished on me,' Dan admitted.

'Maybe it will be,' Milly said.

Dan looked at her quickly. 'I don't think so. I have already had my beauty messed up on his account. It would be tough luck to get worked over for him again.'

Milly picked up the biscuit plate and went to the oven for another batch of hot bread.

The stomach muscles of her guest collapsed as if the floor of a swift elevator had dropped from under him. For against the back of his neck he felt the pressure of a cold round metal rim.

Dan did not look round. He did not judge it wise. He

was aware that the two children were staring at someone back of him out of big frozen eyes.

A voice he knew said, 'Keep your hands right where they are on the table.'

To whomever it might concern, Dan mentioned with what lightness he could summon, 'Someone else at the party.'

Chapter 39

•

DAN LAYS DOWN THE LAW

A HAND reached forward and removed the revolver from its holster on the hip of the marshal.

Ford said harshly, to all present, 'If anyone lets out a sound I'll fill him full of lead.'

The children sat paralyzed with terror. To lessen the strain Dan suggested, in a voice not quite as light as he could have wished, 'After which Mr. Jasper Ford would last about five minutes—maybe ten.'

Milly came back from the stove, a pan of biscuits in one hand.

'Put up that gun, you fool,' she ordered, eyes hot with anger.

'I'll do the bossing,' snarled Ford. 'Think I don't get your game? Think I don't know you're plotting against me?'

'Was Dan plotting against you when he kept you from being torn to pieces?' Milly demanded sharply. 'Take a look at him. He was beaten up and knocked down and trampled on to give you a chance of escape. All he had to do was to stand aside and let you be captured.'

'He's my best friend and I didn't know it,' Ford said, with heavy sarcasm.

'I'll do a little guessing,' Dan put in, his voice even and low. 'Looks to me as if Miss Sutherland has been hiding you. All she had to do was to give a yell for help, or else she could step outside and give a tip to these fellows hunting you. She didn't even tell the kids you were here. A blind man could see how surprised they were when you showed up with your pop-gun.'

Ford began to see that he had made a mistake. Un-

171

graciously he backed down. 'Looks mighty funny you dropped in right now,' he growled.

'I don't expect either of us is any too welcome,' Dan said dryly. 'Our hostess will be pleased to say good-bye to both of us soon as she can.'

The gambler lowered his gun. 'Don't pull any monkey tricks,' he warned.

Dan swung round and looked the man over coolly. 'You seem to have the wrong idea, Mr. Ford. You're the one in trouble, not us. It is your hide the gents outside want to hang up and dry. So far Miss Sutherland and I have saved your bacon for you. If you don't like what we have done, you can open that door and walk out. Nobody is holding you here. But if you stick around with us, my advice would be for you to improve your manners.'

'I can't go now,' Ford told him bitterly. 'You know that. A pack of wolves is waiting around outside ready to jump me.'

'I gather that Miss Sutherland is doing you a favor,' Dan said.

'I'm not denying it, am I?' Ford replied sourly.

'No, you're showing real gratitude by drawing a gun and scaring the children.' The voice of the marshal hardened. 'I'll lay the law down, Mr. Ford. If you want us to do any more for you, put that gun back in its holster.'

The eyes of the men clashed. Slowly, the gambler thrust his weapon back into its place. He knew that this was no time to let his hatred of Clifford dominate him.

'Now I'll take my gun,' Dan continued, holding out his hand.

Ford passed the six-shooter back to its owner.

'Have it your own way if you are scared of me,' he said.

Dan laughed, without mirth, taking in the man with a hard eye. 'There have been times when I have been afraid of you and your gang of killers, but this isn't one of them. You're in a jam. If you were garnished with guns, you couldn't use one.'

'What is the program?' Milly wanted to know. 'Suppose some of these fellows come back and want to search the house?'

'Nothing more likely,' Dan admitted. 'If so, Mr. Ford will be out of luck.'

'And so will some of them,' Ford retorted savagely.

Tom began to cry. He liked adventure, at least in theory, but this was too realistic.

'Don't you cry, son,' Dan told him cheerfully. 'Everything

is going to be all right. We'll get Mr. Ford out of the house soon as we can.'

'How?' snapped the gambler, irritable from anxiety.

'I've got an idea,' Dan said. 'Wait a minute. Let me figure it out.' He drummed with his fingers on the tablecloth, frowning at the sugar bowl.

'They'll keep guards around all night posted here and there,' the hunted man said bleakly. 'As you say, they may search the house. If you've got a plan that's any good, you had better spill it soon, fellow.'

'It might work,' Dan murmured, almost to himself.

'What might?'

'The point is to sneak you out unnoticed,' the marshal explained. 'You can't just walk out. Chances would be ten to one against you. How about your being carried out?'

'Carried out? What you mean?'

Dan turned to Milly. 'The children gather laundry and bring it here for Ah Sin to collect, don't they?'

'Yes,' Milly nodded.

'Mostly he calls for it after supper, doesn't he?'

'Nearly always. But he is not coming tonight.'

'My idea is to see Ah Sin and have him drift up with his cart,' Dan went on. 'All these men see him shuffling around every day. They won't think twice if he passes with his load. Instead of a bundle of clothes he will carry out Ford wrapped in sheets and shirts, dump him in the cart, and wheel him down to the laundry.'

'No,' Ford protested instantly. 'I'll not make a getaway in such a humiliating fashion. Besides, he would have to run a gantlet of dozens of these Mexicans. I might easily be discovered.'

'You might,' Dan agreed. 'But the chances would be against it. Who would take two looks at Ah Sin? As to humiliation— would it be more dignified to be dragged out from under a bed in the next room?'

'If any of these wolves molest me they will go out in smoke,' Ford cried, with an oath.

'But not in this house,' Dan told him sharply. 'I'm looking after the children and Miss Sutherland. There won't be any trouble here. Understand that. You are saying *Adios*. I don't care whether you go on your own legs or on the wheels of Ah Sin's cart. Take your choice.'

'So you claim to be boss here,' Ford sneered. 'That's the way of it, is it?' The man let his shallow black eyes rest on Milly for a moment.

173

The marshal's eyes stabbed at him. 'Be careful, Ford. One more word like that and I'll bring your enemies on you like a swarm of bees.' He added quickly, not to stress the insult of the gambler: 'I'm telling you what you'll do. It will be as I say.'

'How do I know you won't throw down on me and tell these devils I am in the cart?' the harassed man barked. 'You been trying to get rid of me. Here's a fine chance. You claim to be trying to help me. Why would you do that, when I know damn well you hate me?'

'I'm the law in this town. At least I stand for it. That's the only reason I'm in this. If I wasn't marshal I wouldn't lift a finger for you.'

'But you are so conscientious you aim to save your worst enemy. That what you want me to believe?' growled Ford.

'I don't care what you believe. Make up your mind. Do you walk out of the door? Or do we help you get away?'

'The Chinaman might give me away. Those Orientals are so treacherous they would sell their own mothers.'

'I'm not guaranteeing a thing,' Dan answered bluntly. 'I've made you a proposition. Take it or leave it.'

The throat of Ford was dry. He heard in the distance the shouts of men. The sound was like the baying of a wolf pack in pursuit. His eyes darted to the front door and back to the bedroom. No matter what course he followed, he would be in desperate danger.

'I've a right to protection from the law,' he blustered. 'You go get the rangers and bring them here.'

Dan's answer held a touch of malice. 'None of them in town except Lieutenant Page and Obigod Jones. You had the rest of the troop sent to the salt lakes to protect your property.'

'Well, get those two, and pick up some gunmen on Santone Street. We can stand these scalawags off.'

Dan shook his head. 'I won't do it. Half a dozen men would be killed. I'm not going to take the responsibility. You brought this on yourself by your bullheadedness and disregard of the rights of others. I'll help you out of the tight you are in if I can, but I won't sacrifice lives to do it.'

'You go, Miss Sutherland,' the gambler urged. 'You don't want trouble here if you can help it.'

Milly's eyes appealed to Clifford for orders. 'I could go and take the children with me,' she said in a low voice.

'Best thing you can do,' Dan assented promptly.

174

'No,' demurred Ford. 'If you left with them these scoundrels would search the house.'

'That would be likely,' Dan said, smiling grimly.

Ford threw up his hands. 'All right. I'll go in the cart. Hurry up and get the Chink here. If you betray me I'll curse you with my dying breath.'

The marshal reached for his hat. 'I ought to have him back here inside of half an hour. It would be a give-away if I came back to the house myself. I'll hang around near the Buckhorn. Ah Sin had better take the back way down along Narrow Street. It will be darker there.'

After Dan had gone, Ford waited in an extreme nervous tension. His senses were keyed to a high pitch. Every sound startled him. He lit a cigar and puffed at it, then abruptly put his foot on the light and crushed it out. He rose, paced up and down, sat down again. Tom started to cry once more. Curtly the man told him to cut it out.

Chapter 40
•
AH SIN GATHERS LAUNDRY

DAN found Ah Sin sitting in front of the laundry apparently at peace with the world. He sat with his fingers laced together, deep in contemplation.

'Got to disturb you, Ah Sin,' Dan said. 'Miss Sutherland wants you to do her a special favor.'

'Missy ask. Ah Sin do.'

Dan felt his way a little carefully. He remembered that Jasper Ford was no favorite of the laundryman.

'Well, Missy is in a jam. You can help her out if you want to.'

'Me likee Missy.'

'Good. I thought you did. So do I.'

'You mally her maybe,' Ah Sin suggested.

'No such luck,' Dan replied promptly. 'She doesn't approve of me . . . Here's the lay-out, Ah Sin. But before I tell you I want to be sure you won't talk to a soul about this.'

'Me padlocked.'

'Good. I suppose you know the Mexicans are on a rampage tonight. They are looking for Jasper Ford. His men killed two natives at the salt lakes. If they find him, he won't last a minute.'

'Bully. He velly bad man.'

'So he is. But it happens that Miss Milly wants him to escape tonight. She is asking your help.'

'Miss Milly fliend of his?'

'No. Far from it. But it is like I said. She has to help him on her own account. Otherwise she will be in trouble.'

'All light. Me help.' Ah Sin made the promise after his slant eyes had considered Dan for a moment or two.

The man from Canton listened while Dan told him what he must do. He made no protest, did not even mention that there was danger in the task assigned him. He knew the marshal understood the excitable nature of the Mexicans and the chance that they might make an end of the laundryman if they discovered him trying to aid their enemy. In his usual colorless monotone he said 'All light,' and let it go at that. His yellow face was as devoid of expression as the Sphinx.

In his Chinese slippers he flatfooted to the handcart and started up the street. At one or two places he stopped and took on bundles of laundry. Reaching Houston Street, he turned up it toward the home of the Sutherlands.

That the town was full of excitement he sensed. The saloons on San Antonio Street were doing a rushing business. Plenty of white men were in evidence, but they were not interfering with the Mexicans. This was strictly a private feud between Ford's crowd and the Spanish-speaking faction. The Anglo-Saxons were making it clear that they did not regard it as a race war.

After leaving San Antonio Street, Ah Sin began to meet Mexicans. They paid no attention to him. He and his handcart were as much a part of the town's daily life as were the vendors of vegetables and fruit of their own nationality. Before the houses of two customers he stopped with his singsong, 'Laundly! Laundly!'

Presently he pushed his cart down the walk and round to the back door of the Sutherland place. Those inside heard his chant, and at sound of it felt excitement racing in them. They knew that every tick of the clock was bringing them closer to the climax of this adventure.

Milly answered Ah Sin's knock and let him into the house. 'Mlister Clifford say bring cart,' he said impassively.

'Did he tell you what we want you to do?' Milly asked, her big eyes shining like stars.

'He say catchum Mlister Ford and put him in dirty clothes.'

Ford cut in harshly. 'Listen, you damned Chink! If you make a sound to call these greasers I'll put a bullet in your heart. Understand? My gun will be in my hand every minute of the time.'

'Maybeso better not hide in cart,' Ah Sin said blandly. 'Maybe better get fliend help.'

Ford moved forward and took him by the throat, holding him against the wall. The fingers of the gambler closed tightly, cutting off the breath of Ah Sin. The face of the Chinaman became contorted and his eyes popped out.

Milly caught at Ford's wrist with both hands and flung her weight on it, dragging his hand down.

'You brute!' she cried.

Ah Sin leaned against a chair, struggling for breath.

'I know how to handle this kind of cattle, Miss Sutherland,' the gambler said, with an assumption of dignity. 'He would like nothing better than to betray me. Now he knows that if he does I'll rub him out instantly.'

'If you got your desserts Ah Sin wouldn't lift a hand for you,' Milly cried indignantly. 'You come here and ask our help and insult us one after another. You're crazy with fear. That's the trouble. You don't trust any of us and yet you know you have to depend on us to save you.'

'You are mistaken, Miss Sutherland,' answered Ford coldly. 'I have never been afraid in my life. With the greatest pleasure I would fight half a dozen of these swine in the street, but it is impossible for me to stand up to five hundred.'

'You did not assault Dan Clifford, because you know he is a better man than you are, but you jump on this inoffensive foreigner, knowing that he can't strike back. That is what I call cowardice.' The eyes of the girl blazed contempt at him.

Milly had put a finger on the pulse of the cause for Ford's actions. He was trying to fight down his fear and at times it flowed up and filled his throat. His judgment told him that he should attempt to conciliate these people, all of whom had reason to dislike him. But whenever his jumpiness got out of control, he resorted by instinct to his old habit of bullying. This was an effort to dominate a situation in which he knew he was playing a humiliating and unworthy part. The excuse he had given was true enough. If there had been half a dozen of the Mexicans he would have gone out into the night and taken his fighting chance. But the howl of the mob appalled him. More than once the sound of it had been carried to him by the breeze and filled him with panic. If they got a chance they would tear him to pieces.

Even now his vanity demanded expression. 'Not the case,' he retorted roughly. 'I have tried to get your friend to stand up to me and he always finds an excuse for backing down. One of these days I'll show him up.'

'After he has saved your life,' Milly said, with acid contempt. Then, with swift fierce energy she made a stipulation. 'No. We won't help you if Dan Clifford is to suffer for it. Take your choice. Either get along without us or swear that if you escape you will never again try to injure Dan.'

A shot sounded, not forty yards distant. Ford could not repress a start. 'All right. All right. Anything you say. For God's sake get me away from here.'

Milly brought a Bible and pinned him down to a solemn pledge never under any circumstances to hurt Dan Clifford.

The gambler parroted her words, his eyes stabbing at the door and windows through which at any moment might come the attack of his enemies. He was in a desperate urge to be gone. Yet he shrank fearfully from the thought of lying in that handcart while a man whom he had injured pushed him through scores of excited Mexicans clamorous to destroy him.

While they had waited for Ah Sin, his former partner had brought bedding from the adjoining room. Ford lay down on a sheet and was rolled up in it like a ball. Milly opened the door and the laundryman carried the bundle to the cart and tumbled it in. More sheets were flung on top of the hidden man. Ah Sin pushed the cart down the walk and into the street.

Before they had gone forty yards, someone halted them, but as soon as the sentry recognized Ah Sin, he waved the Oriental on his way. The laundryman shuffled along, impassive and imperturbable. Apparently all the excitement meant nothing to him.

Chapter 41

•

FRIENDS OF MR. FORD

DAN met Lieutenant Page coming out of the Tivoli. The ranger officer was a splendid-looking young man of about thirty. His tanned face had a reckless devil-may-care expression. He carried himself with light ease, as if his feet were ballbearing. Broad-shouldered, slim-waisted, and tall, he attracted the eyes of men and women alike.

He grinned at the marshal. 'Liable to be a right lively time in Los Piños tonight,' he drawled.

'Looks like,' Dan assented. 'If they find Jasper Ford or Black.'

'Those gents seem to have gone into a hole and drawn it in after them,' Page said. 'Can't say I blame them. Our Spanish-speaking brethren are real anxious to collect their scalps.'

'Yes.'

'Wonder where that fox Ford is hiding,' the ranger continued. 'I'd give a 'dobe dollar to know. Those looking for him have been combing the town real thorough.'

'Dig up that 'dobe dollar, Lieutenant,' the marshal answered. 'I can tell you where he is and I can show you where I hope he'll be in about ten minutes.'

Page went into a pocket and drew out a Mexican dollar. He flipped it to Dan. 'Does anything go on in this town that you're not on the inside of?' he asked.

'Ford is making a call at the home of Miss Milly Sutherland,' Dan said. 'At least he was a few minutes ago.'

'What is he doing there?' the ranger wanted to know.

'Sneaked in by the back door to save his skin. Miss Sutherland hid him. I've arranged transportation for him to another place. See that outfit?' The marshal pointed to Ah Sin and his cart. The laundryman was shuffling up the street at a leisurely pace. 'I'm hoping to get Ford out of Miss Sutherland's house in that cart.'

The lieutenant rolled and lit a cigarette. 'Glad Ford is taking that buggy ride and not Billy Page,' he said dryly. 'If the Chink loses his nerve and gets scared, friend Jasper will be a gone goose.'

'Or if someone gets suspicious and rams a hand down into the laundry,' Dan added. 'No, I don't envy Mr. Ford his ride. There may be a grave in Boot Hill at the end of it.'

'Ford keeping a stiff upper lip?' the ranger asked.

'Scared to death and snarling at everybody who helps him,' Dan reported.

Page looked the other peace officer over with some amusement. 'The lads certainly worked you over some, Mr. Clifford, while you were fronting for your dear friend Jasper.

'I'm marshal,' Dan said, laconic of phrase.

'That's right. Paid to protect good citizens like Jasper.'

'Paid to help make this a law-abiding town. May have to call on Lieutenant Page for aid tonight.'

'I'll stick around,' the ranger promised. 'If you'll guarantee I don't get caught in a loose blanket stampede like you were.'

'No guaranty. All this hullabaloo may not amount to a hill of beans, or it may run to a riot.'

'Sure enough,' admitted Page. 'These lads will burn powder quick if they once get started. Smoke may fog up this town till it looks like a forest fire. No can tell.'

'Mr. Ford's buggy ride will take him to the *acequia*. The procession will move up Houston Street to Narrow, down that thoroughfare for three blocks, and will then cross to Miss Milly's Laundry.'

'If it is not interrupted,' the lieutenant suggested.

'If not interrupted.'

'I take it Marshal Clifford won't be leading it with a brass band.'

'Not none. But I'll be hovering around not too far away.'

'*Yo tambien.*' Page grinned again. 'We'll be too far away to be of any use to our dear friend Ford if Old Man Trouble breaks on him sudden, but near enough to take charge of the punctured remains of the deceased after the fireworks.'

'Can't tell about that,' Dan said, leaning against the adobe wall. His manner was indifferent, even negligent. He had all the time in the world apparently. An observer would not have guessed that he was holding himself quiet by sheer will power, that all his being was moving swiftly to the little house on Houston Street. He dared not get too close to it, lest the Mexicans guess he was there to protect Ford. His worry was not for the hunted man, but for the brave-hearted girl crowding down her own fear to comfort her children.

180

Dan did not like to think of what might take place if the hunters discovered she was hiding their prey. Very likely they might merely brush the Sutherlands aside as they reached for the victim. On the other hand, filled with excitement as they were, with weapons in their hands, there might very easily be an accident they would regret later. A rush of frenzied men. An impulsive twitch of a finger . . .

Stone drifted across the street to join them. He too had been battered in the human stampede that had poured into Shanley's store after Ford.

'Haven't heard a word about Jas since he hot-footed it through Shanley's,' the deputy said. 'His luck sure stood up fine. I wouldn't have given four bits for his chances about the time fourteen Mexican gents climbed my frame and plowed me under. Looks like he has made a getaway.'

Dan told him what he knew. 'We'll string out along the line of travel,' he added, 'and be handy to jump in to help Ah Sin in case of a rookus.'

'I've heard it claimed that one Texas ranger can take care of one riot,' Stone said, amiably ironic. 'Hadn't we better keep out of this and let Lieutenant Page handle it?'

'This isn't my riot,' Page declined. 'You can't lay it on my lap until you fellows have been killed off. Local authorities get first crack at trouble. We rangers only come in if you can't cope with it.'

Stone had a handkerchief tied around his head. A dark stain showed on it. He caressed the spot meditatively.

'The local authorities weren't one-two-three last time they tried to cope,' he mentioned.

It was arranged by the three men to cover, apparently by chance, the progress of the laundry cart through the streets. Page was to take the Houston Street end of the trip, Stone would meet it as it passed down Narrow, and Dan carry on from there to the laundry. None of them were to hang around the cart or take any obvious interest in its contents.

'Hope they don't hold it against you two for butting in on their little party,' the ranger said. 'Hadn't been for you they would have collected Ford nice. They're probably some annoyed at you. I'd hate to learn that some impulsive Spanish gent had dropped either of you as a substitute for Jas.'

'They know we're marshals of this town,' Dan answered. 'We didn't spoil their show to please ourselves. Likely they will be reasonable. I have always had friendly relations with them.'

'Were they reasonable when they chawed you both up and spat you out of Shanley's?' Page asked dryly.

Dan shrugged his shoulders. 'Well, see you later, gentlemen. I'll be drifting down. Good luck.'

Lieutenant Page had had the advantages of a year at college before embarking on his job of policing the frontier. He flung up a hand in farewell and said something about saluting Caesar.

Chapter 42
•
CURLY UPSETS
THE APPLE CART

AH SIN was stopped four or five times on Houston Street, but was permitted to pass as soon as he was recognized. He shuffled along, not quickening his pace in the least. His shibboleth carried him past the groups of excited men.

'Me catchum laundly,' he explained patiently.

No anxiety showed in his imperturbable manner, no eagerness to get away. He did not do too much talking, but relied on his three-word formula.

All along the line of travel he pushed his cart through groups of voluble Mexicans. Most of what they said he did not understand. His knowledge of the language was limited to a few phrases useful for daily intercourse. But it was not necessary to speak Spanish to get at the emotion which was moving them. They were dangerous, to anyone who crossed them just now.

The laundryman turned into Narrow Street. Progress was difficult here. It was in the old town. Adobe store buildings lined both sides. At intervals were *tendejons*, in front of which crowds milled to and fro. Very little attention was paid to Ah Sin, but he had sometimes to wait patiently before the gesticulating natives would move aside far enough for him to get past.

The deputy marshal Stone sauntered along the cobblestones forty yards ahead of the Chinaman. Tonight the officer was not popular. He moved with a manner of complete indifference, apparently oblivious of the resentment his presence stirred. He had been a partner of Ford. To be sure, he had ostensibly withdrawn from any interest in the Salt Lakes

Company. None the less he had been in command of the men who had been surrounded in the rocks some weeks earlier. Moreover, not an hour ago he had come between them and the enemy delivered into their hands.

There were murmurings in the crowd. Some defended him. It was known he had broken with Ford because he insisted on standing to his agreement. But others guessed there might be something more back of that than had been told. He was working for Dan Clifford, who was supposed to be a friend of their race. But Dan, too, was a Gringo and had helped balk them of their prey. Near the end of Narrow Street the deputy marshal cut to the right along an alley, following the division of patrol agreed upon earlier.

Ah Sin emerged from Narrow into the old plaza and fla'footed across it. He caught a glimpse of Clifford buying a *tamale* at one of the scores of booths. Some cowboys were whooping it up at the door of a dance hall. Curly was one of them. On the opposite side of the square a small group of jabbering *vaqueros* were evidently discussing the marshal, in a hostile mood.

Dan had his back to the *vaqueros* and was aware of the activity of their resentment. He could hear words of obloquy flung at him, could feel waves of anger beating across. The brush riders had been drinking. They were wild reckless youths, and all of them were armed. The marshal had a queer feeling in the middle of his back. He could pick out a spot that seemed the center of the target he offered. It was all he could do to keep from turning to make sure nobody was drawing a bead on him. But to show any apprehension would be a mistake. It was safer to assume that a gunplay was outside the possibilities. The distance between an itching finger and its pressure upon a trigger is a mental stretch that may be shortened by any evidence of fear.

Busy with his *tamale*, obviously interested in nothing else, Dan knew that Ah Sin was halfway across the plaza. He was heading for a lane, flanked by adobe walls, which led toward the *acequia*. The most dangerous part of the journey was past, Dan thought. There were plenty of Mexicans around the plaza, but outside of the *vaqueros* few of them were looking for trouble. Most of those present were owners or patrons of nightstands which sold food, clothing, and other cheap necessities. With any luck Ford's buggy ride ought to terminate safely.

The marshal finished the *tamale* and turned leisurely. Evidently the *vaqueros* were going to take out their disap-

183

proval of him in talk. That was all to the good. Curly and his crowd were crossing the plaza. One or two of them swayed as they walked. Too much tarantula juice.

Ah Sin and the cowboys came face to face. In Curly's mood of stimulated gaiety the temptation was too great. A Chinaman was always fair game, one with a load of laundry was a gift from the gods. Curly reached forward and ripped a sheet from the cart. He waved it above his head like a flag. With howls of joy his companions leaped for the cart.

They jumped back as if they had uncovered a nest of rattlesnakes. For out of the cart a man had flung himself. He faced them, his face a twisted mask of fury and fear, in his hand a menacing revolver.

'Jas Ford!' someone cried.

From the *vaqueros* forty yards away came a yell of triumph. They surged forward. Ah Sin was already flying for the lane, his cart abandoned.

The hunted eyes of Ford swept the plaza. He fired one shot at the charging Mexicans, then turned and followed Ah Sin. A man cut across to join him. He heard the voice of the marshal, warning the *vaqueros*.

'Keep back there! This lane is blocked!'

Ford fled between the adobe walls. The pursuit died away behind him. He reached the open. In front of him he saw the appointed house of refuge. Back of it was the mesquite. He decided to hide in the chaparral and swung to the left. But a voice, speaking Spanish, brought him up short. Men searching the brush, he guessed.

Still in a panic of fear, he made for the laundry. There was no light in it. Ah Sin would hide him if he was there. The gambler flung open the back door and stepped into the house. He closed and bolted the door behind him.

'Hide me—quick!' he ordered, speaking to the soft sounds of someone moving in the next room.

Ah Sin appeared, his outline vague in the darkness.

'Mlister Ford?' he asked.

'Yes. They're hunting the brush back there. Where can you put me?'

The oblique, impassive eyes of the Chinaman fastened on him. Without a word he turned, shuffled into the next room, moved two whipsawed planks from the floor, and exposed a small dirt cellar. Ford drew back. The hole was dark and deep. He made out that it was long and narrow.

'I'm not going down there,' he said roughly.

Ah Sin shrugged his shoulders placidly. 'It fit fine—like a glave.'

Like a grave! The gambler shuddered. He felt as though he were being crowded into his last resting-place.

'You damned Chink, what d'you mean by that?' Ford demanded, his voice hoarse with anxiety.

Even in the darkness the hunted man realized that the Oriental was smiling blandly. 'Mlister Ford no like think of glaves. He send plenty there. Ten—twelve—flifteen maybe.'

Ford ripped out an oath. After this trouble was over, he would make this fool sorry he had tried to be funny with him. Just now he could not afford to resent his words.

'How about air in this hole?' he inquired sharply.

'Plenty air. All Mlister Ford can use.'

Again Ford was troubled by some flicker of irony in what the other said. But he was driven swiftly to decision. Outside he heard the sound of many voices, the beat of many feet.

The gambler looked down into the hole. It was about four feet deep. He lowered himself into it.

Ah Sin joined him. The laundryman explained how best to lie in order to get the most air.

'Get out of here and put the planks back,' Ford ordered, lying down as directed.

The cellar was not more than five feet wide. Perhaps it was six feet long. The sides of it were damp and clammy, as those of a grave might be. The heart of the gambler turned over with fear.

Then he ceased to worry. Ah Sin climbed out and replaced the planks. Cheerfully he called down:

'You be all light there, Mlister Ford.'

Chapter 43

•

DAN ADVISES AH SIN TO LIGHT OUT

'KEEP back there! This lane is blocked!'

Dan did not hurry his words. They rang out like a bell, clear and sharp.

The *vaqueros* came to halt abruptly. His gun was out, pointed negligently toward the ground. But there was no mistaking the menace of it.

'We want that man!' one of the brush riders cried in Spanish.

In the same language Dan answered, 'Can't have him tonight.'

Words gurgled out of them, like water from a narrow-necked bottle.

There had been five of them to start with, at the time of the first pounce toward Ford. Moment by moment the number increased. Dan counted eight—twelve—then gave up counting.

'I'm in this, Sure Shot,' a voice announced cheerfully.

The cowboy Curly was standing beside the marshal, his six-shooter out.

'Agreeable to me,' Dan replied, and in a murmur added, 'No shooting.'

'You got that fixed up with those other birds, too?' Curly asked dryly.

'Keep back—you in the sombrero! No crowding. Not till we have talked this over.'

The anger of the Mexicans beat on him like a heat wave. They shouted—screamed—gesticulated. Dan knew that presently the respect in which they held the drawn guns would be brushed aside, as a dam is by the pressure of increasing water. Then they would sweep over him and the cowboy.

Dan played for seconds. He wanted to give Ford his chance without sacrificing his own life or that of Curly. The point was to hold them as long as he could, but not to try to keep them too long. He could actually see the line sway forward under the push of those in the rear. It was about to break.

He flung up a hand. 'All right. Go get your man.'

The marshal snatched Curly to the wall and let the mob surge past. The Mexicans poured down the lane, as if they had been fired from a gun. A knife blade flashed toward Dan's stomach, struck a cartridge in his belt, and was deflected by it.

'Come on, Sure Shot!' shouted Curly to the marshal. 'Let's go grab us a seat in nigger heaven for the show.'

They followed on the heels of the crowd. At the end of the lane the mob spread fanlike. Dan and Curly headed for Miss Milly's Laundry. Ford had likely escaped into the mesquite, but Ah Sin was probably in the house. They had to get him away from there to a safe place.

The two men met Ah Sin coming out of the back door. For a moment Dan thought he had something in his hand,

186

but he decided he must have been mistaken. Whatever it was, if anything, vanished from sight, perhaps up the wide sleeve of the Chinaman.

'Better get out, Ah Sin,' Dan told him. 'When it gets around you were helping Ford to escape, these fellows may make you trouble. I'd hide for a time.'

'I sink so,' Ah Sin agreed.

'You did fine. Not your fault Curly here knocked our plans galley-west.'

'I sure didn't know what I was going to jump up,' Curly said.

'Any idea where Ford is?' Dan asked.

Ah Sin hitched a thumb toward the house. He explained that the hunted man was hiding in the cellar hole beneath the whipsawed floor of the bedroom.

'Have to get him out of there,' Dan said, frowning. 'They will hunt this house sure soon as they begin to use their brains.'

The Chinaman murmured in his pigeon English that he did not think they would hurt him.

'Hurt him! All they'll do is fill him full of holes as a sieve,' Curly said.

'You had better cut for cover, Ah Sin,' Dan advised.

'Me send good-bye Missy,' her ex-partner told Dan.

'Oh, you'll get away all right,' the marshal reassured. 'Don't worry about that. But light a shuck *pronto*.'

Ah Sin vanished into the night.

Curly went with the marshal into the bedroom. He struck matches while Dan found and lifted out the two loose planks.

'Come on up, Ford,' Dan said. 'You'll have to get out of here.'

There was no answer. An odd chill ran up and down the spine of the marshal.

'Gimme those matches, Curly,' he ordered in a strange, harsh voice.

Dan struck a match, shaded it with his hand, and looked down into the hole. A figure lay stretched at the bottom of it.

'I'm going down,' he announced.

After he had lowered himself, he struck another match.

'Good God!' he cried.

'What's wrong?' asked the cowboy from above.

The throat of Jasper Ford had been slit from ear to ear.

187

Chapter 44

•

A MAN CROSSES
THE RIVER

THE match flickered out. Dan dropped the unburnt end from his fingers and hastily clambered out of the pit.

'When did they get at him?' Curly asked, in startled amazement.

'They didn't . . . Let's find a lamp and light it.'

Dan was shaken. The horror of this finale had jumped at him so unexpectedly. The darkness pressed in upon him. He had an urge to escape into the light.

On a shelf in the kitchen Curly's groping hand found a lamp. He lit it. They found two others on the same shelf. Dan put matches to the wicks of these and replaced the chimneys.

Each of the men carried a light into the bedroom. One of the lamps was put on a table near the edge of the pit. Curly let himself down into the hole carefully. The marshal gave him the other lamp. He set it down where its rays would shine upon the face of the dead man, after which he rejoined his companion above.

Someone came into the kitchen. A voice called softly a warning. 'Page, of the rangers. Don't shoot.'

'Come in,' Dan invited.

The officer entered the bedroom. 'Thought I might find some of you here,' he said. 'Ford made his get-away, I reckon. Otherwise why all the lights?'

He looked down into the pit. For a moment he did not speak; then said, 'So they got him, after all.'

'No,' Dan denied.

'Who, then?'

'Ah Sin.'

'What for?' burst from Curly.

'Ford bullied him and beat him up once. Ah Sin asked me two or three times when I was going to kill Ford.'

'And at last he did the job himself,' Page said. 'We'll have to collect him tonight.'

'Yes,' assented Dan reluctantly. He liked Ah Sin, and he

knew that a Chinaman who had killed a white man would almost certainly pay the extreme penalty when caught.

'Must have been looking for a chance,' Curly said. 'Had the knife up his sleeve likely.'

'I expect he had brooded over this ever since Ford insulted and mistreated him,' Dan suggested. 'Never figured on getting a chance to go through with it, I reckon. Then out of all the men in the world I pick him to help Ford escape. Would you call that Fate?'

'Never can tell what a Chink will do," Page ruminated aloud. 'Chances are Ah Sin thinks he never did anything in the world more right than this. Shouldn't wonder if he won't be satisfied to pay with his life, knowing that he has rubbed out the man he hated.'

'We had better spread the word that Ford has been killed,' said Dan. 'May save other lives. My idea is to invite the Mexicans in to file through the house so they will not have any doubt.'

'Good medicine. That will sure quiet them down.'

It did. The news spread with inconceivable rapidity. Hundreds and hundreds of Mexicans—men, women, even children—filed through the bedroom and looked down on the ghastly exhibit. Early in the procession Dan could not stand the horror of the thing any longer and sent a man down into the pit to put a bandanna around the neck of the dead man to conceal the wound.

He left his second deputy in charge of the building while he and Stone searched the town to arrest Ah Sin. They did not find their man. They never found him. A man on the river had seen him crossing the pontoon bridge into Mexico about ten minutes after he had left Clifford and the cowboy. Then all trace of him vanished. There was a conspiracy of silence. To the Mexicans he was a hero and not a criminal. He had destroyed the evil man who had become their public enemy. So they looked at it. No doubt Ah Sin was passed into the interior of the country by grateful admirers.

There was a sequel to this. Ten years later, Mrs. Daniel Clifford, with two small boys by her side, walked into a Chinese laundry at Los Angeles to find out how soon a bundle of laundry could be washed. She explained she was leaving for Los Piños in twenty-four hours.

The proprietor of the place waited upon her. He was a dignified Oriental clad in modern American attire. His impassive face showed no least recognition. To the young woman he seemed vaguely familiar. While stepping on a

189

street-car half an hour later, it jumped to her mind that the man was Ah Sin.

She showed extraordinary discretion. Knowing her husband's conscience, she buried the suspicion in her heart. Not for several years did she inform Dan that she thought she had seen once more her ex-partner.

Chapter 45
•
ROSES BLOOM

THE death of Jasper Ford cleared the atmosphere of Los Piños. Frightened by the fate of their leader, Black and his associates decided to live up to the paper signed at the salt lakes and relinquishing their claim to a prominent Spanish-American who agreed to hold the property in trust for the public. It became apparent that, though Los Piños was going to remain what is known as a wide-open town, law had come to the community to stay. The worst of the desperadoes who had hailed Ford chief departed inconspicuously for other pastures. The best of the saloon-keepers and dance-hall owners welcomed a clean-up which put out of existence the places of vice that flagrantly violated ordinances for the protection of citizens.

The town began to talk about its new baseball team, the church Philip Washburn was building, the high school for which plans were being drawn. A civic consciousness was in the air. It was time, good people agreed, that the smoke of powder be blown away forever.

Dan welcomed the new era. He felt it would affect favorably his personal fortunes, since he had been a factor in bringing about the change. It pleased him to have the esteem and respect of the town. He felt a boyish pride in the fact that Milly could not help knowing he was far from an outcast in the minds of her friends. If she felt that blood stained his hands and barred him from the love of a nice girl, she was almost alone in that opinion.

But he made no effort to see her. He was afraid she would think he was basing a claim on the help he had given her the night of the riot.

He was not happy. Once she had admitted her love for him, but he believed now that he had caught her at a moment of emotional stress. It was clear she did not love him or she would not be so unfair.

Tom Sutherland brought him a note one day. It was a prim, precise little letter from Milly thanking him for all he had done for her and the children.

Dan put as much time interpreting its meaning as Milly had in writing it, and that was a good deal. On the face of it she said very little. Was it merely an ungenerous duty note? Or was he to read between the lines an emotion she was too shy and too modest to express? He did not know. He did not want to hurt himself by asking for a rebuff. On the other hand, if this was a gesture of friendship, he did not want to ignore it.

Dan compromised. He hung around waiting for a chance to meet Milly apparently not by design. Several hours were wasted staring at the shadows on the blinds of a lighted room from across the road. But on the third evening the door opened and a light, graceful figure came into the garden, perhaps to draw in the fresh clean air of the night.

Now or never, thought Dan. He crossed the street, opened the gate, and walked into the garden. Milly was bending over a rosebush, but at sight of him straightened swiftly.

He told her it was a pleasant evening and she agreed, after which there was a stiff and brittle silence.

'I got your note, Miss Sutherland,' he said at last.

'I wanted you to know—that we are grateful,' she answered in a small voice.

'That's all right. You don't owe me a thing.' He spoke brusquely.

'I'll owe you a great deal as long as I live,' Milly said quietly.

His pulses began to hammer. He told himself not to be a fool. This did not mean anything. A girl had to be polite.

'I've been . . . awf'ly silly,' she went on, finding words with difficulty. 'You were right, and I was wrong. I—hadn't any right to try to—make you do what would have been wrong for you.'

His heart skipped a beat. 'I—had to kill a man,' he reminded her. 'Just as you said I would.'

'You did it in self-defense.' She spoke in a murmur, not looking at him.

He had a lucid interval and took her in his arms. The lips that had lately touched a rose met his.

191